THE
VANISHING
BOOKSTORE

BOOKS BY HELEN PHIFER

THRILLERS

Lakeview House

THE
VANISHING
BOOKSTORE

HELEN PHIFER

Bookouture

Published by Bookouture in 2025

An imprint of Storyfire Ltd.
Carmelite House
50 Victoria Embankment
London EC4Y 0DZ

www.bookouture.com

The authorised representative in the EEA is Hachette Ireland
8 Castlecourt Centre
Dublin 15 D15 XTP3
Ireland
(email: info@hbgi.ie)

ISBN: 978-1-83618-593-2
eBook ISBN: 978-1-83618-594-9

This book is a work of fiction. Names, characters, businesses, organizations,
places and events other than those clearly in the public domain, are either the
product of the author's imagination

For every woman, man and child ever wrongly accused of witchcraft. Your voices will never be silenced.

Real magic is the feeling deep inside of you when you realise that your veins are filled with moonlight and stardust.

Seraphina English, 2023

PROLOGUE
SALEM, 1692

A dense cloak of darkness fell on this night faster than any I'd ever known, bringing with it a heavy feeling of unsettled dread. The sky outside was dark with the threat of a storm, and it felt as if something was approaching at the speed of an unforgiving fox about to strike its prey. I knew it was coming this way, I didn't know what, but I knew it was about to wreak havoc on our little cottage and impact my life forever.

I tried to keep my mind busy, stop it from wandering and fretting. As I swept the ash from the floor around the dying fire that I had no desire to rebuild, my stomach was tight, and a sickness over which I had no control lay heavy in my belly. The rack of drying herbs collected by my mother and aunts filled the air of the wooden cottage we called home with soothing aromas of lavender, rosemary and mint. I inhaled deeply, hoping the familiar scents would calm the sickness. My mother and aunts had gathered the flowers from the large herb garden around the back. I loved everything we grew with a passion that sometimes made my chest swell with pride. To take a dried seed from a pod and plant it in the hard earth, caring for it until a tiny green shoot appeared, was satisfying beyond anything I knew.

My favourite were the tiny mayflowers that grew underneath the pine trees, their delicate white flowers and strong leaves were useful for bathing wounds and treating all manner of afflictions, providing a cure for many women's sicknesses. I often went out on my own to harvest these precious plants with nobody but our pet crow, Hades, for company. Then my aunts would take what we'd lovingly grown and nurtured, turning it into an elixir or tea to help make someone feel better. They were healers and I was learning everything I could so that I could be one too. Weeding and tending the flowers was my favourite chore of all, the freedom working outside under the burning sun gave was like no other. These were happy days.

Of course, I had to keep my head covered with a scarf to protect my silver hair and pale skin, which was prone to turn a deep shade of painful red from the sun. All the English women were blessed with hair the colour of spun silver and emerald-green eyes. The women of Salem village were wary of us, and the men found my aunts mesmerising which we should have known would cause trouble. There is no fury like that of a woman scorned, and although my aunts were not interested in any of those men it didn't deter them from trying to catch their attention. All they cared about was family and taking care of those who asked for their help when they had no other to turn to.

Tonight, they had been called to help in a matter most urgent and had left in a hurry with a large sack of herbs and tinctures.

I had begged to go with them, but someone had to clean up after supper. I did not grumble, what was there to complain about? I lived in a house with my dearest family close to me, we did not want for warmth or food, love or comfort because, despite the house being filled with only women, we all loved each other with a deep family bond that could never be broken and rarely spoke cross words to each other.

My mother and aunts had left earlier to visit the big house on the edge of the common in Salem town and tend to the captain's wife, whose maid had come knocking once the sun had set and the swollen, white full moon had begun its majestic rise in the star-filled sky to light the way back through the woods for my family. I had no idea what was wrong with the captain's wife, and my aunts would not tell me. I did not pry, I knew better, but I knew deep down it must be terrible if all three of them had to attend.

The pounding of fists against the wooden door filled my entire body with a cold fear. Throwing the besom to one side – the sweeping would have to wait – I ran to the door which was bending under the force of the blows to press my hands against it and stop whoever it was from breaking it down. I paused, afraid to open it, then I heard who it was. And the fear in his voice.

'Isadora, Isadora, open up now. You must let me in, we need to go.'

I threw open the door. The look on his face illuminated by the flickering candlelight made my knees tremble and I had to reach out and lean against the doorframe to steady myself.

'What's wrong, Ambrose, why are you here so late?'

He pushed past me. 'No time, Isadora, listen to me, we need to leave. They are coming and have dogs; we need to get far away from here. I heard them making wicked plans at the meeting house.'

'Why?' I stood defiantly watching him as he threw things into the small sack I used to carry things from the market. He didn't answer, grabbing my cloak from the peg and tossing it to me.

'If you stay here, you will die.'

I didn't want to die, of that I was certain, though I knew not why I might. I pulled my cloak on, but as I reached the door I turned and ran back to retrieve my mother's hand-etched, leather-bound journal from the top shelf. Normally, I was forbidden to touch it, but I felt a pull towards it even as Ambrose urged me on.

I followed Ambrose out into the woods. He ran much faster than I could, but he stopped and took hold of my hand. He did not speak, there was a look of absolute fear etched across his face, worsened by the dark shadows cast where the moonlight did not reach, and I knew then that he was telling the truth. If we did not get away from here, I would die, and he might too for helping me even though we had done no wrong. There had been arrests in the village, some of the women were in the gaols accused of being witches by those spiteful, childish girls even though they were no such thing and tensions were running high. I had thought we were safe from the madness since we lived just beyond Salem village; it seemed not.

'We have to hide your mother's book at the bookstore and then get to the cove, my boat, it's the only way to escape the dogs.'

I was panting, I was not cut out for this. I was strong from tending to the garden, but I was not a runner and I stopped, a sharp stitch in my left side taking my breath away. I bent over double, sucking in air to try and ease the pain. I nodded.

Ambrose's bookstore was a small wooden cabin that he had built himself two summers ago. It was hidden by the brambles that grew wild around it and impossible to find unless you knew the hidden trail through the woods to it. Puritans believed every person should be able to read the bible or religious texts, they would have been horrified to find the cabin and its stack of books that Ambrose had traded coin for at the busy port in Salem town. He would speak to the passengers and the crew aboard the sailing ships to barter for the books they sometimes brought with them. It was our special place to spend what very little free time we had in it reading, my favourite had been *Romeo and Juliet*, oh how I'd envied the intensity of their love.

Ambrose had once opened his little bookstore to anyone who was in our circle of friends and allowed them to visit to buy a book if they swore to keep the store a secret from their parents, but the threat of them telling had made him realise it was far too dangerous. It was hidden from view and never talked of again except between the two of us.

Even though I could not run fast enough we carried on until we reached the small hidden doorway. The cabin was in darkness, but I could smell the leather-bound books and the ink on the paper. It soothed my soul what little it could for we had no time.

'Give me your mother's book.'

Ambrose held out his hands and I knew this was dangerous, not just for me, for my mother and aunts, but also for him. I would be sealing his fate if this cabin was discovered, and I didn't know if I could do that.

'Please Izzy, give it to me, we have to be quick. If you don't get to the boat, they will kill you.'

His words hung between us and I looked at him. I was scared and confused. Why did I need to leave my family? We had done nothing wrong. I passed him the soft, leather-bound book that had been a part of my life for as long as I could remember. My family would be furious to know that I had given it to Ambrose. He wrapped it in a piece of linen then pulled out a loose board and pushed it behind it. 'It is safe here, no one but you and I know about this place.'

I nodded and then I heard the hounds, their high-pitched howls filling the night air in the distance.

Ambrose cried out. Taking my hand he dragged me out of the cabin onwards through the brambles, the nettles and overgrown trails where no man had walked, so they could not find the path to our sacred place, and we ran as the thorns tore at our skin, stinging and ripping at the soft flesh on my hands and wrists, but he kept on pulling me. He cut a zigzag path through the dense brambles, but kept moving forwards in the direction of the cove and his small boat.

I looked up at him, my heart breaking that this could be the end.

I began to run faster than I had ever run in my short life, wondering if I had put my trust in the wrong people. I knew the man who was hunting me, and I knew in my heart that I would never escape.

1

LONDON, PRESENT DAY

A cool breeze blew down the narrow, cobblestoned alley, making the fallen leaves dance themselves into a frenzy. The fading autumn sun reflected its burning orange glow in the shop windows before it faded from view. The chimes above the freshly painted, sugared-almond-pink shop door tinkled as the breeze rushed through the gap along with a handful of leaves.

Dora was leaning on the counter, her head resting in the palm of her hand. She had been contemplating what was missing from her life while staring blankly at the page of the latest issue of *Rock and Roll Bride* magazine when the tall man walked into her shop. She looked up at him. He smelled the way a walk through the woods did, tinged with underlying tones of lemon, mint and grapefruit. Dora straightened, pushing the trimmed fresh lilies on the workbench in front of her to one side, along with the magazine. She paused and inhaled deeply, nodding in appreciation of just how good this stranger who had walked into Vintage Rose, her tiny flower shop, smelled. He watched her and she noted the look of mild confusion apparent in his eyes, so dark they reminded her of two pools of melted chocolate. Somewhere deep inside her soul she recognised those eyes, but she did not recognise the rest of his face. He was tanned and cleanshaven with slightly mussed brown hair that was a touch too long for the collar of the heavy white cotton shirt he was wearing.

She smiled at him. 'Can I help you?'

'I hope so, I'm looking for the owner of the shop.'

'Why?'

Dora wasn't usually so blunt, but she hadn't had the best of months and she had barely made her rent.

'Sorry, I mean, that's me. How can I help you?' She righted herself. His cheeks tinged with the tiniest of pink circles that were barely visible underneath his weathered tan. Dora had an excellent nose for all kinds of scents along with an uncanny ability to read people, and she regretted her bluntness – there was something sad and a little mysterious in the man's eyes. She often read people without even trying, which her best friend, Katie Ryan, found infuriating, but that was who she was, and there wasn't a thing she could do about it.

'I was told to come here and speak to her about some funeral flowers.'

'Oh, I'm so sorry for your loss.' That was what she had noticed, she thought. His grief.

Dora held out her hand, and the smallest jolt of electricity ran up the full length of her arm as their fingertips brushed against each other. She let go, lifting her fingers to tuck a stray strand of black hair that had escaped from her messy bun behind her ear.

'I'm sorry about that, I'm Dora English. I can absolutely help you with anything you need.'

He looked around then nodded. 'Good, that's good. Thank you, Dora, I'm George Corwin. My girlfriend died rather suddenly, and I need some flowers for her funeral. A friend of mine told me I should come here and see you, so here I am.' His voice caught a little as he spoke.

'You poor thing, I'm sorry to hear that, George. Why don't you take a seat and I'll show you the book of floral tributes I've made in the past. That's normally what people get for funerals.'

She looked around at the cluttered, cramped shop and rushed towards the small bistro chair that she'd rescued from the builders' skip behind the alley a few months ago. It was now her display stand for the bucket of pastel-coloured roses that were very popular at the moment. As she lifted the bucket down, she caught her fingers on a sharp thorn and it tore at the soft skin of her fingertips, a thin red line appearing instantly.

'Ouch.'

She almost dropped the bucket onto George's toes. There wasn't much room to manoeuvre, and she had to balance placing it on the floor with sucking her finger. George watched her with an amused look on his face and despite his sad situation she could see a glint of humour in his eye. She couldn't decide whether she liked him or not, he looked devilishly dashing in his three-piece, navy tweed suit and he smelled divine, but she knew better than anyone that looking and smelling good didn't count for anything once a person's true personality shone through.

'Please sit.' The words were barked at him, like an order, but he didn't flinch and obliged by doing exactly as she'd asked. Turning away from him, she went to the antique haberdashery drawers she'd found at the market one Sunday. She had bartered the seller down to a price she could afford when she knew she couldn't leave them behind. They served as both her workspace and storage. Pulling out a drawer, she removed a black display book and passed it to him. He took it from her, smiling, and she turned away, not wanting to stand and watch over him, instead she returned to the large bouquet of flowers she had almost finished for her favourite customer's birthday. As she snipped at the long stems, arranging the lilies, roses, eucalyptus and freesias, she ignored the flapping of the pages turning fast and whispered, 'Blue de Chanel' – obviously a little louder than she'd realised because he looked up from the page he was staring at and turned his stare to her.

'I beg your pardon?'

Now it was Dora's turn to blush. 'Oh, nothing, I was thinking out loud. Your aftershave is very familiar.'

'My girlfriend bought it for me.' He stopped talking, as his eyes cast downwards to the page in the book. She assumed this was so he could hide his tears. Dora decided that he was probably okay, he was sad and grieving so there was nothing to worry about.

'She bought you the aftershave. How sweet that whenever you wear it, you'll think of her and that way she's always near to you in your memories. How lovely is that, I think scented memories are the most precious of all – they are stored forever and you will never lose them.'

He stood up and handed her the book. 'Those aren't quite what I had in mind.'

'Oh, I'm sorry. They're the most popular funeral arrangements that I make but I can do a one-off custom order if you like? Is there anything she really loved?'

Shrugging, he fixed his gaze on the tiny pair of crescent moon diamond earrings she was wearing, a gift from her Aunt Lenny on her last birthday.

'Expensive jewellery, designer handbags, champagne, shoes, that kind of thing.'

The smallest of sighs escaped Dora's lips. 'What about a handbag-shaped wreath or a champagne bottle?' She smiled at him, realising just how crass and awful those suggestions were and felt her insides cringe.

'She's dead, I don't think her parents would appreciate me having a huge, flowery tribute in the shape of a champagne bottle on her coffin. They might think I have something to celebrate. Before you know it, I'll be under investigation for murder.'

Dora knew it was going to happen, she tried her very best to stop it, but it erupted quite violently and the laughter that came from inside her belly echoed around the shop. She was equally mortified and stuck in a fit of highly inappropriate giggles. George was staring at her in horror, and she wished the floor would open and swallow her. Managing to compose herself, she whispered, 'I'm so sorry, please forgive me.'

He gave a curt nod. 'Apology accepted. I'll have a think and get back to you, take care Dora.'

And with that he swept out of the shop, leaving behind the lingering scent of aftershave. The door chimes whipped against each other furiously.

She sat down on the chair, which was still warm from his body heat, ashamed of her behaviour. What had come over her?

She looked around; she hadn't felt right all day. In fact, she'd been feeling off for a while now. It was a strange feeling. Not quite anxiety. She felt as if something was missing from her life. As she stood up the skin on the back of her neck began to crawl.

She went back to the bouquet and began to finish it off by hand, tying the stems together. The door opened and her relief was palpable. It was Mabel Hastings, the old lady who lived above the shop, in an equally tiny flat as Dora's shop. Mabel smiled at her and Dora threw her arms wide open and rushed towards her.

'Happy Birthday, Mabel, have you had a lovely day?'

Mabel was the best hugger that Dora knew. Dora's Aunt Lenny, who she lived with, wasn't much of a hugger at all. She was an independent soul, who'd always wanted Dora to be self-sufficient herself. Dora had to make do with stealing hugs from Mabel as often as she could.

'I'm all the better for seeing you. Do you want to come to the bingo later? We could win this time with my birthday luck.'

'Mabel, I love you but I'm not going to the bingo with you even if it is your birthday. You know how rubbish I am, last time I shouted house when I didn't even have a line and I thought the whole room were going to beat me to death with their bingo dabbers.'

Mabel's eyes crinkled as she giggled. 'Yes, you are quite an embarrassment. Okay, how about coffee and cake at the café before it closes?'

Dora picked up the huge bouquet and passed it to Mabel. 'Now that sounds more like it. Happy Birthday.'

Tears pricked at the corners of Mabel's eyes. 'Oh, Dora, you shouldn't have, I can't.'

'Yes, you can and yes I should. Come on, if we take them in the café, they'll realise it's your birthday and they might throw in a free cake.'

She let Mabel out first and locked the door behind her, taking one last look around the shop that she loved so much.

The Café was across the cobbled alley. It was brightly lit against the now gloomy autumn sky. Dora had asked the owner, Mason, why it was called The Café once, and he'd replied he didn't have the time to think up a fancy name for it when that's what it was. She hadn't argued with him, it made sense.

As they walked through the door into the industrial-style shop the aroma of freshly ground coffee hit her nostrils like a steam train, and she smiled. Maybe this was what was missing from her life. Coffee, chocolate and fresh flowers were her favourite scents, and as she navigated Mabel and her gargantuan bouquet of flowers to the biggest table in the corner, she smiled to herself. George's aftershave was now added onto her list of favourite scents. It was a good job she'd never see him again, despite how good he smelled. She had firmly lost his custom with her outburst. Crossing to the counter, she ordered two large hazelnut lattes and the last two slices of Victoria sponge cake. She would just have to console herself with lash-

ings of buttercream and jam after losing out on what was probably the biggest order she'd have taken that week. God knew she
could have done with his custom.

She felt better now that Mabel was here. She liked being
around her; she was wise, with a stoic energy, full of advice. She
was a comfort, not that Dora could understand why. She had
her shop, she had a life here in London. But she always felt a
little lost. If only she could figure out what the missing ingredient was, her life would be pretty perfect.

2

Lenora English, or Lenny to her family, had known early this morning that something was looming on the horizon. It had been the damn rabbit that had started it. She'd been almost out of the car park, driving home from her shift at the hospital, when it had darted across the road right in front of her car. She'd had to slam her brakes on, narrowly missing it. Making sure no one was watching she then had to jump out of the car, make a sign of the cross on the road and spit into it (which was most unladylike), while walking backwards to her car, praying the security guards weren't watching her strange behaviour on the CCTV monitors in the office.

When she got home and decided to make herself some scrambled eggs for breakfast, the lid had fallen off the salt grinder as she'd taken it out of the cupboard, spilling salt all over the gleaming white marble worktops. Of course, she'd thrown a pinch over her left shoulder with her right hand, but it had unsettled her even more. Then a few hours later came the phone call she had been dreading.

She was sitting on the sofa, her legs tucked under her as she whispered down the phone to her sister Sephy, afraid that Dora may walk through the doors any moment and hear the conversation that wasn't for her to know about. At least not yet.

'How poorly is she, Sephy? Give me a timeline. What does she have left? Months, weeks? For the love of God do not say days.'

'If you answered your mail occasionally, Lenny, you would have known this was coming. What's taking her so long this time, why is she not even the slightest bit suspicious of her heritage? It never usually takes her this long, has something gone wrong, do you think? Has she forgotten everything? Lost her memories completely? Maybe sending her away was a bad idea. I hoped this time it would make the difference.'

'How long has Lucine got, Sephy?' Lenny replied, her tone firm.

'You're the doctor, if you were here, you would know. I can't say for certain. Come home, Lenny, you can't avoid it forever. I think you're using Dora as an excuse not to come back. Well, it's no good. I think she may have a couple of months if we're lucky, she's holding on to see Dora.'

'But she hasn't even started the process. Do you remember the last time we did it, when she wasn't ready for it, and how difficult it was to get her to escape from that dreadful asylum? It gives me the shivers just thinking about that place, those poor people covered in lice and screaming from dawn until dusk. She's a lot more fragile than the rest of us. More important.'

'I know she is, and it was so horrid that she ended up locked in that awful place for months. It was lucky for her that you found her and managed to help her get out, but what are we to do? Each time it takes her longer to come back to us, I fear it's not right. Something is awry.'

Lenny sighed, thinking that you could take the girl out of the 1600s but you'd never take the 1600s out of the girl. 'Tell Lucine I'll be there in a few days; I'll bring Dora too.'

'What will you tell her?'

'I don't know, I'll think of something.'

The door to the luxury penthouse apartment that Lenny owned swung inwards, and she whispered, 'Got to go,' then hung up the phone.

Dora walked in and looked at her. Lenny knew that Dora suspected something was going on, it was always this way and had been since the beginning of their time.

'Evening, Aunt Lenny.'

'Good evening, Dora, busy day?'

Dora shrugged. 'Not particularly, how about you?'

Lenny nodded. 'Chaotic would be a good word.' She walked over to the huge American-style fridge in the open-plan kitchen and took out a cold bottle of Pinot Grigio, waving it in Dora's direction.

'Would you like a glass?'

'No, thanks. That bad a day, eh?'

Pouring half of the bottle into one of the fine crystal gin glasses that she favoured over a simple wine glass, Lenny took a large gulp and gave her the thumbs up.

'Did you lose a patient?' Dora asked quietly.

'God, no, my patients are all just fine, I had to go shopping when I realised, we were almost out of wine and you know how that stresses me out, all those people it gets too much.' She kicked off her black Louboutins and shrugged off her Gucci suit jacket, hanging it on the back of one of the bar stools, then, carrying her glass, went and sat on the sofa. 'Anything exciting happen today at the shop then? Come on, give me something to cheer me up, Dora, you usually have the best snippets of gossip that make me smile.'

'Not really. It's Mabel's birthday so we went for coffee and cake. She asked if I wanted to go to the bingo, but I said no.'

Lenny grimaced at the thought of the bingo hall, it wasn't her scene. It never had been and never would be. It was too much like a meeting house full of gossiping Puritans ready to point fingers and see innocent people hang for no good reason. It brought back bad memories.

'Oh, and this really nice-smelling man came in the shop just before closing. I mean, he smelled so good.'

Lenny sat up; this was interesting. Dora had always had a strong connection with smells and memories.

'Really, who was he, what did he want?'

'Well, this is the awful part, I was so rude to him. His poor girlfriend died, and he wanted a floral tribute for her funeral.'

'How could you possibly mess that up?'

'He didn't like the standard stuff out of the book, so I asked him what she liked, and he mentioned handbags and champagne. I offered to make him a champagne tribute wreath for her coffin without even thinking of the implications.'

Lenny choked on the mouthful of wine; she started coughing. 'You did what?'

Dora shrugged. 'It just came out, then he told me that he didn't think her parents would appreciate the sentiment and I started to giggle, well actually I was laughing, and it was awful, but you know when you know that you shouldn't be laughing but then it makes it even funnier, so you laugh harder? Yeah, well that.'

Laughter from her normally serious Aunt Lenny filled the apartment and Dora smiled. It was so bad that it was funny.

'Dora, what are we going to do with you?' Lenny replied. She needed to introduce the idea of the trip to Salem, but what would convince Dora? 'It sounds like you need a break, and I need to go away for work for a few weeks to the States. How do you fancy coming with me? We could turn it into a holiday, drink cocktails, hang out in seedy bars, find us a couple of cowboys to ride, visit Salem, that kind of stuff.'

Dora looked thoughtful. She seemed to react to hearing the word Salem; perhaps it was triggering some memories.

'What about the shop?' she said. 'I can't just shut it and

disappear for a few weeks; things are a little bit tight at the moment. I could have really done with that sale.'

'Yes, you can, I can float you some cash to make up for your loss of earnings and pay this month's rent. You always say no to any financial help, which is very honourable of you, but come on, I want to help you and we both need a break. What about your friend Katie, isn't she between jobs? Couldn't she cover for you?'

'She's not a florist, she wouldn't know where to begin with orders and deliveries.'

'Well, this is important, I can't miss it. I have to leave Monday at the latest, that gives you three days to teach her how to do it. It can't be that hard, can it, I mean you manage it.'

An expression of hurt filled Dora's face and Lenny realised she shouldn't have said that. It was plain mean of her.

'What I mean is of course it's not easy, but maybe you could teach her how to make basic bouquets and she could always tell customers there's no delivery service while you're away? Come on Dora, we could have such fun. Salem is a wonderful place. There are all these museums and gift shops – you would love it; look how much you love Halloween, we could get lots of goodies to bring back for the shop to display.'

Lenny was lying through her teeth. Yes, Salem was an amazing place, but the thought of going home filled her with a cold shard of fear. It ran the full length of her spine and left a terrible taste in her mouth that no amount of Pinot would ever remove. When she'd first lived there it had been the most god-awful place in the whole world. But they always ended up back there. No matter how many lives they lived, they always gravitated back to Salem. It was the human equivalent of an elephants' graveyard to the English women.

'I'll think about it, thanks.' Dora disappeared into her bedroom, closing the door behind her, and Lenny took another large sip of wine. How was she going to convince her niece she needed to come with her? It was a big ask; perhaps the mention of Salem hadn't even sparked the tiniest of memories inside her? She had hoped that sending Dora away would help them break the curse. The curse that had bound them for hundreds of years. They all knew Dora was the key. That there was a way to save her life.

She laid her head back against the soft velvet sofa and closed her eyes. Maybe it was time they all let it go, and accepted the curse forever?

3

SALEM, PRESENT DAY

Sephy sat with her eldest sister, Lucine, and read to her. She liked to listen to stories and was particularly fond of the current book they were reading: *Where the Crawdads Sing* by Delia Owens. Her sister was enjoying being whisked away to the marshes of North Carolina.

A gentle snore filled the room and she looked at Lucine who was dozing, her shoulder-length silver hair glinting in the candlelight. She looked as if she was in her late forties, not sixty-one, and had gone grey prematurely, but her emerald eyes were losing their sparkle, the light inside them dimming. It was always the same. It was the eyes that gave the English sisters away, all of them had the same vivid green eyes and hair like spun silver. Except for Dora; her eyes were a slightly paler shade of green, her hair a raven black. They had also been blessed with skin that didn't seem to age the same as most women, although she also credited the cold cream she had been making since time began with helping to keep the wrinkles at bay. The cream along with her herbal teas were her most in demand at her little shop.

Closing the book, she placed it on the nightstand next to the bed. Standing up, she blew out the candles. She couldn't go to the shop and leave the house with them burning even though Lucine preferred candlelight to the harsh electric lights. There was a small nightlight and she switched that on, so she wasn't in the dark. She hated leaving her sister when she was so tired and frail, but they had made a promise a long time ago that as long as the townsfolk needed help they would provide it. Which Lenny thought was ridiculous. It was the townsfolk who had persecuted them for doing just that back when the Salem they knew was nothing more than a farming village. It was tradition though and if there was one thing the English sisters were good at it was keeping the family traditions alive.

The small shop Sephy owned on the corner of Essex and Summer next to the tattoo shop was a profitable one. She could stare over at the Witch House all day if she wanted, which she didn't because she didn't need the constant reminder of what had happened to them that first time around. She did love watching the tourists dressed as witches standing out front having their photographs taken and often wondered what that brute Judge Jonathan Corwin would think of it now. There was no bigger screw-you than having thousands of wannabe witches standing outside your own front door where you once lived after sending innocent women and men to the gallows accused of witchcraft.

Out the front of the store she sold all the usual things that visitors who came to Salem expected to buy: tarot cards, crystals for every occasion and situation, spell books, candles, books on witchcraft, mugs with pictures of witches on, tiny little pink cauldrons; you name it, she sold it. What the tourists didn't know about was her consulting room at the back, and her beautiful apothecary. The English women had sold teas, potions, creams and soaps for as long as they could remember, and the townsfolk loved them. Even the men would come after dark when the consulting room was open if they needed something.

But the women, well they came in droves to see Sephy whenever they needed something that Doctor Parish couldn't give to them; oh how times have changed, she thought to herself.

Downstairs she tugged her cloak around her shoulders and heard a loud miaow from behind her as Ophelia, their black cat, strode towards her and began to rub herself against Sephy's ankles, demanding to be fed.

She stared at her. 'I fed you not an hour ago, are you still hungry?'

When she was a child, she used to think that the cats they'd always kept would answer in a perfectly formed human voice and had been bitterly disappointed that, despite the years of living with the Englishes, they had never quite mastered speech. She hurried back into the kitchen to see the bowl. Opening the fridge, she took out some milk and poured some into a saucer.

'Be a dear and go keep an eye on Lucine for me. She's asleep so don't go waking her up but if you could keep her company, I'll give you sardines when I come home. Is that a deal?'

The cat looked up at her and let out a long purr which Sephy took for a yes. She let herself out of the front door. The porch light was out again. That was another thing to add to her never-ending list of jobs. If Lenny was here, she could shoulder some of the burden for a change. Life never used to be this complicated. She remembered with great fondness the times when they grew their own vegetables and herbs, spending time together of an evening after a hard day working the land. They would be tired but talking among themselves and enjoying each other's company, unlike now when everyone was glued to their cell phones.

She grabbed her bicycle which was leaning against the fence, snapped the buckle on the helmet and began the short ride into town. It was easier to cycle, although her cloak was sometimes a nuisance if it was particularly blowy, but she tucked it under her bottom. The large wicker basket on the front was just big enough for most of the things she had to buy from the shops, and it saved her many lost minutes trying to park the van.

The shop was one of the oldest still standing in Salem and always had been since as long as she could remember. Lenny used to say they should shut it, move with the times and work online, but Sephy much preferred meeting people face to face. There was so much coldness and indifference through buying your goods online; it was great if you needed things that weren't readily available in town and that was it. How could she read what a person really wanted if it was all carried out through a computer? There was no personal touch to it. The English women all had special gifts: Sephy was a natural at healing and knowing exactly what a person needed before they could tell her themselves, while Lenny had the gift of seeing things before they happened – although it was a dreadful shame it hadn't kicked in before they'd found themselves the victims of a vicious witch hunt in 1692.

Sephy shuddered at the memory of the awful time they spent cooped up on the stinking, dirt floor covered in urine-stained straw in the dark, dank dungeons below the county jail. Sheriff George Corwin, the judge's nephew, had taken a liking to Lenny, much to their horror, which had been the start of his wicked persecution of them all.

She shuddered, pushing thoughts of Corwin out of her mind for now. For the last few lifetimes Lenny had been a skilled surgeon so she was more of a modern-day healer than Sephy was. Lucine, their elder sister, had the gift of natural healing too, she'd taught them both everything they knew, how to grow, pick and dry the herbs they needed to make their potions and creams. It was Lucine who knew a lot more about things than they did and she was the one who had kept a beautiful spell book that had been gifted to her full of everything they should need. They had never seen it since the first time they died. She could talk to the animals too, Sephy was sure of that; they all followed her around almost fighting for her attention.

Lucine had always had a pet crow called Hades who would come and go as he pleased; he'd sometimes disappear for months then turn up out of the blue. He'd come back two days ago; he was always around when the end was near for Lucine which she found a great comfort. The crow is known for its links to the other side and said to be able to cross over from the living to the dead, Hades' name came from the Greek god who was the king of the dead, which was a pretty appropriate name for a bird with feathers as black as the night. Hades and Lucine were as thick as thieves and Sephy was convinced there was something more to their relationship or knowledge but who was she to ask.

Then there was Dora, or Isadora as she was called in her first life. It was funny how all of their names except for Lucine's had been shortened over the centuries to something less dramatic. Sephy had loved being called Seraphina; Lenora, however, had loved shortening hers to Lenny. Dora's special power was being able to grow anything, no matter what or how shrivelled and dead it might be. If she picked it up and whispered to it, before you knew it blooms would appear and the shrivelled-up plant that had been about to be thrown into the trash would be living its best life on someone's kitchen windowsill. She was as good with scents as she was plants and could remember a person she'd seen for even just a fleeting glance with her sense of smell. She spoke the language of flowers, which was a beautiful gift, and Sephy thought that she also had the most powerful magic out of them all if only she could figure out how to tap into it. All their gifts and ability to do good in the world hadn't stopped them from that treacherous persecution and horrific death at the end of the hangman's noose the first time around and she let out a long, drawn-out sigh at the thought of it.

She leaned the bike against the shop wall and locked it to the drainpipe. Sephy didn't trust many people – the local kids were a nuisance, always messing around with stuff they shouldn't be. They called them witches, but no one took the slightest bit of notice these days. Hundreds of years ago it had been a death sentence, but now, well it seemed as if everyone on the internet was calling themselves a witch. To Sephy this wasn't a bad thing, it was nice that they had come full circle from doing what nature intended them to do, to dying for a noble cause, then being reborn again and again. Each time the stigma surrounding what they were had got weaker and weaker until nobody really cared one little bit, except for the hunters. They didn't forget.

'Can you help me?'

The voice jolted Sephy from her memories. She had a tendency to forget where and what she was doing, which was the main reason she didn't drive very much – she was far too easily distracted and there had been a few close calls with a ditch and a couple of signposts. Turning to look for the owner of the voice, she couldn't see anyone but could sense them hiding in the shadows close by.

'Who said that, where are you?'

She stood tall against the night, looking quite the figure. She was the tallest of them all, Lenny much to her disgust was shorter and spent a small fortune on designer high-heeled shoes. Sephy preferred her boots, she'd always had a passion for red boots which had been replaced with pink once the world caught up and started using colours other than red, brown or black. Looking around, she couldn't see anyone but could feel their vibrations in the air, wavering like a mirage and giving them away. She knew they were out there.

'Well, if you don't show yourself there isn't an awful lot I can do to help you, is there? I'm here for a couple of hours and then I'm off home so you best decide how badly you need my help because I might not be open the rest of the week and I'm not doing house calls or taking visitors to my home.'

Turning back, she took the key for the shop from her pocket and opened the back door, switching on the outside light as she did. It filled the evening sky with warm white light, a beacon of hope to all who were in need. She knew that they would come, they always did, and eventually the owner of the vibrations would pluck up the courage to tell her what it was they so badly needed.

4
SALEM, 1764

Ambrose Corwin had been restless on this voyage in a way he hadn't been during any of the previous ones. As the schooner he was captain of sailed into the port of Salem town, he had been hit by such a strong sense of having been here before it caused him to bend over double as all the air expelled from his lungs. A rough hand clapped against his back, almost tipping him off balance.

'What's up with ye, captain, a little late to lose your sea legs now?'

He straightened up, adjusted his shoulder-length hair that was tied back with a piece of thin ribbon and straightened his tricorne so the hat looked as respectable as it should. He smiled at John Beckett, his lieutenant and second in command.

'I have never felt better, Beckett.'

'Seems to me you are telling lies, captain, but I'll not argue with you over that one, your face is as white as the driven snow.'

Beckett walked away, leaving Ambrose staring at the portside. He closed his eyes and was there walking up and down it, a lad of maybe sixteen or seventeen waiting on the merchant ships to dock. He saw himself bartering with sailors and passengers, exchanging coins for books, he saw a forest and somewhere in that forest was a small, rough cabin with lots of books. The memories so real, so vivid, he lifted the back of his hand to feel his brow in case he was coming down with a fever. It was then his gaze fell upon the most beautiful woman he had ever set eyes on. She had hair the colour of a black bird, hanging down her back in loose curls, and a lace cap on her head. Tucked under one arm were some books and she was smiling at a small girl who was staring up at her with her palm outstretched. This beautiful lady took out a small purse from the pocket of the emerald gown she was wearing and passed the child some coins. The child did a small curtsy then ran off before her kind benefactor could change her mind. As the lady looked up, she saw Ambrose watching her and gave him a coy smile and a small wave of her gloved hand, then turned and walked out of his life, taking his heart with her at the same time. Ambrose knew that woman even though he had never set eyes on her before in this lifetime that he knew of, and pushed to get to the gangplank as the ship was being tied to its moorings along the dockside. He looked at the deckhands who were being too slow.

'Put your back into it, lads, I need to disembark now.'

No sooner had the narrow planks settled than he was off running, his cap in his hand to stop the sea breeze that was blowing across the churning waters of the bay from taking it. He knew he was acting irrationally, but he could not let her get away from him, he must speak with her. He looked around; she was nowhere to be seen, but the child was there on the corner of the wharf with a younger boy.

'You, did you see where the woman went who gave you the coins?'

She shook her head. 'What woman?'

'I do not want your coins, and I do not want anything other than to know how to find her.'

The girl looked at the boy, who shrugged his shoulders as he held out the palm of his grubby hand. 'I can show you where she lives.'

Ambrose pushed a hand into his pocket and pulled out a small foreign coin that he doubted would be of much use to the boy and handed it over. The boy lifted it up to his face and studied it, decided it would do and pushed it into his pocket.

'Follow me.'

'Thomas.' His sister's voice was stern. 'You better not, her aunts will curse you.'

Thomas laughed. 'Those wild ladies will not, they like me, Bridget, so mind yourself.'

Ambrose watched the children intently, wishing he had siblings he could bicker with, then he reminded himself why he was watching them.

'I am in a hurry.'

'Follow me then, captain, and do not listen to my sister.'

The boy took off much faster than Ambrose had expected, who followed as best as he could through the bustling crowds. Turning back to take a look at his ship, he saw Beckett watching him, hands on his hips, head shaking from side to side but with a grin on his face. Then Ambrose was pushing through the people to keep up with Thomas, the crowds thinning out as they got inland, and he found himself following the boy through a maze of narrow streets.

'Are you leading me a merry dance or do you know where she lives?'

'I know. I have better things to do with my time than take you on a chase through Salem for no good reason.'

Ambrose smiled. Young Thomas reminded him a little of his younger self. Eventually he found himself on a large expanse of hilly grass. There were several houses dotted around the edges of it. Thomas stopped and pointed to one furthest away with a white picket fence around it.

'That's where she lives, her mother and two aunts live there, and they will likely chase you away unless you know them or need their help.'

He turned to Thomas. 'What kind of help?'

'If you are sick, they can make you better, they can give you a spell to make you fall in love, they can give you the pox too if you are a bother to them.'

'Can they now, are you telling me that they are witches?'

Thomas lifted a finger to his lips. 'Shh, we do not use that word here in Salem. Any person called a witch is sure to suffer a terrible fate. They used to swing anyone like that from the end of a rope and it is all very terrible. We call them healers, but never, ever witches.'

Thomas gave a quick bow to Ambrose then turned and ran away, back to his sister no doubt, and Ambrose found himself walking across the grassy field to reach the house that seemed familiar, yet he knew he had never been here.

Before he even reached the gate to the house the woman of his dreams appeared, her emerald gown replaced with a simple grey linen dress and her beautiful curls tied back in a manner almost identical to his. She stared at him for a few moments, her striking green eyes narrowing slightly.

'Why have you followed me home, sir, I do not know you?'

He paused; how could he say what he wanted to say to her when he did not know her either?

'I am Captain Ambrose Corwin, at your service.' He performed a bow similar to the one Thomas had made minutes before.

She laughed and it was the most beautiful sound he had ever heard.

'And what service would that be?'

He stumbled, he did not know and found himself staring into her eyes, mesmerised as if in some kind of trance. The sound of flapping wings broke his gaze as a big black crow swooped down to land on her shoulder, making his entire body jolt backwards.

'Shoo, get away, bird.' Ambrose waved his hands at the crow, which made the woman laugh even more.

'You cannot chase him away; he is not scared of you, and he is my pet. Hades, this is Captain Ambrose, he is at our service.'

Ambrose stared at the woman. 'You have that wild bird as a pet?'

She pulled a face at him, lifting a hand to stroke the bird's glossy black feathers and whispering, 'Hades, he means no harm. I think Captain Ambrose is under a spell of some kind.'

'What kind of spell would that be, miss, I do not even know your name.' But a voice inside his head whispered *Isadora* and he wondered what her answer would be.

'My name is Isadora English and, forgive me, but have we met before? You do seem familiar the longer I look at you.'

Ambrose could not lie, he had never met her before, yet he knew her name, he knew her beauty and he wondered perhaps if he was enchanted. If she was a witch as Thomas had claimed, had she put a spell on him when their eyes had locked down by the port?

'I feel as if we did know each other perhaps in a different time. This may sound strange, and forgive my forwardness, but I think I am in love with you, Isadora English.'

Ambrose smiled to himself at that particular memory, which he had managed to store at the back of his mind forever, releasing all the others he hadn't realised he had, he had indeed known this woman and loved her more than life itself. He had kept his promise to Isadora and not told a soul about her mother's spell book. After Dora had been taken from him the first time in 1692, six months later he had gone looking for his hidden bookstore to see if there was a way to bring her back, but things had changed. The woods were much denser, thicker and the brambles so thorny they had taken over all of the old paths he'd known, making it impossible to find. He had spent days searching for the right path; he needed that book, perhaps it could make things right.

5

LONDON, PRESENT DAY

Dora was awake early. She liked to peruse the flower market at Columbia Road. Taking in its heady scents and beautiful blooms never failed to chase the cobwebs away. She hadn't slept very well; she'd had vivid dreams about being chased through the woods by men with dogs and had woken several times. Eventually, she'd given in and got up for a cold shower to wash the lingering memories away.

The thought of grabbing a hazelnut latte and wandering along the road through the bustling stalls was already making her feel better. The smells were overpowering, but in a good way. She could have taken her van, but she didn't really need any stock unless something took her fancy. She just wanted to be out there doing what she loved in a place that made her feel warm and fuzzy.

As she dressed, Lenny's offer of a holiday to the States lingered on in her mind. She was tempted. How amazing would it be to visit Salem? She'd always had this deep longing inside her to go visit there though she'd never told anyone about it. It was strange that Lenny suddenly had a work trip that was going to involve a visit to Salem. She got off the tube at Queensbridge

Road and headed for Queens Deli to grab her coffee. Waiting in the queue, the faintest whiff of Bleu de Chanel filled her nostrils and she tried to ignore it. There must be thousands of men in London who wore that particular brand of aftershave. It didn't mean anything at all. Ordering her coffee and a cinnamon roll to go, she couldn't ignore the sensation of eyes prickling the soft skin on the back of her neck and she knew she was being watched and gave in. She turned around slowly and saw him sitting at a table not too far from her. She wouldn't say he was staring at her, but he was looking in her direction. She smiled at him then turned away, wondering what he was doing here. Of all the places he could be eating breakfast in a city the size of London, what were the chances that he just happened to be here?

'Hazelnut latte, warm cinnamon roll to go.' The barista shouted so loud it made her jump.

'Yes, please, that's me.' She took the cup and warm bag and, turning around, she realised that she couldn't avoid him, he was sitting at the table nearest the exit. He looked up again at her and this time she waited until their eyes met, he smiled.

'Dora, isn't it? From the flower shop.'

She nodded. 'Yep, guilty as charged. How are you, George?'

'I'm okay, why don't you take a seat and eat your breakfast. Or are you in a rush?'

Dora couldn't think of anything worse than having to eat in front of a complete stranger. She wasn't sure if she could make small talk without mentioning his recently deceased girlfriend and the awful mess she'd made of yesterday, but she was a pushover and didn't want to offend him, so she pulled out the chair opposite and sat down.

'I don't want to disturb you.'

'You're not, so what are you doing here? Let me guess, this place makes the best coffee in London.'

She laughed. 'Well, it's pretty good, but not even close.'

He looked perturbed. 'Oh, do you live around here then? It's quite some way from your shop?'

It was an innocent question, but it prickled at her skin, like some uncomfortable needle scratching at the surface. She shook her head.

'I've come to take a look at the flower market.'

'Of course, I'm such an idiot. I completely forgot it was Sunday.'

'Well, that's understandable, you have a lot going on.'

She sipped at the coffee, inhaling the aroma deeply before each sip and savouring it. He was attractive, there was no doubt about it. She burned her lip on the hot coffee and managed to spit it all over herself in the most unladylike manner. He pushed some napkins towards her and she blotted the brown liquid off her cream scarf.

'I'm so clumsy. Sorry, did I get you?'

He laughed. 'No, I'm good but thanks for asking.'

She stood up, feeling the heat radiating from her cheeks in waves. 'Well, it was lovely to see you again, take care.'

'You're not going already, are you? How about I come to the flower market with you? I need a change of scenery and some fresh air.'

Dora wanted to say no, she was happy on her own, but he was already standing and downing the last of his flat white. She should refuse. She didn't know him; she had come here to clear her own head and now she was going to be stuck with him making awkward conversation until she could get rid of him.

'Of course.'

Leading the way out of the shop she forgot her cinnamon roll, but he followed her out waving the brown paper bag at her. 'Your breakfast, it's the most important meal of the day.'

Nodding, she took it from him, opened her handbag and dropped it inside. She began walking towards Columbia Street and he followed.

'How long have you been a florist?'

'Since I was four, possibly younger.'

He stopped walking. 'What, how can you have been one then?'

'I've always loved flowers and plants. Lenny used to let me grow seeds on the windowsill and choose the plants and flowers for the apartment, it's something we used to do together, and I loved it. I'd even grow those little pots of chillies and peppers.'

'Lenny, is he your father?'

Dora laughed. 'God, no she's my aunt, although sometimes I wonder because she can be so strict.'

'That's a strange name for a woman.'

'Not really, it's short for Lenora which she hates because it's so ladylike, she shortens it to Lenny. If you saw her, you'd realise that she is definitely not a Lenora.'

He grinned at her. 'She sounds like quite a woman, I'd like to meet her.'

She nodded, wondering at his strange reply. Why would he want to meet Lenny because she disliked her name? 'She's quite something.' She decided not to tell him anything else about her family.

An abundance of floral scents filled Dora's nostrils, making her sneeze and signalling their arrival at the flower market. She led the way among the stalls, pausing to look at everything but not buying anything at all. George stopped at a stall selling cottage garden plants and flowers and picked up a bunch of beautiful periwinkles and forget-me-nots so blue they looked out of place against the gloomy sky. Plucking up some fern leaves and sprigs of rosemary, he passed them to the vendor, and Dora wondered at his strange choice of blooms. When they reached the end of the market, he handed them to her.

'What are these for?'

'Pretty flowers for a beautiful lady.'

'Thank you, but there's no need.' She tried to pass them back to him, but he held up his hands.

'I insist you have them; I have no need for them. I have no one else to gift them to and I thought that they suited your personality just right.'

'Thank you, that's very kind.' Dora was wondering what peculiar behaviour he was exhibiting for a recently bereaved boyfriend, but she didn't say it. She had heard that grief made people do all sorts of weird things, maybe he was in denial.

'How about I come back to your shop with you, and we can try to think of a more appropriate floral arrangement for the funeral?'

She thought George was handsome, and he definitely smelled good, but there was something about him that she couldn't put her finger on, and she shook her head.

'I'm sorry, I'm meeting my friend. The shop isn't open until tomorrow, it's Sunday, I don't work them, got to have a day off now and again.'

'I'll pay you double, triple, what the cost of the arrangement is.'

Dora paused. The money would be very handy after the month she'd had and it was tempting, but her heart never listened to her head.

'Don't be silly, come tomorrow morning and we'll sort it out then.'

He stared at her a little too intensely with his big brown eyes but nodded.

'Of course, sorry. I keep forgetting what day it is, tomorrow it is then.'

He turned and walked away. She finished her latte and threw the cup into the recycling bin outside the tube station. Looking around to see where he was, she couldn't spot him, but she felt as if he was still there somewhere, and he was watching her. A cold shiver ran down her spine, and taking out her phone she rang Katie.

'Hey, what are you doing right now?'

'Dora, it's not even nine o'clock and it's Sunday morning. I'm not doing anything, I'm in bed.'

'Oh, sorry, I forgot it was so early. I wanted to ask you a favour, but I'll speak to you later.'

'No, you never ask for a favour. What do you want?'

'How do you fancy running the shop for me for a few weeks while I go on holiday?'

Laughter filled her ear. 'You're funny, you never go on holiday, and I know nothing about flowers. You're not being serious, are you?'

'Yes, I am. Lenny has to go to the States for work and I thought I might tag along if you could manage the shop. I can show you how to make basic bouquets and arrangements, I'll put a post up on Facebook and Instagram saying collections from shop only while I'm away. What do you think?'

'I think you're nuts, Dora, but does this position pay?'

Dora smiled. 'Of course.'

'Then I'll give it a go, but don't turn around and blame me if it all goes horribly wrong and your customers start buying their flowers from M&S online. I'm not ashamed to tell you that I will honestly only be doing this for the money, not because of some weird friendship loyalty that I owe you.'

Dora laughed but at the same time hoped to God that Katie wouldn't be that bad at basic flower arranging. She was always the arty one at school so she should be okay.

'I won't and you'll be fine. When can you come to the shop so I can show you?'

'Ooh, in an hour. I need to shower and eat something, is that okay?'

'Perfect, thanks, Katie.'

Katie hung up and Dora wasn't quite sure what else was

going to happen to her today because up until to now it had been the strangest Sunday morning that she had ever spent. What was it that Lenny was always saying, *Be careful what you wish for?* Hadn't she been wishing for her mundane life to be more interesting and to maybe meet a handsome man, go on holiday? What she hadn't wished for was a handsome man who was grieving, not to mention a little bit weird, plus a holiday with her aunt, but she supposed she'd take what she could get and be thankful at the same time. She didn't know how she felt about George and his strange behaviour but at least if she went on holiday, he would lose interest in her. He would be a distant memory.

6

Dora unlocked the shop door and stepped inside her tiny world of bliss. She smiled whenever she first walked inside, it was hard not to. She loved her little slice of heaven. She placed the flowers George had bought for her on the side. She didn't really stock any of the flowers that were bunched together, there wasn't much call for them in the bouquets she made, but they were very pretty. She did stock tiny herb plants – rosemary, lavender, bay and mint were her most popular sellers. But not in October, in fact she wasn't even sure that forget-me-nots and periwinkles were in season. She went out the back into the tiniest kitchen in London and filled the kettle, thinking Katie would no doubt need a large mug of tea to get her in the mood to pay attention. Dora took two mugs out of the small pine cupboard and placed them on the draining board. The bells above the door tinkled.

'Blimey, this is early for a Sunday. I hope you've got the kettle on, Dora.'

Dora turned, took three steps and held up the large mug that Katie used whenever she came to the shop, waving it in the air.

'Your wish is my command, thank you for coming.'

Katie looked as effortlessly beautiful as always. Her honey-coloured hair was in a high ponytail and she was wearing jeans, a black polo neck and a pair of Gucci trainers, teamed with simple gold hooped earrings. She crossed the room and gave her a brief hug. They had met at college, Dora taking art classes and Katie business skills, both of them bonding over a love of horror movies and cheese salad baguettes.

'You're my friend, if you need help then I'm here for you. Although I'm not sure our friendship will survive you leaving me in charge of your shop for a few weeks.'

Dora laughed. 'I'm sure it will, what's the worst that could happen?'

'Let's not even think about it, just promise me you'll still speak to me when you come home.'

'I promise, honestly, you'll be fab. I have no weddings and if anyone needs funeral flowers you can tell them to go to Ivy & Rose down the high street. Oh, actually.'

'Actually?' Katie rolled her eyes at her.

'Actually, there may be a funeral, but hopefully it's before I leave, and I'll get it sorted. Although to be honest the guy is a little weird.'

'Weird?'

'He's lost his girlfriend.'

'Don't be so mean, Dora.'

'I'm trying not to be, but he acts strange. He was at Queens Deli this morning when I called in on the way to the flower market.'

'What's weird about that? He might be grieving but he's still got to eat.'

'I don't know, I can't be specific, but he walked through the market with me and bought me those.' She pointed to the flowers she'd put on the side. 'He said pretty flowers for a pretty lady or something like that. Grieving boyfriends don't move on that fast, do they?'

Katie laughed. 'Oh, Lord. Dora, you do know how to pick them. Bless him, maybe he's just being kind.'

'Thanks, what are you trying to say?'

Katie nudged her. 'Nothing, leave the guy alone, grief can make people act strange. Right, pass me my tea then you can talk me through the basics while I drink it and then we'll get started making up the bouquets.' She let out a loud squeal, making Dora jump.

'Jesus, what's that about?'

'Nothing, I'm just excited. I've always fancied myself a florist. Having a little shop like yours is a dream come true for me.'

'Oh, well that's great then for the both of us. You've never said before.'

'No, I suppose I hadn't but that was when I thought the world of being a PA was my calling, especially the lunchtime sex with the wealthy boss...'

Dora shook her head in amazement. 'Before you found out about his wife...'

Katie shrugged. 'Not my finest moment.'

'Well, let's hope nothing as exciting happens while you're here. I think you could do with a little time out from all the drama.'

'You and me both. Right then, show me all your secrets.'

'Erm, I'm not showing you all of them, there isn't enough time. Let's just start with the basics, okay, and take it from there. Once you know them you can begin to expand and be more creative.'

Katie nodded and Dora set about talking her through all the different flowers she had in the shop. They spent the rest of the day laughing and making up bouquets ready for the next few days.

'Well, I think you're a natural. Look at how easy you've taken to it.'

'Dora, I love it. I can't explain but it gives me such pleasure to see the flowers all arranged and put together in a pretty bouquet.'

As Dora began gathering up all the cut stems, the chimes above the shop door tinkled. She looked up to see who had walked in, catching her thumb and finger on the sharpest of thorns and tearing her skin open again.

'Ouch.' As blood ran from the deeper wound, this time the sharp pain took her to a place she didn't know, a distant memory of another time maybe, but she saw herself running through a forest, breathing hard and fast, her arms and legs covered in cuts from the brambles.

'Dora, are you okay?'

She heard Katie's voice, but it seemed so far away and for a split second she didn't know if she was okay. And then she heard his voice, which brought her back from wherever she was.

'Hey, I thought you weren't open. This is the second time I've been past today, and the lights were on.'

George was standing there, smiling. She'd known it was him or she smelled it was him before he'd even spoke.

'I'm not open, I told you this earlier, why are you here?'

Katie looked at her open-mouthed. Dora knew she was being incredibly rude but there was something about him that unsettled her.

'Oh, thanks, I just wanted to say hello again.'

Katie was smiling at him. 'Hello, I'm Katie. Dora's friend. We're not open, she's been teaching me how to run the shop.'

Dora glared at Katie, who stopped talking. George walked towards Katie, holding out his hand, and she giggled and held hers out. Without a second's pause he took it in his and lifted it to his lips, brushing his mouth against the skin in what Dora could only describe as a seductive way. Every hair on the back of her neck began to prickle with unease.

'Oh, how lovely and very exciting. Not only is this the sweetest little flower shop, it's also run by two of the fairest maidens of them all.'

He tilted his head ever so slightly, staring at her, and Dora felt such a strong wave of déjà vu rush over her that her knees buckled, and she had to lean against the counter.

'I'm sorry, George, like I said I'm not open. In fact, we've finished up for the day and going home.'

'Even better, let me buy you two ladies supper. I know a lovely little Italian place tucked away behind Belmont Road, it takes you back to a time when food was simple and life a lot less complicated. The ravioli is to die for, and they do a house wine that tastes as good as an expensive bottle of Chianti.'

He was smiling at them both and she knew that Katie was smitten. It didn't take much for her to fall in love; she'd been this way since college.

'I'm sorry, we can't. Another time perhaps.'

Katie turned to stare at Dora, then turned back. 'I'm not busy, I'd love to, but I completely understand if it's Dora you're trying to ask out even though you're doing a terrible job at it.'

He laughed then; a deep laugh that sounded so familiar.

'Well, that would be lovely, and no, I'm really not asking anyone out. This is just me being a gentleman. Dora, maybe another time.'

He winked at Katie and held out his hand. Katie practically tore the apron off over her head and threw it on the counter as she crossed towards him. Taking her hand, he led her to the door, leaving Dora feeling as if she shouldn't let her friend go on her own with him. Katie blew her a kiss with a huge grin on her face.

'See you tomorrow, Dora.'

Dora nodded, not sure what was going on but feeling as if

she was sending her friend away to be eaten by a great white shark. George turned back to look at Dora and winked at her, then they were gone. Dora rushed to the window and peered out. They were walking down the alley, George's arm linked through Katie's as if they were old friends. Part of her wanted to rush after them and join them. What if he asked Katie about her? Katie couldn't hold her own water – after a couple of glasses of wine, she'd probably tell him everything about Dora including her bra size and her last disastrous boyfriend. She didn't like the feeling of not knowing what they were going to talk about, especially if it involved Katie telling him Dora's darkest secrets.

Grabbing her coat, she tugged on her hat, picked up the flowers George had bought her earlier to show Lenny and locked the shop. She could just make out their shapes as they were about to turn the corner and Dora did something she had never in her life done before, she followed them. She knew the Italian place he was talking about, why hadn't he said he was taking them to Marco's? They'd be lucky to get a table at this time of day anyway, it was always packed with the teatime rush. She hurried after them, wondering if she should tell them she'd changed her mind. But did she really want to sit and make polite conversation for the next couple of hours?

When she reached the narrow side street where Marco's was situated, she peered around the corner like some under-cover cop or private investigator. She'd expected to see them queuing to get a table but they were nowhere to be found. Now she was torn. Did she walk past and check they were inside, maybe join them, or did she go home? She had to check he'd taken Katie where he said he would, so she strolled past the busy bistro and there they were, sitting at the bar waiting for a table, a carafe of house wine in front of them. George was sitting particularly close to Katie; in fact, his knee was pressing against hers and Katie had her hand on his thigh. Dora carried on walking, deciding to leave them to it. What kind of man behaved that way when their girlfriend wasn't even buried? What a creep, she would tell Katie tomorrow... And then she stopped herself. Tell her what? Katie was a grown woman just like her, she could do whatever the hell she pleased. This was nothing to do with Dora, if George wanted to flirt with her best friend there wasn't much she could do about it, was there? So why did she have a feeling that something was wrong?

7

Dora let herself into Lenny's apartment. It didn't matter how many times she did this, it always felt as if she was an intruder. Even though she'd lived here as long as she could remember, it was expensive, luxurious, and she often wondered how Lenny could afford such a beautiful home that overlooked the Thames and the South Bank. She could see the London Eye, its neon pink lights in the distance. She loved the South Bank; spending time browsing the second-hand book market was one of her favourite things to do. She had a passion for books that rivalled her love of all things floral.

Opening the wardrobe door, she kicked her shoes inside, hanging up her coat and hat, then took the flowers George had given her to the sink. Forget-me-nots were for true love, periwinkles for everlasting love. Did he know about the meanings of the flowers he'd chosen or was it just a coincidence? Filling the sink with water, she put them in it until she'd had a quick shower. Her thumb and finger were throbbing where she'd torn the skin and she felt as if she needed to soak the day away under the hot jets of spray and a good dose of disinfectant. There was something rather disconcerting about George and she couldn't make up her mind what it was.

She stopped mid-removal of her leggings. *Disconcerting*, where on earth had that come from? She never used words like that, she hadn't realised that she knew words like that. Stripping off the rest of her clothes, she stepped into the shower enclosure, which was almost as big as her bedroom, and under the multiple warm jets that sprayed from every angle possible. She closed her eyes and sighed; this was far better than bathing in an icy-cold stream. 'When have you ever had to bathe in a cold stream, Dora?' she whispered, her voice drowned out by the noise of the water.

When she had steamed the bathroom up sufficiently, she wrapped a fluffy black towel around her head and slipped her soft, cosy dressing gown on. She was hungry so she wandered into the kitchen where Lenny was bending over the sink, her fingers holding the flowers. Lenny straightened, letting go of them.

'Strange choice of flowers, even for you. Where on earth did you find these this time of year?' She was pointing to the forget-me-nots and periwinkles.

'They were a gift.'

Lenny turned, her green eyes staring directly into hers. 'Oh really, a gift from who?'

'The guy who I put my foot in it with about his dead girl-friend yesterday.'

'Hang on, a customer came to see you about a wreath but ends up bringing you flowers. How odd.' There was a look of concern on Lenny's face.

'I'm glad you think so too. He's weird but he smells divine. And anyway I refused his offer of supper at Marco's, so he took Katie instead.'

A look of alarm crossed Lenny's face and Dora was suddenly piqued to know why.

'What's the matter?' asked Dora.

'Nothing, it's just a bit strange. Has he said anything to you?'

'About what? Come on, I'm not a gifted psychic. I haven't got a clue what you mean.'

Her aunt shrugged. 'Nothing, I'm just being silly. That was nice of him in a peculiar way. Did you speak to Katie about the shop?'

'I did better than that, I've spent all afternoon supplying her with tea and showing her how to run it and make up simple bouquets.'

'Really?'

Dora grinned. 'Really.'

Lenny laughed.

'Phew, what a relief then, you're coming home with me.' She began walking towards the bedroom and Dora shouted.

'Coming home, I thought you were going on a work trip to Salem?' Lenny turned around; her normally alabaster cheeks were tinged hot pink. 'Where exactly is home?'

'Did I say home? Blimey, I must be more tired than I thought, it's just a slip of the tongue, dear. I meant Salem, it's my turn to talk rubbish.'

She smiled at her then disappeared into her bedroom, closing the door behind her. Which was a signal to Dora that she was not to be disturbed. Her Aunt Lenny didn't have many rules, but the main ones were: do not enter her room if the door was shut; do not tell lies; and do no harm to anyone. Dora had always found that last one a little odd, but she obliged. She wasn't the harming kind of person anyway. Her aunt had been the mother she'd never known so there was no chance she was going to upset her and make her mad enough that she'd tell her to pack her bags and leave.

Crossing to the fridge, she took out the milk and poured some into a pan. Warming it on the hob, she added a couple of

squares of white chocolate, a dollop of fresh cream and a few
drops of vanilla essence. As she stirred it slowly, she remembered a time she used to stand over an open fire, tending a cast-
iron pot over the flames. Closing her eyes, she could feel the
coldness of the air around her in the wooden shack she called
home. It was draughty, old and had barely any furniture, but it
smelled wonderful, the aroma of lavender, mint and rosemary
filling her nostrils. And then she smelled burning milk as the
hot liquid boiled over the side of the pan and onto the electric
hob, sizzling loudly.

'Aaah, bloody hell.'

Lenny's door opened and she popped her head out, her
nose wrinkling at the stench of burning liquid. Satisfied the flat
wasn't on fire she shut the door again. Dora moved the pan off
the heat and surveyed the mess. Her hot chocolate was definitely hot and if she was lucky she'd have half a mug instead of a
full one. Grabbing a tea towel, she wrapped it around the
handle and tipped the boiling mixture into her mug, then
placed it out of reach while she set about cleaning up the mess.
Opening the cupboard, she took out the cleaning spray her aunt
insisted on making by hand and sprayed it liberally all over the
hob. It sizzled along with the burnt milk, but when she ran the
dishcloth under the hot water tap, added a dollop of washing-up
liquid and swiped it over the offending hob the burnt milk lifted
with ease, leaving the hob clean.

'It's like magic,' she whispered, smiling to herself that she'd
cleaned up without ruining anything.

Taking the mug, she went into her room and lay on the
super-sized bed without closing the blinds. She stared out of the
window at the twinkling lights across the South Bank. She had
no idea what was going on or where these sudden jolts of
memories were coming from, or if they even were memories, but
it was making her tired. She was excited to go to Salem, just the
thought of going on an actual holiday was what was making her

stomach churn with nerves, that and the worry that Katie might
have made a mistake in going out with George. Picking up her
phone, she rang her friend's number.

'Hey, what's up, Dora? You should have come to Marco's, it
was delicious and free. You know free food is the best, it tastes
divine.'

Dora sat up. 'Where are you?'

'At home, why?'

'Alone?'

'Yes, of course, what do you think I am? Do you think I give
out on a first date?' Katie's laughter filled her ears and her shoulders relaxed; she lay back on her bed.

'You didn't take him home with you then?'

'Dora, no I did not. And besides, it's quite clear he's a little
besotted with you.'

'Why?'

'It was like the Dora show for the whole time we were
eating. How old are you, where do you live, have you got a
boyfriend, what kind of guys do you like, blah, blah, blah. To be
honest it got a bit boring. I downed the wine, finished my
carbonara and made an excuse to leave.'

Dora's entire body had gone bone-chillingly numb. 'Katie,
what did you tell him?'

'Not a lot. I told him you were single, but I never gave him
your address or anything really personal. I told him you liked a
hazelnut latte, were partial to a chicken pad thai and would
happily munch on a bag of prawn crackers all night rather than
eat at a posh restaurant. I'm not stupid Dora, I thought that
maybe he might be a bit of fun. But it turns out if he wasn't
talking about you, he was staring into space.'

'Blimey, he sounds odd. Did he talk about his girlfriend?'

'Not a peep. You'd think someone who's grieving would do
nothing but want to talk about their dead girlfriend. You know,
for a guy who looks as good as Luke Evans did in *Dracula*

Untold he's pretty crap at the whole romance thing. Even I would tell you to stay clear of him and I'm not that fussy.'

'What about you, are you going to? I'm worried he might keep coming into the shop when I'm not there and bothering you.'

'Honey, if he buys me expensive meals, plies me with wine then eventually screws me, I'm never going to turn him away. I'll take it for what it is.'

'Katie, that's awful, please don't. And what do you think it is?'

'I'd say it's working his way in to getting to know Dora English without having the balls to ask her out directly. Look, I have nothing else better to do, I can scope him out for you, and if he starts getting all crazy then I'll phone the cops and tell them he's a nutjob. It's what friends do.'

'No, it's not, I don't want you to have anything to do with him, Katie. I mean it, he gives me this weird vibe that he's up to something. He could be like one of those guys off the documentaries on Amazon, *The Serial Killer Next Door*.'

Katie's laughter filled her ear. 'Night, Dora, I love you. You're funny, you know that, don't you.'

The line went dead, and Dora stared down at her phone. She wasn't being funny, she was being serious. She wanted to escape London more than ever now, get away from George with his strange personality and forget that he'd ever come into her shop.

Lenny paced up and down her bedroom. Those flowers were not the usual choice for a man trying to impress a woman... unless you were a hunter. And High Sheriff George Corwin was certainly that. She clenched her fists. Those flowers were a message to her. And this time, Dora knew nothing about what was happening.

How had he found them again? This time they had been so cautious, she had left Salem when Dora had been a few weeks old. They had to go home quickly. They had never been able to find the journal that was the key to Dora's powers. There was a time when they'd thought Dora wasn't ready; they'd made her swear never to touch the journal. It had been their biggest mistake.

Lenny had no idea how they'd beat Corwin. But one thing was for certain, they were stronger together. At home.

8

Dora had never been to the airport before. She had an irrational fear of flying and she had no idea where it stemmed from. When she was younger and Lenny had tried to get her to go on a holiday she'd scream and cry, begging her not to make her fly. As much as Lenny must have been frustrated about missing out on a trip abroad, she had never pushed her. They'd had some lovely holidays in the UK. Dora loved Edinburgh, had been fascinated with the castle and the gothic monuments, so Edinburgh was where they went when it all got too much for Lenny.

Now, as they were lining up to go through security, Dora was beginning to get all clammy. Her stomach was in knots, and she wanted to throw up the bagel she'd eaten for breakfast. Lenny, who was staring into the distance, turned to look at her.

'Dora, you look as if you're about to commit some terrible crime. Why are you acting so shifty? I thought we were over this fear of flying, you had enough hypnotherapy to cure a whole busload of fearful flyers.'

'I'm fine, it's just a little bit of nerves.'

'A little, my dear? If they pay any attention to you, they'll cart you off to get strip searched to make sure you're not concealing a kilo of heroin.'

Dora smiled.

'Look at me. This, all of this, is the reason why it's safe to fly. We are going on a seven-hour direct flight to Boston, it will pass quicker than you could imagine. By the time they've brought the drinks cart around, then the food, then the coffee, then more drinks, you'll be nicely chilled, and we'll be landing at Logan before you know it.'

'I know.'

Lenny grabbed a plastic tray off the conveyor belt, took off her shoes and placed her hand luggage inside it. Dora copied her, kicking off her trainers and dropping her backpack in her own tray. They passed through security without a glitch.

'Come on. I think a stiff drink might help you calm down a little and then a spot of duty-free shopping.'

Dora didn't disagree although she had no money to waste on duty-free. Lenny had given her a credit card and told her to buy what she wanted. Dora thought that she was the sweetest woman on earth underneath her rather grouchy exterior, but she wouldn't take advantage of her aunt's kindness, she would only use it when she needed it. She followed Lenny into the huge waiting area and found herself staring at the multitude of designer shops. Lenny was striding ahead to the rotunda bar and Dora followed, feeling more like a small child than a thirty-three-year-old woman. She tried to avoid looking at all the people and kept her head down, her gaze directed at her feet.

Although her feet seemed to have other ideas. They felt as if they didn't belong to her and at one point when she was trying to keep up with her aunt she thought for just a moment that they were no longer touching the floor, but that was wild, she wasn't levitating in the middle of Terminal 3, it was impossible. Lenny found two seats at the bar facing away from the gates and Dora wanted to kiss her. She didn't though, knowing her aunt wasn't fond of public shows of affection. She sat on the high stool next to her and before she could open her mouth Lenny had ordered a bottle of rosé champagne and a Welsh rarebit toastie.

'What do you want darling, you need to eat something in case the food on the plane is terrible.'

Dora shook her head. 'I'm good.'

Lenny shrugged. 'Make that two toasties, thanks.'

The waiter smiled and went to get their champagne.

'Trust me, a bit of stodge in your stomach will help quell those nerves. The fizz will help too.'

Dora didn't think it would, but she did trust her aunt more than anyone else in the world. She had nobody else. Her parents had died a few days after she'd been born, in a tragic car accident. Lenny had stepped up and taken over. Her aunt had always been there for her, taking care of her, teaching her, supporting her and loving her when no one else would. She'd taught her everything she needed to know, but the subject of her parents' deaths had always been out of bounds. Lenny had said it was too painful for her to talk about it, but one day she would when the time was right. Even though this part of Dora's life had been blocked since she could remember, she wouldn't press her aunt too much, not if it was so hurtful for her. Dora was respectful of everything Lenny did for her and tried her very best not to upset her too much.

When the waiter popped the cork and passed her a glass, she began to sip it, pretending she hadn't seen the price of the bottle and food on the menu. Lenny wasn't usually so extravagant, and she wondered if she was nervous about flying too. Lenny's emerald-green eyes settled on Dora's slightly paler ones, and she shook her head.

'I'm not nervous, I'm celebrating finally getting my niece on a plane to go on holiday. It's been a very long time coming, Dora, I'm proud of you.'

Dora stared at her aunt. Her normally wavy, wild, silver hair was in a sleek chignon, and she was wearing a black trouser suit. She was the essence of pure style and Dora thought that she'd look quite at home in a *Vogue* photoshoot. It was then that she realised her aunt had read her mind, something Lenny was annoyingly good at.

'Did I say that out loud?'

'No, you really need to work on hiding your emotions. You're like an open book, Dora, anyone can see what you're thinking.'

'They can?'

Lenny tipped her glass to her lips and drained it, then lifted the bottle out of the ice bucket and refilled it.

'Yes, they can. It's such a lovely innocent trait but it's going to get you into trouble when you don't want people to see inside your soul who have no business looking. And, my dear, there are people out there who love to look into innocent souls, they thrive off it and take great pleasure from trespassing into our most intimate selves.'

Dora took a sip of her champagne. 'See into my soul. You say the strangest things sometimes, Lenny, where do you get this stuff from?'

Lenny laughed. 'I do, when you've been around as long as I have you get a little muddled, it's to be expected. Sometimes I forget how little you remember. I can't wait to show you Salem. Thank God it's a gorgeous place now, it wasn't always. At one point it was a pit of human depravity and bitterness, but those days have gone. I have some, actually, *we* have some family over there who I want you to meet.'

'We do? Since when? And why have you never mentioned this before? Who are they?'

'I didn't mention it because there was little point when you wouldn't travel on anything other than a bus, car or train.'

Dora felt a stabbing pain inside her heart at this somewhat

casual revelation. Why had she not known she had other family members? Why had Lenny felt the need to keep this important information from her? She had missed out on so many years of getting to know them. But it did explain the feelings she'd had since she was a child of never quite being alone, the occasional flashes of her doing impossible things she knew she never had. When she had told her aunt about the two women who looked like Lenny that she sometimes saw in her dreams, Lenny had told her it was her overactive imagination. But had those been actual memories she'd blocked out now resurfacing?

This time it was Dora who drained her glass. 'You really are full of surprises, Lenny; all this time I thought it was the two of us and now you're telling me I have more family. Who are they?'

Lenny smiled, reaching for the bottle and refilling Dora's glass. 'Honey, you have no idea. You have another aunt.' Dora raised her eyebrows in surprise. 'But that's all I'm saying until we get there, okay?' Dora nodded her head, intrigued. 'It's far easier for you to meet them in person than me try and tell you about them,' Lenny said.

The waiter interrupted them with their toasted sandwiches and Dora's stomach let out a loud growl. She hadn't realised how hungry she was. Maybe the fizz had loosened her up, or had it been Lenny's revelation that they had family out in Salem? She had thought it had been her and Lenny against the world, no one else but the two of them. As she nibbled her toastie she glanced at her aunt, wondering how many more secrets she had kept from her and what this other aunt was like. She knew better than to keep asking Lenny because she would clam up and not say another word. If her aunt was anything it was stubborn.

9

SALEM, PRESENT DAY

Sephy lovingly peeled and chopped the squash, carrots and onions, grinding the freshly picked herbs from the garden. She put them all into the pot ready to make a hearty autumn broth for Lucine. Humming to herself as she worked, she felt lighter knowing that Lenny was bringing Dora home, where they both belonged, where they had always belonged. No matter how far the pair of them ran, Salem always drew them back.

As she stirred the vegetables into the slow cooker, she smiled, remembering the days she would cook in a huge cast-iron pot, over an open fire of wood chopped from the forest and brought back to their cottage by the armful. Electricity had been a welcome necessity, but food cooked over an open flame would always win on the taste test. Closing her eyes, she whispered her intentions for the broth – filled with love, healing and warmth it would be delicious as long as she didn't overcook it.

This life so far had been the most peaceful yet lonely. She counted on her fingers. The year 1692 was the first time they died, well were murdered. This was their eighth life. They had lived through so many changes, had seen so much history, some good, some dreadful, but they always died young. They always lost Lucine first, and then Dora. Dora was cursed never to live past thirty-five years old. It didn't matter what they tried, Corwin eventually tracked her down again and again, leaving Sephy and Lenny to live until they were sixty if they were lucky, then usually dying in some terrible accident. He had cursed them with this in 1692 – promising to never let them rest, never let them be happy. Life was supposed to be a wonderful thing, but sometimes life was not as good as you imagined. Especially not if you spent most of it without your family, or watching your niece, who had all the potential in the world, die far too young.

They had always known Dora was the key to breaking the curse. But year after year nothing had changed. They'd forced her away from Salem this time, hoping it would bring her memories, her powers, back quicker – and stronger. But if anything the opposite had happened. Still, Dora had no idea who she was. Of the power she held. Of the curse on her. Of the time running out.

Mrs Pitcher was coming over to sit with Lucine for a while so Sephy could meet Lenny at the airport. She didn't particularly enjoy driving into Boston, especially the airport, which was such a busy, horrible place, but she couldn't leave them stranded and she knew how much Lenny disliked the train. Plus she was too excited to see Dora.

There was a knock at the door. Sephy looked at the cat who was lying on her side and purring on the rug. *Be nice to Mrs Pitcher, Ophelia, no jumping on her and no scratching. You know she doesn't like cats.* Ophelia glanced at Sephy then turned away and began cleaning herself which Sephy took as a direct refusal to be nice. Wiping her hands on her apron, she rushed to the front door and opened it wide, smiling at her neighbour. Well, Mrs Pitcher lived a few houses down but still she was the closest neighbour who would come into Sephy's home, and as far as Sephy could tell she didn't have links back to the witch trials, which meant she trusted her.

Mrs Pitcher looked around the hallway, peering around Sephy.

'The cat is on her best behaviour, she's been warned.'

'She is?'

'Absolutely. I'm sorry about the last time you were here, and she caught your pantyhose. She's a playful thing at times.'

Mrs Pitcher didn't look convinced and Sephy didn't blame her. Ophelia had purposely clawed the woman's calf when she had sat down on her favourite armchair. The scratch had bled, a long thin line of blood. Not today. Mrs Pitcher was prepared, wearing thick black corded trousers and a long-sleeved jumper. Sephy led her into the kitchen.

'Please help yourself to anything, except the jars of tea in the end cupboard. They haven't been labelled yet and the wrong one could give you an upset tummy. There is a box of store-bought tea bags in the cupboard and a jar of coffee. Lucine is fast asleep and probably won't wake up before I'm home, but if you could make sure she's okay and has everything she needs if she does, I will be eternally grateful.'

Sephy knew that the wrong tea could give Mrs Pitcher much worse than an upset tummy, but she didn't want to scare her timid neighbour more than she had to. Smiling at her, she grabbed her bag, then untied her apron and hung it over the back of the chair.

As she walked past the lounge where the cat was sprawled out, she pointed at her, then was out of the front door and walking towards the white van she used when she needed to restock the shop.

Turning to look up at Lucine's bedroom window, she felt better to see Hades sitting on the windowsill proudly preening himself. He never neglected his duties when it was getting near to the end. He could watch over Lucine better than any mortal could.

She climbed into the van with a swish of her cape, her pink boots glinting in the early morning sunlight, and Sephy felt an overwhelming feeling of both sadness and happiness. Their lives were always this way, the joy and the sorrow walked hand in hand with the English sisters and always had done. She longed to hold Dora close, she'd almost forgotten her smell. It had been so long since she'd cuddled her niece and sung her nursery rhymes.

She had the book of everyday English spells ready should they have to resort to giving Dora a helping hand remembering the past, but she wished, not for the first time, that she had the original. She remembered the leather journal of Lucine's she used to hold in her hands, and the last time she had seen it. They'd been called out to the captain's house as a matter of urgency to help his wife and had gone without question.

As they had entered the garden in front of the large, two-storey, stately home near to the common, all three sisters had stared up at the criss-crossed windows of the gables on the second floor. Each window bore a cloak of darkness over it that should not have been there. The moon was full in the sky and had illuminated their path all the way there, yet the house was shrouded in shadows.

Seraphina had put a hand on both Lucine and Lenora's wrists. 'I fear this is something that may be out of our control.'

Lenora had nodded in agreement; they heard the anguished moans of pain coming from the second floor and Lucine whispered, 'We have to help her regardless of whether we can save the baby or indeed Sarah. We are here now and to walk away would be unforgivable.'

She stepped forwards and walked into the hallway. Seraphina glanced at Lenora, fear making her eyes wider and her lips so tight they were no longer visible. They followed their sister inside, unable to do anything else. They would not leave her to do this alone, no matter how much the voice inside Seraphina's head was telling her to run. Once they were inside, the house became unnaturally still, the painful moaning stopped and all three of them feared they were too late. As they rushed up to the large room that was Sarah's, darkness filled the hallway behind them. Lucine pushed the door open and all three women saw Sarah standing in the corner of the room. She looked afraid, but she was not about to birth a child. Next to her was the captain, his hand on her arm, and standing in the corners of the room had been six of the men that Corwin used to round up his accused witches. But there was no sight of Corwin himself.

'A trap,' whispered Seraphina, fear making her voice tremble.

'Where is the beast you answer to and why are you here?' asked Lenora, her voice bold despite the desperation of the situation.

'We're here to take you women in,' said the captain. 'You have been accused of witchcraft by the afflicted girls and it is our duty to take you to the meeting house to be examined.'

Lenora pulled her shoulders straight and stared into his eyes. 'On whose authority?'

'Judges Hathorne and Corwin. The sheriff has the warrant.'

'If you are here to take us, why do you not have it?'

The men looked at each other, they could not answer.

'I shall ask again, where Sheriff Corwin is?' Lenora stood tall with her arms crossed and Seraphina had never felt prouder of her sister. But it occurred to her that if Corwin wasn't here, he was busy somewhere else, and she cried out, 'Isadora.'

Lucine's head snapped in her direction at the same time as Lenora's and all three of them realised that the reason the despicable sheriff was not here was because he had gone after the most precious thing in their lives. The men pounced, two for each woman, manhandling them out of the door to the sound of Sarah's heartfelt cries.

'I'm sorry, this is not me, 'twas my husband who agreed they could bring you here. Please forgive me.'

Seraphina had managed to turn back to her and nod. What choice would Sarah have had? Men ruled this world, which was the reason she avoided them at all costs.

Sephy shook her head, pushing those memories out, they were too painful. Those following days in the dank dungeon of the jail had left Lucine unable to talk. Lenora had been angry, and had cried so many tears her skin had chafed, but it had done them no good. They had been doomed the moment they arrived in Salem town that night and now here they were, centuries later, still trying to put right the wrongs of that terrible time.

The spell book had been gifted to Lucine but they had never used it, too afraid of the consequences because it contained old, powerful magic. They had kept it out of sight, hidden from Dora, for what reason Sephy didn't know because it hadn't made a difference in the end. Even though they had never in their first lifetime been practising witches, they had still been accused of it.

Sephy's blood had run cold when Lenny had sent the picture of the forget-me-nots. She couldn't have been more disappointed when Lenny had phoned up to confirm that Corwin had found them again.

Some of their memories were happy, and some were terribly sad. Each time they lived it was different yet the same. This time, though, Sephy had known something was wrong. Lenny had ignored her warnings, brushing them off with indifference, perhaps believing it was easier to bury her head in the sand than to actually fix the problem she was hiding from. Now, though, they would put it all right because Lenny and Dora were on their way home, where they belonged. It was time to end it. The English women were stronger together than worlds apart and no one could deny that.

10

Dora followed Lenny off the plane, through the airport and customs with minimal fuss, as if they were invisible. She'd thought it would be a long, drawn-out process, but it wasn't, at least not for them. She turned her head and saw the huge queues behind them, wondering how they had managed to get to the front so fast. Neither of them spoke, the row of cubicles with the customs agents sitting in them waiting to approve the arriving passengers' entry into the US was the most daunting thing Dora had ever seen.

She leaned forwards and whispered into Lenny's ear, 'What if they don't let me in?'

Lenny turned her head to face her and muttered, 'Don't be ridiculous, Dora, you've faced far worse than this. Just smile and don't make any jokes. Unfortunately these people have no sense of humour.'

'Next.'

Lenny snapped her attention to the guy calling her forwards and strode towards him. He scanned her passport, looked up at her and smiled, then asked her reason for visiting before telling her to put her fingers on the electronic pad so it could take her fingerprints. Then he curled his finger and beckoned Dora forward. Lenny thanked him and walked away. Dora gave him her passport and he did the same although he didn't smile at her like he did her aunt. He handed it back and she heard Lenny hiss, 'Come on girl.'

She did, walking away amazed at how easy it had been. She couldn't believe it, she was in the States after all these years of dreaming about what it would be like. If she hadn't been with Lenny she'd probably have squealed with delight, but her aunt wouldn't take kindly to her making a fool of herself.

Next was the baggage collection. Lenny had insisted they take one case only, so they weren't waiting around forever. They found the carousel and, like a dream, the first cases to come around were theirs. Lenny grabbed them both in the blink of an eye and Dora marvelled at her aunt's strength, considering she never went to the gym as far as she knew. Passing Dora her case, Lenny smiled at her.

'Sorry if I've been grouchy. I've never really liked flying or at least not this kind where everything is so damn complicated.'

She turned and walked out towards the exit, then stopped dead. Dora was worried something terrible was wrong, but a huge grin broke out on her aunt's face.

'We have a visitor waiting for us. I told her we could manage but she's come anyway. I wanted to prepare you before you met her, but I guess the best thing for you to do is see her for yourself.'

'Who?' Dora's imagination was running wild, who was Lenny talking about? Some friend, or was it her aunt that she had only discovered lived here just before they boarded the flight?

'It's complicated, probably best not discussed here where we are blocking the exit for thousands of tired travellers. Come, you can see her for yourself and, trust me, you will know it's her.'

'Who are you talking about, Lenny?'

'Your Aunt Seraphina.'

Dora felt her mouth fall open. Her aunt? Before she could say another word, Lenny was out of the huge frosted-glass doors and walking into the arrivals hall. Dora rushed to catch up to her – it was so busy, there were so many people waiting for loved ones and friends to walk out – but then she saw her. Standing alone, her hands crossed in front of her, a tall woman with hair the same colour of spun silver as Lenny's. She was dressed from head to toe in black, with a cape around her shoulders, her hair hanging down in soft curls, whereas Lenny's was much wilder when loose. Lenny was walking towards her, and the woman was jumping up and down, her reflective pink boots looking as if they were hovering off the floor. Dora thought she was the most beautiful, striking woman she had ever seen. She was the image of Lenny but somehow softer around the edges.

'Isadora.' The woman squealed her name and Dora couldn't help but grin, despite the fact that she had never met her before. Seraphina ran towards her, arms open wide, and scooped her into a hug so warm and loving that Dora felt as if she was melting into them and she felt a happiness settle over her that she couldn't explain. Dora hugged her tightly. She smelled of caramel apples, cinnamon and something else she couldn't quite put her finger on. Then it came to her: she smelled like home. But not Lenny's apartment. No, this was a memory buried deep in the depths of Dora's mind. One she had hidden away and being so close to Seraphina had woken it up, or at least a little because Dora still had no idea where exactly home was.

'Let her go, Sephy, you'll scare her to death.'

Sephy bent forwards and kissed Dora's head. She whispered, 'She's such a grouch and a sourpuss, take no notice.'

Dora laughed, not meaning to, but it was true that Lenny was a sourpuss at times. Her aunt let go of her and suddenly Dora felt lost. She wanted to stay wrapped up in those soft arms forever. Sephy smiled at her, and her emerald eyes that were identical to Lenny's crinkled as they lit up. She stepped forward, closer to Lenny.

'Come on sister, you know you want to.'

The two women hugged briefly and huge tears began to form and fall down Sephy's cheeks. They were a sight to behold, both women were stunningly beautiful and tall, and every single person who walked past them turned to stare. It was Lenny who drew away first, but for the first time in her life Dora thought that her aunt looked relaxed. Sephy sighed, then reached out and took hold of both Dora and Lenny's hands.

'Come on, we have so much to catch up on and I've missed you both dreadfully, it's been far too long. Don't you ever do this to me again, I want you both to promise that it won't happen next time. I'm not waiting a lifetime to see you both, ever again.'

Dora didn't understand what she meant but nodded, realising that now she had met this glorious woman she didn't want to ever let her go. As they walked along hand in hand, Lenny and Dora pulling suitcases behind them she caught sight of their reflection and smiled. She was like a raven in between two white doves, her black hair and tattoos making her the complete opposite of her silver-haired, beautiful, unblemished aunts. They had one thing in common though: they were all dressed from head to toe in black, except for Sephy's pink boots. People were still turning to look at the trio as they made their way outside to where Sephy had parked.

The white van was almost identical to the one Dora had for the shop only much bigger. All the cars parked outside in the pick-up area were huge. Sephy ushered them towards the van, opening the rear door and releasing a strong scent of lavender into the air. She threw their cases inside then led to them to the front cab, which had three seats. Dora climbed in and sat in the middle of her aunts, still a bit shocked to have discovered that Lenny had a sister who was so beautiful and that it wasn't just the two of them against the world anymore. She had so many questions for Lenny, but they could wait, she didn't want to embarrass her in front of her sister.

'Seraphina, that's such a pretty name.'

'It is, thank you. But it's also a huge mouthful so everyone calls me Sephy. I want you to call me that, Isadora.'

Dora laughed. 'On one condition.'

'What's that, dear?'

'You call me Dora.'

Sephy laughed, so loud it filled the cab of the van. It was an infectious laugh and even Lenny joined in.

'Same old Dora. I'm glad to see you haven't changed too much, although the tattoos and septum piercing were a little unexpected. But I like them, they're modern and you've put a stamp on yourself that means something to you.'

'Same old Dora... I'm sorry if this sounds rude, but I don't remember you at all. Have we met before?'

Lenny glanced at her sister, who gave the slightest nod of her head.

'I realise this is all a shock for you, honey, so we're going to take it slow. I haven't seen you since you were a baby. You were a feisty little thing then, born with a head full of black curls and skin the colour of beetroot. You practically came into this world shaking your tiny fist in the air.'

Dora closed her eyes; she didn't understand. How had Sephy been there when she was born? Why had Lenny kept everything such a huge secret? When she opened her eyes, Lenny was looking at her with what she thought was trepidation. Was her aunt worried about how she was going to respond to all these secrets and lies?

'Can we maybe talk about this at some point? Why I had no idea about you, Sephy, why it's all been some big secret?'

'Of course, my darling, we will talk about it until you know everything and feel as if you have the answers you seek. First, let's go home and relieve Mrs Pitcher who is watching...' She paused, glancing at Lenny, who gave a slight shake of her head.

'She's watching the house for me. Hades will be so happy to see you, he's missed you so much.'

'Hades, is he your son?'

Sephy giggled. 'He is most certainly not my son; he feels like an errant child at times but he's far wiser.'

Lenny was still watching Dora's face and she didn't know if her aunt was expecting her to have some kind of medical episode. Sephy composed herself.

'Sorry, that really made me giggle. I'm so childish at times. I was hoping you might have remembered him, it would have at least been something. Hades is our pet crow; his wings are the colour of your hair and you two were inseparable when you were a baby. He is just the best watcher that we could have ever asked for.'

'We have a pet crow, one that used to watch me? How did he watch me? Didn't he want to peck my eyes out? I thought they were vicious things.'

'Good Lord not at all, Hollywood has given birds such a bad name, that film especially. I mean, some birds are not very nice, but it depends how you treat them. Not Hades, he'd sit on the end of your crib, or your stroller when I walked you, he'd fly above us, sometimes he'd sit in the stroller with you. He would chatter away to you, and you would babble back to him. He always brought you little gifts too, a sprig of lavender if you weren't sleeping too good, rosemary to make you smile if you were upset. He's such a sweetheart, we are lucky to have him as our watcher.'

Dora didn't speak. She couldn't have even if she'd wanted to because she was too busy trying to recall if she remembered a pet crow that would sit on the end of her crib and bring her gifts when she was sad. She should remember that, surely, she should. Why would she want to block it out and repress those memories? None of this made any sense to her. An over-whelming urge to close her eyes made Dora feel exhausted. She felt so drained she could have curled up in a ball and gone to sleep. The confusion was weighing heavy on her too, and her stomach was in knots, making her feel queasy.

Sephy glanced at her. 'It's okay, we're almost home. The tiredness will wear off once you've been here a couple of days. It's always this way when we've been somewhere and return. People talk about being homesick and missing the place where they live, but this is what real homesickness is. I'm afraid the longer you're away the worse it is, but I have some tea that will help soothe the sickness and exhaustion.'

Dora smiled at her aunt. She was so like Lenny, it seemed they both had the ability to know everything she was thinking or feeling, and it was beyond weird. Her brain felt as if it had been overloaded and she decided to keep quiet until they reached home, wherever that was.

11

LONDON, PRESENT DAY

Katie had thoroughly enjoyed her first day being the sole employee at Vintage Rose. She had sold far more bunches of flowers than she'd imagined possible, and it looked as if Dora might not come home to a locked shop with a sign that read, 'Out of Business'. She smiled as she sipped at the lukewarm mug of tea. Maybe this had been exactly what she'd needed, a complete break from the world of being a personal assistant. Something had sparked deep inside her when she'd made her first bouquet for a customer who wanted a gift for her wife; no wonder Dora loved being a florist so much and it smelled divine in here. Taking out her phone, she wondered if the plane had landed yet and whether she should let her friend know that today's takings had been far more than she'd expected. Mid-text the small bell above the shop door jangled and Katie looked up to see the vision of male godliness called George standing there, smiling at her. She managed to slosh tea all down her front and was relieved she was wearing Dora's black apron to hide the stain.

'Hi.'

He nodded. 'Hello again, how are you, Katie?'

'I'm good, yourself?'

She thought to herself that now was the time he was going to say he was distraught over the death of his girlfriend. Especially because he had never once mentioned her when he took her to Marco's on Sunday evening. He must have been in denial maybe.

'Never better, thank you.'

She was wrong. What was the matter with him? Surely he should be in the throes of grief by now. She understood that everyone reacted differently to death, but to not acknowledge it was weird.

'Have you come about the funeral flowers? I'm afraid Dora isn't here to make them for you. I'm not able to help you either, sorry, I can barely tie a bouquet.'

'I don't need flowers.'

'You don't? Oh, that's okay. Then what do you need?'

He closed his eyes and inhaled deeply; Katie felt a chill run down her spine. He reminded her of someone, but she didn't remember who. When he opened them, his gaze met hers and he stared deep into her eyes. Those brown eyes were much darker today, they were almost black.

'Are you wearing lenses?'

'Am I wearing what?'

'Contact lenses. Or maybe you were wearing them the other day?'

'Why do you ask that?'

'Your eyes aren't as brown; they look totally different.'

He smiled at her and moved a few steps closer to her.

'No contact lenses. My eyes are changeable depending upon my mood. Now where is your friend Dora, I'm disappointed she's not here. I keep visiting and she rebuffs my offer of friendship at every opportunity.'

The air in the shop had become chilly and Katie wrapped her arms around her midriff trying to warm herself up. She had a bad feeling about George, she didn't know what it was because yesterday he had been so charming and gentleman-like. Today he was completely different, and she decided that maybe he had one of those split personalities. Whoever he was today she didn't like him one bit. He made her skin crawl and gave her the urge to run out of the door and not look back at him.

They stood there in silence. He smiled at her as he took another step forwards and she realised he'd blocked her in. She couldn't escape if she wanted to. Not unless she vaulted over the shop counter and made a run for it – which she would if she had to. Dora had told her he was weird and Katie had laughed at her. Who was laughing now? Not bloody her. She watched as he picked up the pair of secateurs she'd used to trim the stems of the roses down with.

'Where is the elusive Dora?'

Katie eyed the shop phone; it was a wall-mounted vintage eighties phone in bubble gum pink. If she couldn't reach her phone, which she'd left on the counter when he'd walked through the door, she could dial 999 on that.

'She went on holiday.'

Confusion filled his eyes. Katie watched, sure they'd turned even darker at the news she'd just given him, but how was that even possible?

'Where to?'

'I don't know, she never said. It was a last-minute thing. You know, one of those getaways that the travel agents stick on a piece of card in the shop window.'

'Hmm, that is very interesting and quick thinking by yourself but I'm not entirely sure that I believe that.'

'It's true, it was so last minute she had to ask me to step in and run the shop. I know nothing about running a flower shop.' She laughed, but it sounded so wrong – high-pitched and on the verge of hysterical.

'And who did she go on this last-minute holiday with?'

She shook her head. 'No one, she went on her own.'

He breathed out a long sigh that seemed to fill the air and last forever. When he put the secateurs back down Katie let out the breath she'd been holding in herself.

'I guess I'll have to wait until she comes back. When will that be?'

'I don't know, she didn't say.'

'For her best friend, I get the impression that you don't know an awful lot about her, Katie. Now, you are either a complete airhead who hasn't got a clue or you are lying to me to protect your friend, which I must say is very, very honourable of you. Far more honourable than I would have given you credit for, but I can't always be right.'

He smiled at her. 'Now which is it, are you stupid or lying?'

She glanced at her phone. She could grab it and run for the toilet. It had an old-fashioned hardwood door that was always getting jammed. If she locked herself in, she could phone the police and get the arsehole standing in front of her arrested or at least escorted out of here. Katie lunged for her phone, startling George who jumped a little and stepped back, giving her a precious few seconds to run to the toilet. She turned and pumped her legs hard, she had to get away from him because she had this awful feeling that if she told him where Dora had gone that he might actually try to follow her. She made it to the toilet, running into the small space she slammed the door shut, catching her own finger in it and screaming, then yanking it out and pushing her shoulder against the wood, drawing the small brass lock across. It wouldn't hold him if he started to kick it down, but it might give her a few minutes. She dialled 999 and shouted, 'The police are on their way, you arsehole, get the fuck out of here.'

Katie looked down at her phone and the back of her throat filled with hot vomit as she realised there was no signal in the tiny room. She slid down the back of the door, her knees drawn up to her chest as she pushed against it with every ounce of strength she had.

'Katie, what's the matter with you? Why are you acting like this? I'm not here to hurt you, I'm here to talk.'

She realised that the end of her finger was bleeding, and felt a hot pain inside it so intense it made her eyes water. She loaded Messenger to try and get hold of someone to ring the police for her, anyone would do. The door moved slightly as he shoved against it and she pushed harder against the wood.

'Get out of here now.' She tried to scream the words at him but all that came out was a weak, pathetic whisper.

'Well, I have nowhere to go, so I'll sit out here and wait for the police to come. Then I can explain to them that this is all some misunderstanding. And when you've had enough of sitting on that cold, damp floor maybe you could open the door and I'll take you to Marco's for a bottle of wine where we can laugh about this little episode and eat creamy pasta smothered in mozzarella and garlic.'

Katie's stomach let out a loud groan at the thought of a penne al forno from Marco's. She'd been so busy today she had forgotten to buy lunch. As her finger throbbed, she wondered if she had lost the plot. Had she acted irrationally because Dora had warned her he was strange?

'What do you want, George? Why are you so obsessed with Dora?'

There was a slight pause. 'I'm not, I just have this feeling that I knew her once what feels like a lifetime ago and I've been really stupid by not telling her this. Do you believe in déjà vu, Katie?'

'Yes.'

'Well, I do too. I also believe that sometimes we are born to find each other and become soul mates. That our destiny is written in the stars long before we even know about it and sometimes you can't fight it, you have to follow it.'

Katie stood up. He sounded sad, and she felt stupid. Maybe he wasn't a psychopath, maybe he was a sensitive soul who believed in past lives and true love, which was kind of corny, but sexy as hell.

'Are you going to hurt me if I open the door?'

'Why on earth would I want to hurt you? I have no desire to do that to you.'

She wiped her eyes, which had tears rolling from them, and tore a strip of toilet paper off the roll to blow her snotty nose. As she ran her finger underneath the cold tap, she never heard him whisper:

'I won't hurt you; I'm going to kill you, but only after you've told me what I need to know.'

Katie turned off the tap, dried her hands on the soft pink towel and ran her fingers through her hair, then she slid the lock across and opened the door.

12

As Sephy drove into Salem, Dora perked up. She looked at the plain white welcome sign on a board on the side of the road and felt something stir deep inside her. Sephy navigated the warren of streets, driving past Dairy Witch Ice Cream store towards Essex Street. The ice cream shop was busy; there was a queue outside with kids hanging off their parents' arms, huge cones clutched like prizes as they licked the drips. Dora had to admit the ice cream looked pretty good and she realised she was craving something sweet. The sign above the shop was her first glimpse of a witch, she was flying on a broomstick and clutching an ice cream cone in one hand. It wouldn't be her last though; as Sephy drove farther every available signpost was adorned with orange and black flags with a silhouetted witch on them.

'They're so cute,' she said, pointing towards a prominent one outside a dry cleaners. 'Are there witches everywhere in Salem?'

Lenny side-eyed Sephy, who laughed. 'There are witches on every street corner, dear. This whole town isn't called witch city for nothing.'

'Not like the old days at all. Back then, you murmured the

word witch and before you knew it Corwin would have you rounded up and put in those stinking cellars of the county jail in a room so small you couldn't bend at the knees.'

'Lenny, you have to let it go. It's been a long time, we never expected things to turn out like they did, but it worked out.'

'Did it? Look at this place, Sephy, all these people cashing in on the horror and heartbreak brought upon those poor souls by that Betty Parris and Abigail Williams. Those little girls started the whole crazy panic. They have a lot to answer for. And for what? Because they got scared their father would find out poor Tituba had told their fortunes as a joke when they were bored out of their tiny minds with their strict Puritan upbringing, desperate for some attention they never were given.'

Dora had never seen her normally cool, calm and collected aunt so angry.

'I can't let it go and neither should you.'

'Then you're going to have a simmering pot of anger inside your chest for a long time to come. I'm just as angry about it as you but I've learned to make my peace with it. You know, maybe it's time you did too, Lenny.'

Lenny tutted and turned to look out of the window. Sephy smiled at Dora and shrugged. Dora had no idea what Lenny was so angry about. It wasn't as if she'd been there. They turned onto Chestnut Street, filled with beautiful old Federal-style mansions, all of them three storeys high with huge entrances in the middle, some with double doors. There was a mixture of styles of houses, many with gardens to the side that wrapped around to the rear, filled with beautiful blooms of roses and lush greenery.

Dora sighed. 'Oh wow, these are amazing.'

Sephy nodded. 'It's nice. I prefer it here, it's steeped in so much history. It was built as a haven for the wealthy mariners who wanted to escape the hustle and bustle of the busy waterfront.

Plus, the houses are mainly single family homes and the neighbours keep mostly to themselves, it's a little more refined than some
of the streets. The neighbours are so busy doing their own thing,
they don't care what anyone else is doing. That's always a good sign
if you want good neighbours. How are you feeling now, Dora?'

   She'd momentarily forgotten her sickness, but the mention
of it brought it back with vengeance, and her stomach suddenly
ached so much she wanted to either be sick or lie down with a
hot water bottle.

   'Not too good.'

   Sephy nodded. She pulled up in front of a quirky pale pink
house with a pristine white picket fence. It was like something
out of a fairy tale and Lenny growled.

   'You didn't?'

   'I most certainly did. And what's it to you? It's not like you
live here.'

   'Pink?'

   'Pink is my most favourite colour after black. I would have
painted it black but that black house a few blocks away in Salem
is enough in this area, don't you think? I didn't want the tourists
mistaking this for that fool Corwin's house and standing outside
all day and night in fancy dress while taking photos of each
other for Instagram.'

   At this Lenny laughed. 'Well, I suppose pink will deter
them although it still stands out.'

   Dora thought it was the most beautiful house she'd ever
seen; it wasn't like the others along the street, this one was set
back from the rest. There was a huge oak tree in front of it and
behind the white fence was a front garden full of pretty pink
roses, lavender, rosemary, basil, thyme, every single herb she
could name and some she couldn't. There was a turret that
looked like a pointy witch's hat, with white windows and sills.
Intricate trellis work adorned the house and the white arch that

led into the front garden was covered with an abundance of the smallest but most fragrant tiny blooms.

'Mayflowers,' Dora whispered to herself. A beautiful porch wrapped around the front of the house, on it a swing and a couple of rocking chairs. She sighed. It was like a real-life gingerbread house. Whenever she'd pictured living in America this was the kind of house she'd imagined.

Sephy opened the gate and stepped through. Dora could smell the flowers and the scent was intoxicating, although there was something else as well. A distant memory of planting the seeds for the herbs, working the ground on her hands and knees, singing while she raked her fingernails through the crumbly, fertile soil. She shook her head; she had as far as she knew never planted a garden in her life but something about this place was so distant, yet familiar. Sephy came back towards her, linking her arm through Dora's, and leaned close to her ear.

'Welcome home, Dora, we've waited a long time to see you.'

At that moment, Dora was almost overwhelmed by such a strong sense of love for the woman standing next to her, even though as far as she knew she was a complete stranger. Lenny was already dragging the two cases from the boot. Sephy walked Dora through the arch, smiling.

'A garden planted with love is sure to bloom for all of eternity. Look at how these lilacs bloom; they knew you were coming home and opened in time for you to marvel in their beauty.'

Dora looked at the lilac bush, its branches so heavy with blooms they were bending in the breeze. They looked as if they were bending towards her. She stepped forwards and gently lowered her face to the flowers, inhaling their sweet, heady smell, and whispered, 'Thank you for being so pretty and flowering for me, you are incredibly kind and beautiful.' A low sigh of pleasure filled Dora's mind. She looked around to see Lenny was already at the front door and Sephy was standing back, nodding her head with the biggest smile on her face.

'Was that you who sighed?' Dora asked.

'No, although I could have. You speak the language of the flowers and it's a rare and beautiful gift. They were sighing in appreciation of your thanks and also, I think, because they've waited as long as I have to have you here. They should have bloomed in April or May, but they didn't, they held on. I think the flowers knew exactly when you'd be coming home.'

Home. Dora felt tears prick the corners of her eyes. Yes, this was what it felt like. She had come home to the place she belonged, despite having had no knowledge of it until five minutes ago.

Sephy reached out her fingertips, trailing them across the delicate petals. 'Did I not tell you she was coming home; I thank you for this glorious display too.' She hooked her arm back through Dora's.

'Magic is truly everywhere. If you open your eyes and your heart you will feel it deep inside of you. It will also find you when you're ready to accept that and let it in.'

A loud squawk from above them made Dora jump; she felt as if she had been intoxicated by the heady scent and Sephy's words. She looked up to see a bird, with midnight-black feathers like her hair. It flew down from the upstairs windowsill it had been perched on, landing softly on one of the branches of the twisted hazel tree next to them.

'Dora, this is Hades. He is our watcher, a very wise and a much-loved member of this family, aren't you, Hades.'

She held out her arm and he swooped towards it with such grace that Dora was mesmerised. He perched on Sephy's arm and stared at Dora, his two shiny black eyes watching her every move.

'Hello, Hades, it's lovely to meet you.'

Hades looked at Sephy and tilted his head to one side. Sephy laughed.

'Of course she remembers, don't you, Dora? He's very sensitive for a bird, aren't you, Hades?'

Dora had always been a little scared of the pigeons that were everywhere in London and would swoop down to land on your head if you weren't careful. But she held out her arm. Sephy nodded at the bird, and he hopped across to sit on Dora's forearm, making Sephy clap her hands in delight.

'Oh, look at you two, you always were inseparable.'

Hades bent his head towards Dora and, before she could stop herself, she bent hers and kissed his small head. He squawked loudly then took off circling around them both.

'Did I scare him?'

'No, you just made an old crow very happy. He's showing off.'

Lenny appeared at the door smiling, her head shaking, showing two different emotions at the same time.

'Will you get Dora inside; I'm sure the neighbours are wondering what's going on. It's like a scene from Harry Potter out here.'

Sephy rolled her eyes. 'My dear Lenny, trust me, the neighbours have seen much worse. Come on, Dora, let's do what she says before her head implodes. She's such a mortal at times it really is hard to understand that she's a bloodline witch through and through.'

Dora laughed and followed her aunts into the picture-perfect pink house wondering if she was ill or if this was all a dream. Would she wake up any minute now with a stiff neck from the plane seat and a broken heart, longing for the life she had just been shown that could not possibly exist? Sephy talked about magic as if it was a very real thing, like it was a part of her daily life, and Dora wanted to believe that it was, more than she'd ever wanted to believe in the tooth fairy or Santa Claus.

13

The inside of the house was as beautiful as the outside, but it was the kitchen that stole Dora's heart. It wasn't as big as Lenny's open-plan kitchen in her penthouse, but what it lacked in size it made up for with everything else. There was an old-fashioned drying rack adorned with bunches of flowers and herbs above a well-worn, but much-loved pine table. There was a matching dresser that filled one entire wall of the kitchen, holding rows of jars with neat, handwritten labels filled with everything under the sun. Dora could read some of the scribbled black handwriting from afar: there were dry flowers of all varieties, herbs and spices. It truly felt as if she had stepped into a fairy tale about good witches – there was even a black cat sitting on the bottom tread of the staircase watching her. She smiled at it, wondering if she knew the cat also. Its eyes narrowed and it turned its head away, and she let out a little sigh; maybe this wasn't a fairy tale after all.

A woman appeared at a doorway and Sephy rushed towards her.

'Mrs Pitcher, thank you. Is everything okay?'

The woman was staring at the cat. 'Yes, she's fine. I tried to check but the cat didn't let me go up to the very top again. I'm sorry but I wasn't arguing with it.'

'That's fine, it's okay, Hades was there too. Thank you for coming over.'

Mrs Pitcher was staring at Dora, and she didn't know if it was her tattoos, nose piercing or just general curiosity.

'Forgive my manners,' Sephy said hastily. 'This is my niece, Dora, and my sister Lenny; they've flown in from London.'

'London, I've always wanted to go there, it looks so exciting on all the TV shows.'

Dora smiled. 'You should, it's great, lots to do.'

Lenny nodded. 'It's a busy place, a lot more exciting than Salem.'

Mrs Pitcher looked at Lenny. 'Most places are a lot more exciting than here, except for this month when it turns into a full-on circus show. But, you know, it keeps the town busy and brings the money in. Are you here for Halloween?'

Dora looked at Lenny. Halloween was three weeks away. As far as she was aware she wasn't going to be away from her little shop for that long.

'It depends,' Lenny replied. 'I'm not sure whether it will be warm enough for dancing naked in the forest under the full moon and sacrificing a child.'

Mrs Pitcher gasped. Sephy glared at Lenny then took the woman's arm.

'Forgive my sister, she has the worst sense of humour. I think she's lived in the UK far too long.'

Mrs Pitcher glanced back at Lenny, who was now studying the jars on the dresser. As they walked past Dora noticed the cat hiss and reach out a paw, all of its claws extended. Sephy pulled the woman out of the cat's reach, turning to wave a finger at it. Sephy ushered the woman out of the door then closed it, letting out a sigh of relief.

'You know better, Ophelia. How are we ever going to have

nice neighbours if you insist on attacking them every chance you get?'

The cat jumped off the bottom step and made her way over to sniff first Dora and then Lenny's leg. She barely gave Dora a passing sniff but when she rubbed her nose against Lenny she dropped to the floor, lying on her belly purring loudly. Lenny grinned and bent down to stroke the cat's tummy.

'I thought you had forgotten me, my old friend. It's good to see you too.'

'Ahh, that's more like it. She's missed you as much as Hades has missed Dora.'

'I like that she's getting feistier in her old age, a bit like me.'

Sephy laughed. 'A bit, you've been grouchy since you could talk.'

'And you've been sweetness and light. We can't all be as happy as you, it's just not possible.'

An overwhelming feeling of sickness and tiredness washed over Dora again, and she pulled out a chair to sit down. She put her arms on the table and laid her head on top of them.

'Forgive me, Dora, in all my excitement I forgot that you needed the anti-homesickness tea.'

Sephy filled a pan with water and lit the gas ring for it to boil. Lenny shook her head.

'You can take the girl out of the sixteen hundreds but you can't take the sixteen hundreds out of the girl. Where is your kettle?'

'This is my kettle.'

'No, it's not, you have an electric one. I bought you it.'

'It's in the box somewhere, you know I prefer to boil my water this way.'

'Well, you better find it because I am not waiting around for a pan of water to boil every time I need a hot drink.'

Sephy tutted but carried on. Dora watched fascinated as her aunt took a jar filled with all sorts of herbs from the middle of the shelf and put two heaped teaspoons into a small tea pot, then she tipped the pan of boiling water into it and stirred. Taking a clear glass teacup, she picked a tea strainer out of the drawer and poured the liquid through it, adding a spoonful of honey before passing the mug to Dora.

'Sip it gently, it will help, then it's best if you go and lie down in your room and have a little nap. When you wake up you will feel much better and more like yourself.'

Dora lifted the mug to her nose and sniffed. She wasn't sure what she'd expected but it didn't smell very nice.

'The worse it smells then the better it is for you, it's the same with modern medicine isn't it, Lenny?'

Lenny nodded. 'It will help, Dora; I promise she isn't trying to poison you even though it looks that way.'

Dora trusted Lenny more than she trusted herself, so she blew on the liquid and sipped, grimacing a little, but it didn't taste as bad as she'd expected. Lenny and Sephy were standing shoulder to shoulder watching her and she was struck by how similar yet different they looked. They both had beautiful skin with no age spots, freckles or blemishes and the only lines they had were tiny laughter lines around their eyes. Dora knew that Lenny was sixty next month, yet her forehead was as smooth as her own and she was half her age. She had always thought that Lenny had work done, but somehow, she didn't see Sephy as the kind of woman who would inject toxins into her skin to make her look young and she looked as ageless as Lenny.

'What are you thinking about, Dora, you're frowning?' Lenny asked.

She smiled. 'Just how beautiful you both are and whether you've had Botox?'

Sephy laughed. 'Good God not at all. We are blessed with good genes, Dora, as are you, and I make a pretty good skin lotion that keeps the lines at bay, which I'll share with you when you're ready because you're never too young to start.

Dora let out a huge yawn. Her eyes were getting heavy and Sephy was right, she needed a nap. She heard Lenny whisper, 'What did you put in that tea?'

Sephy whispered back, 'Just a little something to ease the sickness and help her sleep. We have a lot to discuss.'

Sephy came and took hold of Dora's arm. 'Come on, flower, let's get you comfortable in bed and you'll wake up feeling like a new woman. Lenny, a hand would be appreciated. Maybe I was a little too generous with the valerian root.'

Lenny softly took hold of Dora's other elbow and they both lifted her to her feet. She smiled at them and murmured, 'Please tell me I'm not dreaming; I want this to be real.'

'You're not dreaming, sweetheart.'

They led her up the first flight of stairs, down a corridor where they passed several doors, all painted in different shades of pink. Sephy pointed to the door at the far end, and they helped Dora inside. She could barely keep her eyes open, but the bed was huge, a white cast-iron frame with a big soft mattress on it. Dora sank into it when her aunts lowered her down, managing to kick off her boots as she lifted her legs and closed her eyes. She felt the weight of a heavy cotton throw being placed on top of her and the soft touch of lips as they brushed against her forehead.

'Sweet dreams, sleepyhead.'

And then she sank into a darkness so black she couldn't see anything, but she knew she was safe and loved. She was finally home, which was all that mattered.

14

SALEM, 1692

The small boat cut through the water with ease with Ambrose using the oars and not even breaking a sweat. He was a skilled sailor and spent his days fishing and helping out in the harbour, when he was not scouring the boats to procure new books for the bookstore. His boat and face were not out of place, giving no one cause for concern around the wharf. Isadora lay under the thick, scratchy blanket that he had thrown over her and did not move, trying her best to breathe deeply. The ocean gently lapped at the side of the boat, lulling her into a dreamlike state, and she had not realised that she had fallen asleep until she felt the salty sea air on her face and heard Ambrose's voice whisper her name. She opened one eye and looked at his handsome face, then lifted her hand and gently trailed her fingers across his cheek.

'We are far enough away from the farms for you to sit up now,' he said.

'Where are we?'

The sky was midnight black now, it had been dusk when Ambrose had come to get her.

'The south fields, no one will bother us here.'

She nodded. 'I am weary, Ambrose; it seems a life of adventure does not agree with me.'

Ambrose laughed. 'Izzy, 'tis not adventure that has tired you so, it is running for your life.'

A look of sadness crossed his face that made her heart almost tear in two.

'Why is this happening? I do not understand, all we do, or all my aunts do, is try to help the villagers in their times of need and ask for nothing in return that they cannot offer.'

He let out a sigh so loud it felt as if it enveloped her shoulders with the weight of it.

'It is those girls, they are afflicted and laying the blame on any person who may have crossed them. Those Putnams are the worst, but the Parris girls and Mercy Lewis are just as bad. They have been pointing their fingers at anyone who they have taken a dislike to, and they dislike Lenora very much. She called them out and said it was they who were bewitched after they accused Goodwife Nurse. I thought perhaps they would leave your aunts be because of Lenora, but they are gathering strength in their numbers and accusations. I think that my uncle may have had a hand in it too.'

Isadora looked at him. 'How so?'

'I heard him talking, he is angry that Lenora will not accept his offer of marriage. He is also aware of the size of your homestead and that you have no men to run it for you.'

'I do not understand. Why would she marry him, she loathes him. And what about the size of our homestead?'

Ambrose took hold of her hand. 'You are women who live without the guidance of any man. You keep a distance from the village and the reverend has been excusing your aunts from the sermons at the meeting house because of Lucine's illness. Those girls turned around and pointed their mean, horrid fingers at your aunts and now my uncle, who has been looking for any excuse to get revenge on Lenora for turning his offer of marriage down, has been rubbing his hands together with glee. He has waited for this day to come; I would not be surprised if he prompted those Putnam girls to name your aunts at the meeting house in front of the whole village.'

'Where does that put me?'

Ambrose took her other hand in his; they sat opposite each other, knee to knee.

'When they find you, they will arrest you as well, for if your aunts and mother are witches then are you not one too?'

She pulled away from him. 'Nay, I am no witch, and neither are my mother or aunts, and you know that, Ambrose Corwin. Take me back to the village now and I shall tell them this, I will tell everyone that it is all lies. Those girls are the ones who are in a pact with the devil, just let me get my hands on Ann Putnam, I will show her what 'tis like to be bewitched when I pull every hair from her head with my fingers. How many innocents have already been hanged because of them? Goody Bishop was no witch, not one of them were. They even accused the Reverend Burroughs – 'tis madness.'

He grabbed her hands again. 'I know this, Izzy; I know they are making mischief of the worst kind. I was trying to explain to you what it is like in the village, it is as if they are all scared of each other and pointing fingers at any person that may point them back. And my father is sitting as a judge on the trials, enjoying every moment of it. I hear him talking to the other judges late into the night. Judge Stoughton is enjoying the trials and the fuss that goes with them. My uncle is even worse, I have heard terrible tales of the things he does to get the accused to confess, he hath no shame or no morals. They say they are doing God's work but cannot one person see that only the devil himself would want to see innocent women and men tortured and hanged for crimes they have not committed.'

Izzy began to sob, unable to stop the tears from falling freely down her cheeks. Ambrose stood up and, balancing precariously, managed to lay the blanket on the bottom of the boat.

'Come, let us rest. We can lie here and think about what we can do about it all on the morrow.'

She realised that the fear and the running through the woods had exhausted her, and she did lie down. She patted the space next to her. 'Lie with me, Ambrose, I do not know how long we have together. Let us spend this time as wisely as we can.'

She held her breath as he lay next to her, the boat rocking from side to side with the movement. It soothed her soul; Izzy rested her head against Ambrose's shoulder, glad of the warmth from his body so close to hers. This could be her last night on this earth if the sheriff caught up with her. If she was to die accused of witchcraft she may as well add sinner to her list. Puritans were forbidden to touch one another unless they were married. They may as well stamp 'fornicator' onto her forehead with a branding iron before they hanged her as a witch. Isadora knew she was neither, she was a good girl with a family of strong women who needed no man to make their lives better. They farmed what they needed and grew herbs and flowers to heal the sick. How had it come to this?

'Look at the moon and the stars, how they twinkle so brightly for you, Izzy.'

She looked into the night sky. The clouds had cleared and there was a full moon high above their heads and hundreds of tiny stars. ''Tis so pretty, it looks as if they are shining for us both.'

Ambrose turned to look at her. 'Not as pretty as you. I love you, Isadora English, and I have done ever since I laid my eyes on you when I was four years old.'

He leaned closer, making Izzy's heart thrum with both fear and passion. Their lips were almost touching, and she wanted that more than anything, to feel his gentle kiss. She filled the gap and crushed her lips against his, expecting him to pull away but he did not, he pulled her closer and they lay that way, lips pressing against each other's, hearts racing. Izzy did not want it to stop but Ambrose broke the kiss as if he knew she could not.

She reached out and clasped his rough, warm fingers in her delicate, cold ones and squeezed. 'I have loved you since that day too, Ambrose Corwin, even though you did laugh at me when I fell into the pond and had to be dragged out by Lenora covered head to toe in sticky mud.'

He laughed. 'Oh, yes. You were more mud than girl that day, but still I loved you and I love you now even more than all of those stars up in the sky. I am scared for you; I do not think I could live a life without you in it or your aunts – they are more family to me than mine own.'

She realised that his shoulder was damp, yet it was not raining, and then she lifted a finger to her cheek and saw that it was her tears that had made it that way.

'If they find us together you will hang too, Ambrose. They will not care who your father and uncle are, they will make an example of you. If they catch me, please take care of the book, I know it's important – I just don't know why. The only thing I can do for my aunts and my mother is to keep it safe. I fear if your uncle got hold of it, he would use it for things that he should not.'

'Then they shall hang us together for I shall not leave you alone. We have hidden it in a safe place so they cannot lay their dirty hands upon it. I have never told another soul about the bookstore since the day we let our friends come to buy books. When they asked about visiting again, I told them it had been torn down in a storm and the books ruined by the rain. It will forever be our secret.'

'And I have wished deep in my heart for it to vanish so it will stay hidden forever, it will be our secret for all of eternity.'

Her heart felt as full as the sky full of stars with her love for this boy who was almost a man lying next to her. She could not let him hang with her for no crime other than loving a woman wrongly accused as a witch. She would not let that happen. She knew he must be tired, he went out at first light in his boat to fish. When he wasn't fishing, he was down at the marina buying and selling books that merchants brought in on the boats. Ambrose loved books as much as she loved flowers.

'Let us try and sleep. We may feel better and find some kind of way to get out of this trouble that we have both found ourselves in through no fault of our own.'

Ambrose squeezed her hand gently and let out a loud yawn. 'At least we will have tonight, just the two of us.'

He closed his eyes, and she listened as his breathing began to slow. Her heart was broken despite how full of love it was. There was one thing Isadora English was not and that was a coward. She would not let her mother and aunts face the gallows alone and she would not let Ambrose swing with a rope around his neck because he was foolish enough to fall in love with an English woman.

After enough time had passed that she could move away from him without waking him, she did. Soundlessly, she slowly undressed until she was in nothing but her shift. Rolling her dress into a ball she drew back her arm and tossed it as hard as she could towards the shore, which was not too far away. The boat rocked and she held her breath, for if Ambrose was to wake and see what she was doing he would try to stop her. The dress landed on the stony shore, mere inches from the water, and she removed her boots next, throwing them onto the stones. As careful as she could she put one foot into the cool water lapping at the sides of the boat. Expecting it to be bitterly cold she was thankful it was not. It was chilly but she could wade through it without too much difficulty to get to the shore. The fish tickled her skin as they darted around her legs, her undergarments held high above her. She felt the soft sand move between her toes; it was not as unpleasant as she had thought and for a moment she wondered if it would be better to lie down in this water and let herself drown. It would be kinder than Sheriff Corwin's rope around her neck. But then she thought of her aunts and mother. They should be together; they were stronger together. She would not leave them alone – if she could not save them, she would join them.

As she reached the shore there was a crow perched on a rock, watching her, and she smiled. 'Hades, my old friend, have you come to guide me home?'

The bird let out a gentle caw and took off, swooping towards her and landing upon her shoulder.

'Thank you, take me to them and, when you are done, please take care of Ambrose for me.'

She felt foolish speaking to a crow the way she would to a person, but Hades had been in her life since she could remember and been there for her through the best and the worst of times. She knew he would not let her down.

15

SALEM, PRESENT DAY

Sephy led Lenny to Lucine's room. She knew her sister didn't want to go in and face Lucine alone, she could deal with anything except their elder sister dying. It broke her every time and was the reason she'd run off to train to be a doctor, swearing to give up the old ways that couldn't stop Lucine from dying and instead focusing on learning as much about modern medicine as she could to see if there was a cure there. How devastated Lenny had been to find out that there wasn't, there was no way they could stop what happened to Lucine every lifetime, just as they couldn't stop Dora from growing more distant in hers and dying before the age of thirty-five. Unlike with Lucine, they never knew when it was Dora's time; the curse of the English sisters was not the dying, it was the living through it again and again, being helpless to put an end to it.

There were only two things that might make a difference: if Dora truly embraced her power and they had the book that had been lost to them since that fateful night they had been arrested and Dora had run away.

The book had incantations written inside it that made it possible to call upon the true goddesses of witchcraft. It had been given to Lucine by a man she once loved. She told Sephy he was a circus performer, that he'd left her with child, stole her heart and never came back to return it.

They had never started out to be powerful witches, only healers, but things had taken a turn when Lucine had discovered her talent of talking to the animals and birds. Hades had been the one to bring the spells to Lucine, who had written them down, adding them to the book, all the time pining for the man who left her with child. In the beginning they had never understood why they might need it but she felt compelled to keep a record of them anyway. Hades, the wise and clever bird, had known that evil stalked the English sisters since the day they'd been born on this earth, and that was the reason he had been sent to watch over them. Sephy hadn't yet figured out who had sent him, but was grateful that he had arrived in their lives to take care of them.

Their fate had a way of catching up with them over and over, no matter how far they ran. This time it had been Sephy's decision to run no more, and she'd come back to Salem where it all began, where the High Sheriff George Corwin had ruled so cruelly. But if she wasn't mistaken, he had found Dora, hunting her to her beautiful little flower shop in London, somewhere Lenny had never expected him to find. It didn't seem to matter where in the world they hid, he would track them down eventually and, just like them, gravitate back to Salem to inflict as much misery on them as he could, just like he had back in 1692.

There had been some fierce battles over the years, but Sephy knew that if they could break the curse that wretched soul Giles Corey had inflicted upon Corwin and Salem town as he lay dying, his insides crushing slowly to death from the weight of the stones placed upon him, then just maybe they could put a stop to Corwin and his relentless chasing of their souls through all eternity. What Corey hadn't realised was that by cursing Corwin he'd given him the same immortality that had been bestowed upon them, and Corwin was able to live forever, hunting the hunted.

The English motto was 'Do no harm.' They never used their magic for anything other than love spells, beauty spells to a certain degree, healing minor ailments and generally making the world a better place. Although even harmless spells could have negative results: beauty spells could lead to the beholder becoming self-centred and focused on their looks and not their loved ones. For each spell the English sisters gave out, they always issued a little caveat about the possible consequences. Not that anyone cared about anything other than getting what they wanted; in a way they were all selfish.

The book had never been used. But every lifetime, Sephy, Lenny and Lucine had wondered: was it destined for Dora? Should they have given it to her all those years ago?

And Corwin's own will to destroy Lenny had connected them to his own fate.

That terrible day when Lenny, Sephy and Lucine had been dragged from the gaol into the blinding light and manhandled into that rickety old cart by none other than George Corwin with a smirk on his face had never faded even the tiniest bit from Sephy's memories. The indignity and fear they shared was horrific and, as bad as it was that they were to hang for no good reason at all, they had all been relieved that at least Dora had been saved. Until they'd reached the makeshift gallows up on the ledge and saw Dora already there, hands and feet bound, staring defiantly at her guards. Sephy's heart had truly broken in two at the sight of her beautiful, strong niece positioned with a noose around her neck. She could still hear Lucine's silent screams as they tore through her mind. Before being dragged out of the filth and blackness, all of them had agreed that they would not make a sound and give Corwin the slightest satisfaction, but my God it had hurt their hearts so much to see Dora standing there defiantly.

'Sephy, what's the matter?'

She looked down to see that Lenny had hold of her arm and was gently shaking it.

'Nothing dear, I was just thinking about the bad old days, all of this and how we could put a stop to it.'

'Do you honestly, hand on your heart, think that we could? Our plan hasn't worked – she's more distant than ever.'

'The more I think about it, the more I think it's about that damn book. We need to find it.'

'How do you suppose we could do that? We've tried, we've looked for it. Dora doesn't remember where it is.'

Sephy shrugged. 'Is this why you didn't want to come back? Have you given up?' Lenny was looking downcast. 'A plan has been hanging around the edges of my mind, I need to draw the pieces in and slot them all together.'

'She doesn't even know a fraction of who she is. She's come here and thinks she's in some sugar-coated, candy-pink fairy tale, with talking flowers and animals. Just how much valerian root did you give her, Sephy?'

'She's brighter than you give her credit for. She knows that all fairy tales have a wicked witch in them, what she doesn't know is that in ours we traded the wicked witch for a witch hunter. I only gave her enough to cure the sickness and let her sleep well while we discuss what needs to be done.'

Lenny let out a sigh, so long and deep it was tainted with centuries of pain-filled sadness.

'How is she?'

'I'll let you judge for yourself, you're the expert. Thank you for coming home, Lenny, I've missed you, we've all missed you terribly.'

Sephy opened her arms and Lenny fell into them, tears flowing freely down both their cheeks as they held each other close.

Lenny whispered, 'Your plan, what does it entail so far?'

'It has to do with him. With Ambrose. I can feel him. I think that maybe in keeping Dora away we've made a difference this time. Perhaps her reappearance will help jolt his memory of what they did with Lucine's book too.'

'God, I hope so.'

Sephy reached out, her slender fingers gripping the door-knob. She thought of the boy who had been so in love with Dora. He had been cursed too. Forced to relive his life and to lose Dora just before they fell in love. But maybe this time, when they finally met, he'd remember where the journal was.

'Not a word to Lucine, no false hope or wishes made of star-dust. She's tired and ready to give in, she's only hanging on for Dora. This time it seems to have been much quicker than the last and more aggressive too.'

Lenny nodded, brushed her tears away with the sleeve of her shirt and inhaled deeply. She twisted the brass knob then pushed the door open, gasping to see her sister, sitting up in bed, a huge smile on her face and her arms open wide. Lenny rushed to her and fell into them as gently as she could, and then she was on the bed, lying next to her and sinking into the soft mattress, cocooning her beautiful, frail sister in her warm arms.

Lucine whispered into her ear, 'You came, and Dora?'

'She's fast asleep, in bed recovering from her bout of home-sickness.'

A happy sigh escaped Lucine's lips. 'Thank you.'

Sephy clambered on the other side of the bed and all three of them lay there hugging each other. Finally, Lucine laughed. 'I needed that more than you could ever know but now you're squishing me.'

Both Lenny and Sephy loosened their grip of their sister who instead took hold of each of their hands. All three of them lay there on the bed, silver hair glinting in the sunlight that filtered through the branches of the huge oak tree and through the window, Lenny and Sephy dressed in mainly black while Lucine wore a long white cotton nightgown. She chuckled.

'I always was a rose between two thorns.' Then she let out the biggest sigh of all as she squeezed their fingers. All three of them stared up at the intricate Milky Way on the ceiling that Sephy had spent hours painting by hand so Lucine could always see the stars.

'The English sisters back together, it makes me so happy. It's fate, you know.'

'What is?' asked Lenny.

'That we were always supposed to be like this, whole, a family unit. I've missed you, Lenny, and life seems to be getting shorter each time around.'

Tough, sassy, independent, confident Lenora English crumbled into one loud sob. Lucine reached out and stroked her forehead.

'Don't be sad, I know you have your life to live and that you take the best care of Dora I could ever wish for. I'm not complaining, I'm just saying that I think this is where we are at our best. Do you remember when we were at kindergarten and those boys were always terrified of us?'

Lenny laughed; she did remember. Every fresh school year, they told everyone they were triplets with magical powers and could turn them into frogs if they were mean. They did have magical powers, but they never got strong enough for major spell work until they reached their sixteenth birthdays.

'Those little fools were terrified of us.'

'They were, but they also were very mean, which upset me more than it ever did the pair of you.' Sephy had a tear in her eye, but Lenny knew her sister wouldn't waste it on those childhood memories.

'Sephy, all little boys are mean to some degree. It's a rare thing to come across one with a gentle soul.'

'We do occasionally though. Look at Ambrose. He was meant to be with Dora from the very beginning. He always watched out for her, took care of her and saved her life that day when Corwin went after her and sent his men to the captain to take us to the meeting house to answer those ridiculous charges. Ambrose tried to get her to safety, he is pure goodness through and through.'

Both Lucine and Lenny nodded. Ambrose had indeed been a perfect, rare specimen of a boy, with the cutest curls and the biggest blue eyes. He had protected Dora when they had been unable to. He was the son of Jonathan Corwin, judge in Salem in those times, and the nephew of the witch hunter. His position in their household had allowed him to warn Dora of what was happening. Of Lucine, Lenny and Sephy's fates. Not that it had stopped Dora rushing to their aid eventually, wanting to be with them no matter what the consequences of standing together meant.

They knew that Dora had hidden the spell book that night and had tried over the years to find it, but to no avail. It had simply vanished.

Lucine sighed, 'I can't wait to see Dora. How much does she know, has she remembered anything?'

Lenny shook her head. 'It's the worst she's ever been. There are little bits and pieces that seem to be breaking through and of course she's absolutely awestruck with Sephy and her pink obsession. Just as she will be when she sees you again. It's funny how much you don't realise that you needed the things you never knew about.'

Sephy screwed her face up. 'Good God, Lenny, don't write any poetry, will you, please spare us from that.'

'Are you saying that I'm not poetic or that my words have no meaning, sister?'

Sephy laughed. 'In a nutshell, yes. They're all a bunch of gobbledygook.'

'Gobbledygook. You still speak like that and have the nerve to criticise, really, Sephy, that's mean.'

Lucine smiled. 'You know what we need?'

Both Lenny and Sephy giggled, wide grins on their faces. 'A little black magic.'

Sephy jumped off the bed. 'I'll be right back; I have some already baked and I'll mix up the cocktails.'

She left them to it; Lenny sighed. It was good to be home, she had missed her sisters and this place was far more comforting than she remembered. Lucine rested her head on her shoulder and whispered: 'Thank God you are here, I've been asking for some black magic for weeks and she keeps telling me it's not good for me. I love her more than anything but I'm dying. Who cares what my sugar and alcohol intake consists of?'

Lenny laughed. 'Seems like I came back just in time. You shall no longer be wishing for cake and cocktails. I'll take care of your every need.'

Five minutes later the door burst open and in walked Sephy carrying a wooden tray with a large jug of the blackest-looking liquid that shimmered in the light and three huge slices of an equally black cake with frosting the colour of Hades' wings. There were three martini glasses balanced precariously next to the jug and Lenny jumped off the bed to clear a space on the small bedside table. Sephy placed the tray down and lifted the jug to pour the swirling, shimmering mixture into the glasses. Lenny helped to make sure that Lucine was sitting up and as comfortable as she could be to hold a martini glass. Sephy handed Lenny a glass with a small straw in for Lucine and a glass without one for her. They sat back down on the bed and clinked their glasses together, a little of the cocktail sloshing onto the front of Lucine's nightgown, which made them all giggle.

Lenny raised her glass. 'To the English sisters, our magic

and our lives. Here's hoping there are many more to come and that one day we might actually figure this shit out.'

This set Lucine off into a fit of giggles and soon all three of them were laughing. When they contained themselves, they sipped at the cherry-flavoured vodka drink and sighed in unison.

Sephy smiled. 'This always reminds me of the good times, we should drink it for breakfast every day.'

Lucine nodded. 'Haven't I been saying that for at least the last two lifetimes?'

Lenny downed hers then refilled the glass. 'It's been a hell of a day, but we're home, we're together, and I don't think there is anything else I could ask for.'

Sephy nodded, then passed out plates of cake. 'We shouldn't drink on an empty stomach, eat some cake. I spent hours baking that yesterday, I wanted it to be just perfect. And you're right except for maybe one thing.'

'What's that?'

'Putting an end to this blasted curse. It's gone on far too long. If we can stop that vile man from chasing us across all of our lifetimes, stop Dora dying before she's had the chance to fall in love with Ambrose, well then it would be perfect.'

All three of them nodded, raised their glasses and chanted, 'Here's to stopping the curse and living one more life without fear. One more life where Dora gets to grow old with the man she loves.'

16

Dora had no idea where she was, she lay in the darkness wondering what had happened to her. The bed wasn't hers, it was far too soft. The room smelled of lavender and lemon, and there was no daylight, just a soft blackness that for all of its strangeness wasn't the least bit scary. She remembered the flight to Boston, but not much after that.

Yawning, she closed her eyes. Her stomach didn't feel as if it had been tied in knots, that was one thing. She no longer felt queasy either. A tapping on the windowpane startled her, but she had no idea what it was, so she ignored it. Whatever it was didn't want to be ignored though, and tapped harder. She sighed. What was that – or *who* was it? She really didn't want to leave the warmth and comfort of the bed but whoever was tapping was becoming more insistent by the second.

Lowering her feet to the wooden floorboards, she crept towards the window, her heart beating a little too fast. She had no idea what could be so determined to capture her attention. Pulling one of the soft drapes back a little, she jumped to see a beady glass eye staring at her, then realised it was a bird. Not just any bird, it was... she couldn't remember. What was it, what had her aunt called it? Unlatching the window, she opened it a little and the bird shook its head at her so she pushed it wider. It hopped straight in, making Dora stumble backwards a little.

'Hades, you're my watcher. Or you were my watcher.'

She sat down on the edge of the bed. It was her turn to watch, and she did with great interest. She had always thought birds were scary, too fluttery, but not this one. He didn't flutter his wings much at all. He was staring at her just as she stared at him, and Dora laughed.

'What is this, some kind of crow staring contest? I think you might win; your eyes don't have heavy semi-permanent lashes like mine. So, in reality, I don't stand a chance against you and to be honest I'm quite happy for you to be the winner.'

Hades cackled and tilted his head. 'Winner, winner, chicken dinner.'

Dora's mouth dropped open. 'You can talk? Like, really talk? Oh I must still be dreaming.'

She bent down and pinched her own arm hard enough to sting; she felt it, she wasn't asleep. The bird hopped down onto the floor then strutted across towards her, and she thought that maybe she should get out of here but before she could move Hades flew up onto her leg, staring up at her.

'I don't know what you want, and if I'm honest I'm a little scared too.'

He bent his neck and rubbed his head against Dora's hand, which was folded in her lap. His feathers were so smooth and she lifted a finger and stroked the top of his head.

'Can you talk, or do you just repeat phrases?'

'Dora's home, she's home, she's home.'

'Am I home? I'm sorry, Hades, but I don't remember this place at all. I don't know what is going on.'

He hopped onto her arm. 'Dora's home.'

She laughed. 'Well, if you say so then I'll take that as a yes. I must be home, how long have I been away?'

'Forever and a day.'

'Yes, it kind of feels that way.'

They sat that way for some time, Dora and the pet crow she never knew she had, reunited with each other after how many years? How was she going to explain all of this to Katie? Oh God, she never even rang her to see if she was okay with the shop! She looked at her phone. It was almost seven. She had no idea what the time difference was. Instead of phoning she sent her a message.

Hey, hope today was okay for you and there were no problems. You wouldn't believe what's going on, but I'll tell you over the phone tomorrow, it's far too complicated over Messenger. Thank you for looking after the shop, speak soon Xxx

The message was sent, but the log didn't show that it had been delivered. She decided she would ask Lenny. And then it came flooding back to her: Sephy and her pink boots, meeting her at the airport, the gorgeous house, the warmth and feeling of coming home to a family she couldn't remember. Maybe she wouldn't tell Katie about Hades just yet, it might be too much for her. Blimey, it was too much for Dora.

She yawned and stretched. 'Sorry, bird, I need the toilet and I'm starving.'

As she opened the bedroom door, she heard laughter coming from a room down the hall, proper full-on giggles, and it made her smile. She hadn't heard Lenny laugh like that for a long time and she liked it. Not wanting to intrude, she made her way to the bathroom. She still felt a little out of it, but at least she no longer felt queasy. She splashed cold water on her face to wake herself up then lifted her head and screeched to see Lenny standing in the doorway. Her eyes were shiny, the pupils huge, and she had a smile on her face. For once she looked relaxed although Dora could tell she was also a little drunk.

'Dora darling, how are you feeling now?'

'Much better thank you.'

Sephy came out of the room behind Lenny, softly closing the door behind her with one hand while balancing a tray with an empty jug and three used martini glasses.

'Dora, you look much better. You must be starving. Let's go down and eat.'

Dora stared at the door, there had been several different tones of laughter. Lenny saw the direction of her gaze.

'Whose bedroom is that?'

'Mine,' said Sephy. 'Sorry, did we wake you? We were having a little celebration; it's been so long.'

'Why did you need three glasses?'

'In case you woke up and felt like a little drink, but we were greedy and drank the lot. I'll make some more if you feel like it.'

Dora smiled, she didn't acknowledge that the spare glass had the tiniest amount of black liquid in the bottom or that it had a straw. She didn't want her aunts to think she was being rude, but she knew they were hiding something from her. It was quite obvious.

'Hades. He can talk.'

Sephy smiled. 'That bird used to be such a chatterbox, but he hasn't been like that since you left. He can sulk for England. It must be seeing you again, Dora.'

'How old was I when I left? Because I don't remember any of this. There are tiny memories, from what seem like a very long time ago, just bits and pieces really. I must have been young?'

Lenny gently touched her sister's arm.

'You were a tiny little thing, and you didn't speak much except to Hades and then you babbled to him in a language that no one else understood, but he did. He'd listen and chatter back to you.'

'Why did I leave?'

Sephy's cheeks had been flushed pink and now they were a deep red.

'Is that the time?' She was staring at the large grandfather clock on the landing, the ticking of which had soothed Dora's sleep. 'I really must be going; I have to open the shop tonight, I have a couple of customers who will be waiting for me. Please excuse me, help yourself to whatever you want, and Lenny knows the recipe to make you a little black magic.'

Sephy turned and rushed down the stairs, leaving Dora staring after her. Lenny breathed out the loudest sigh Dora had ever heard.

'Always runs away from anything slightly confrontational, always has done and always will do. I have no idea how her plan is going to work if she can't even face her own niece.'

'What plan? Please Lenny, can you just tell me what is going on? I feel like Alice in Wonderland when she fell down the rabbit hole. Everything is beautiful, strange and it's really making me feel weird that out of the blue I have this whole other life and family that I can't remember.'

'I need more alcohol, then I'll tell you what I can, but you have to trust me that it's not for me to fill in the blanks. I brought you home because you need to remember yourself, Dora, you need to dig deep inside of your soul and find all those memories you chose to forget this time around.'

'I was only a baby, how am I supposed to do that?'

Lenny walked down the stairs and Dora followed her. 'If you don't, this lifetime will end. I can't let that happen, we won't let that happen, but you have to work with us, Dora. On the next full moon Sephy and I can perform a ritual that might help you to release what's buried inside of you, but you have to do the work, we can't do it for you. All we can give is a helping hand.'

Hades, who was watching the women from the banister, called out.

'You have to work; you have to, Dora.'

Dora stared at him. 'I have no idea what's going on. What do you mean, *this* lifetime? We are born, we grow up, we live, we get old and we die, end of story.'

Lenny shook her head. 'That's not technically true, at least it isn't in this family. It's not been that way for the English women for hundreds of years. Don't get me wrong, most mortals do exactly that.'

'Mortals?'

Her aunt waved her hand in the air dismissively, her blasé attitude to all of this making Dora a little perplexed.

'If we are not mortals then what are we?' Dora held her breath, afraid of what her answer would be.

'Immortals. And I'm not discussing this any further until tomorrow. It's been a hell of a long day.'

'What about me? I'm not tired, I just had the world's longest nap.'

'You will sleep once your head hits the pillow. I'm afraid Sephy was a little too generous with the valerian root and lavender.'

'Lenny, am I dreaming or am I going mad? Because I don't understand what's happening.'

Lenny's face softened in the glow from the warm light above her and she stopped at the bottom of the stairs, waiting for Dora to catch up to her.

'No, Dora, you are not going mad, at least not this time. Although you did a very long time ago and that was a terrible time for you, but right now you are as sane as I am. I can't speak for Sephy though, she's always been a little out there, you know.'

She opened her arms and Dora fell into them. 'I'm scared that I can't remember all of this.'

'You will, a little helping hand from me and Sephy when the time is right is all you need. For now, I want you to relax the best that you can. I know this has all come as a huge shock to you but, trust me, you can handle this and everything else that is going to get thrown in your direction the next couple of days. For tonight at least, let's just enjoy being here. Why don't I take you for a little walk down Essex Street, that will take your mind off things and the fresh air will do you a world of good. For all of its faults, Salem is a wonderful little town. Who knows, they might be showing *Hocus Pocus* on the common, it's your favourite film.'

Dora laughed. 'You know, you remind me a little of Winifred Sanderson, probably the same amount of grumpiness but you save lives, not steal them.'

Lenny grinned at her. 'Funny you should say that. I think those Sanderson sisters were probably based on the English sisters, only we didn't and never would steal children's souls to make ourselves look younger, not when there is Sephy's magic cream.'

'Are you saying that the English women really are witches?'

Lenny rolled her eyes. 'What do you think? We come from Salem. Sephy has the oldest apothecary in the city, you have a pet crow that talks to you, and you come from a strong bloodline of English women who were far too ahead of their time for those Puritan bastards who ruled with an iron fist yet were the biggest hypocrites of all. I'll let you work that out for yourself, Dora. Now, come on, I'm getting cabin fever. I need to walk those cocktails off and clear my head before you ask me a gazillion more questions.'

Dora smiled at her aunt. She loved her more than anything and she loved Sephy the same even though she'd only met her a few hours ago. Lenny was right, she felt as if she'd known Sephy forever and maybe she had. She had to trust both her aunts. Everything would be fine. She had all the time in the world to work this out. Didn't she?

17

Salem was alive, the air practically fizzing with excitement, and Dora could feel the energy as she walked through the pretty streets, her boots crunching on the fallen leaves that covered the uneven red-brick sidewalks. The crowds of people dressed as witches, ghosts and ghouls outnumbered the people dressed like her and Lenny. She felt positively underdressed. There was a queue thirty people deep outside a black house with a wooden sign swinging in the breeze that read 'The Witch House'.

She glanced at Lenny who didn't even look in that direction, purposely keeping the pair of them on the opposite side of the street. 'What is that place?'

'It's the only surviving house in Salem from the witch trials. And the bastard that lived there.' She stopped herself from saying anything more, but Dora couldn't tear her eyes away from it. They continued down Essex Street, past a Pennywise, a huge Frankenstein and lots of witches. There were so many shops selling all manner of witchy things that Dora knew her mouth was open in awe at the sights and sounds. They reached what Dora knew, or at least suspected, was the common. The large expanse of grassy park had trees lit up with thousands of orange fairy lights and a huge bandstand in the centre, with lots of small white tents with vendors selling their wares. There was a large hotel called The Hawthorne just before the common with blue and gold canopies adorning each ground-floor window and a giant golden eagle above the entrance. As they walked among the stalls, Dora spotted one selling broomsticks.

'Look. If we are what you say we are, we could get a couple of those broomsticks and fly around.'

'Besoms, Dora, we don't call them broomsticks and, unfortunately, flying's never been something any of us could master. It would be perfect when the streets are this crowded, I'd forgotten how much I dislike other people's body odour mingled with scent of popcorn.'

Dora could smell popcorn, toffee apples and hot dogs but not anything else. She stopped in her tracks as a terrifying Pennywise walked towards her and Lenny, his mouth all bloody, jagged teeth and a handful of red balloons clutched in one fist. Lenny hissed, 'I hate that clown.'

Pennywise stopped in front of them, then did a theatrical bow to Lenny who shook her head. He offered Dora a balloon which she took from him, and he smiled.

'Well, it's been a while, Ms English, how are you keeping? I've missed you.'

'I was good until I saw you, Brandon. A scary clown, really?'

Lenny shook her head and he threw back his and laughed so loud the people around them stopped and stared, shocked to see Pennywise laughing so hard.

'Your Aunt Lenny is such a spoilsport; I have no idea why she won't put on her costume and give the crowds what they want.'

Dora smiled. 'What do the crowds want?'

'What does anyone who comes to visit Salem want? A witch, a real witch, one who can levitate and do magic. They want to know that they exist. Your aunts are the real deal, it's a shame they spend all of their lives in denial. They could work it for all that it's worth and then some.'

He took hold of Dora's hand and raised it to his cherry-red-stained lips, gently kissing it.

'Miss Dora, you need anything you come find me over at Crow Haven Corner. I live above the pub next to it at the end of the pedestrian walkway. I am always at your service, I'm so happy to see you both.'

He let go of her hand and turned to the crowd watching them.

'Want a balloon?'

Lenny pushed Dora away from him. As the crowd opened up to let them through, Dora handed the red balloon to a small boy who was smiling at her. They were walking back up Essex Street now, or at least attempting to but there were so many people. As they passed one shop doorway Dora jumped to see the most life-like Freddy Krueger standing still, in his dirty red-and-green jumper and brown fedora. Lenny kept on leading her on. Dora lost count of the number of Sanderson Sisters that they walked past, but she knew she was falling in love with this strange, beautiful little city. Everywhere she looked there were witchy shops selling spells, trinkets, hats, costumes, books and everything else an aspiring witch could wish for.

'Is it always so crowded?'

'October is the busiest month of the year; I do think it's great for the local businesses but dreadful for the people who live here. We have a mutual friend, Ambrose, who usually opens Sephy's shop up around ten a.m., it's not really busy until after lunch. I recommend you pop in first thing and introduce yourself to him.'

Dora nodded, and wondered why her aunt was so desperate for her to meet this Ambrose guy.

'Where are we going now?'

'To Sephy's shop. You need to know where she spends most of her time when she's not home.'

Lenny stopped and Dora knew she was hiding something.

'What is it with the big secrets you two keep hiding? And who have you got cooped up in that bedroom? I heard you earlier, there were three voices.'

Lenny kept on walking so fast that Dora had to almost jog to catch up to her. They rounded the corner and there was a quaint, very pink shop. Lenny muttered, 'Oh God, she didn't.' Dora laughed; it was even prettier than the front of Sephy's house. There was a garland of pink and white flowers surrounding the door with tiny pink pumpkins and silver witches attached to it. Wind chimes tinkled as Lenny slammed the front door open and stepped inside. Dora was almost disappointed to see the inside of the shop wasn't the slightest bit pink. It was full of old wooden glass cabinets and shelves upon shelves of glass bottles, there were beautiful crystals in baskets and on the huge pine dresser that filled an entire wall, lots of dried herbs, tarot cards, cups and mugs galore, but not one book in sight apart from a few leaflets. Above the counter was an old-fashioned wooden sign that read, 'English Sisters & Co.' Sephy appeared from behind a black velvet curtain and grinned to see them both standing there.

'Welcome Dora, what do you think of the shop?'

Dora wasn't quite sure. 'It's beautiful, but why don't you have a sign outside so people know what shop it is?'

Sephy gave Lenny a knowing look.

'I don't need a sign, dear. People who need my services know where to come, there is no need to advertise.'

'Oh, that's good then.'

She smiled at her. Lenny had crossed her arms and was staring at Sephy.

'What did you do to the front of it?'

'What can I say, I like pink and whimsical. I think it suits the shop rather well.'

'I have no words; I mean, I literally have no words.'

'Well, that's good because it doesn't matter if you do. This is my shop, you left a long time ago, Lenny. Dora, would you like to take a quick peek inside the heart of the place before my next customer arrives?'

She nodded and Sephy held back the soft black velvet curtain for her. She walked around the counter and past the curtain just as the shop door tinkled and three women all wearing pointed witch hats walked in.

'Lenny, be a dear and cover for me.'

Lenny gave Sephy a death stare and she let the curtain drop, cupping a hand to her mouth to stifle her giggles. Dora smiled; she adored her Aunt Sephy's happy manner and light-hearted way of looking at things.

'She's going to kill me,' Sephy whispered. 'But, you know, she is half owner, it won't hurt her to do her part and serve a few customers. Besides, they will buy a jar of tea and a couple of crystals then leave, this isn't what they're looking for.'

'How do you know?'

'I just do, I have a gift of reading people deep inside of their souls. Something tells me that you want to know about the person in the bedroom because you heard us, or you're very astute?'

Dora nodded, unable to find her voice. She pointed to the round table on which sat a Ouija board on a black velvet cloth, next to that a spread of tarot cards.

'Are you not scared of that thing?'

She shook her head. 'It's just a tool, one of the many tools I use. If I'm honest I don't tend to use it very much, I don't need to, but it gives the customers a bit of satisfaction to see it sitting there. The damn thing is as reliable as the newspapers, it's always getting things wrong and sending messages from the wrong people.'

'What about the bad spirits and demons?'

'They can only come through if you let them, dear, and I am very strict about it, I chase them away if they start to try and get through. After you've been around as long as I have, you realise those needy little pests are just attention seeking.'

'Oh.'

Sephy laughed. 'It's all a matter of perspective, Dora. I have been on this mortal plane more times than I care to remember and over the years I have met some horrid humans far worse than anything that board could conjure. Now, I suspect that Lenny will not want to be the one to tell you this, but there's somebody else you need to meet.' Sephy's tone was light and breezy, but she looked down at the floor, and Dora felt a wash of sadness come over her.

'Someone else? I have two aunts, one who lives in the most beautiful house and owns the most wonderful apothecary, and I didn't know about any of this. It's kind of hard to believe. What about my parents? Would my mother have been a third English sister?'

'No, dear...'

Dora felt confused. 'There are more than three?'

'There's just the four of us. You, me, Lenny and Lucine...'

For a moment Dora didn't understand what Sephy was saying. And then it clicked. Her mother was alive.

'My mother's alive?' Dora felt her stomach twist. Everything she knew had been turned upside down. The shop door closed, and Lenny stepped through the curtain, her face aghast.

Sephy looked at her and shrugged. 'We have to tell her sooner or later; we don't know how long Lucine has left.'

Lenny sat down heavily on one of the chairs, her head bowed. Dora looked at her, then back to Sephy.

'Why have I been living with you in London instead of here

with my mum?' Dora exclaimed. 'What do you mean "has left"? Are you saying she's dying? I don't even know her, why would you never tell me about her, this is unfair.' Her stomach had knotted itself so tightly that she could hardly breathe. 'Why were we kept apart from each other, and what about my dad, where is he? Is he not dead either?' She glared at Lenny. 'Why have you never told me about her? Why have you kept me from Salem? You lied and told me my parents were dead?' Dora was pacing up and down the small room, the shock and betrayal making it hard to focus.

Lenny sighed as if the weight of Dora's questions was physically pressing down on her shoulders, her face looking pinched and even paler than it usually did.

'It's complicated, Dora. I took you away to keep you safe. As for your father, he was nothing but trouble and I knew it the moment he breezed through the village on that dapple grey horse of his with his bag of tricks. He stole your mom's heart and her virginity, leaving her pregnant and alone in the most unforgiving place on earth. All he gave her was that blasted grimoire, full of spells that he swore would change her life for the better, only we knew that doing any of them would put all of our lives at risk. It was him who brought the magic into our lives and left us alone to face the wrath of George Corwin's noose.'

Dora felt as if her mind was about to explode. How was it even possible that she had a whole other life she'd known nothing about?

'Keep me safe from what?'

Sephy was standing with her hand clamped on Lenny's shoulder, she spoke directly to Dora.

'From him. From the witch hunter.'

Dora closed her eyes, this all sounded like some Grimms' fairy tale.

'The witch hunter? What does that even mean? Have I just

fallen down a black hole and found myself inside "Hansel and Gretel"?'

'Unfortunately, no, sweet child. That is what George Corwin is and always has been. He chases us. He hunts us. He never gives up; he stalks us no matter where we run to, which is why we decided to keep you away from Salem this time.' This time? Dora could barely understand what Lenny was saying. 'But I fear he found you in London anyway. He used to leave sprays of forget-me-nots for me, and when that man gave you some I realised that he might have found you anyway.'

A cold chill settled over Dora's shoulders that seemed to envelop her in a cloak of ice so cold it made her shiver.

'What do you mean, he might have found me?'

Lenny looked at her. 'Those flowers, he gave them to you. The ones that you and I both know are out of season this time of year.'

'He said his name was George Corwin.'

Sephy looked at Lenny. It was her turn to look horrified.

'He came to my shop for some funeral flowers, his girlfriend had just died.'

Sephy took both of Dora's hands in hers.

'Did he seem familiar; did you recognise him perhaps, his voice, his manner?'

'I thought I knew his eyes; they were so dark, and I remember thinking that I'd looked into them before, but I didn't recognise his face.'

Sephy turned to Lenny. 'Did he know who she was or was he just guessing?'

'I think he would have moved fast if he'd been sure it was her. He can't have been convinced.'

'Erm, could you please not talk about me like that, it's very weird and unsettling.'

Sephy stood up and patted her arm. 'Of course not, Dora. It's difficult there's so much to talk about and do, but we need to put it in order of priority. Did you tell this man you were coming to Salem?'

'No, I did not. There's only my friend Katie who knows. Oh God, she's running the shop. Is she safe? Would he hurt her to find out where I am?'

Panic filled Dora's voice and she pulled her phone out of her pocket to text Katie. She checked her messages and felt a wave of sickness rush over her. Katie hadn't read the message she'd sent earlier, and Katie always replied to messages even in the middle of the night. She never put her phone on silent, always telling Dora she was too nosy to miss any gossip.

'I have to go back to London and check on her.'

Her aunts screeched at the same time. 'You can't, you simply can't.'

'Until today I had no idea any of this existed. And I don't understand half of what you've told me. But one thing is certain, Katie has been my best friend since I went to college, and I can't leave her in danger.'

'Honey, it's almost one in the morning in London, she might be out or exhausted after working the shop. Can you phone someone else to check on her, what about Mabel?'

Dora nodded. 'I can ask Mabel to check the shop, she has a spare key; will I be putting her in any danger though?'

Lenny nodded. 'Possibly. Why don't you ask her to check the shop when it should be open in the morning? You could phone Katie's parents or the police and ask them to check on her for you.'

'I can't drag her parents into this, they're elderly and live too far away. Seriously, what are the police going to say when I tell them my friend is in danger from a witch hunter?'

'Not a lot, I should imagine they may tell you to stop wasting their time.'

Sephy looked down and Lenny nodded. 'Good, that's good.

Maybe ask Mabel to check her in the morning but for now I need you to turn your phone off, just in case.'

'Just in case what?'

'Please, it's been a long day. Katie is fine. There's a lot going on and we don't want to worry about anyone tracking your phone. Turn it off and we'll get you a new one tomorrow. Let's go and say hi to Lucine, she's been waiting a long time to see you again.'

'Okay.'

Dora felt all her anxieties draining away at the thought of meeting her mum. Just then, the shop door tinkled again.

Sephy smiled at them both. 'Perfect timing, my customer is here. I'll catch you both at home – try not to tire Lucine out too much and have fun.'

She walked through the velvet curtain, leaving Dora staring at Lenny, who shrugged.

'Come on, we'll go out of the back door and take the long way home to avoid all those people outside the Witch House.'

They left, Lenny softly closing the door behind them. It was dark, the alley a lot more peaceful than the mayhem they'd walked through on the way here. Dora realised that after all these years of wishing she'd known her mother that she was finally about to meet her, and she wasn't sure how she felt about that.

18

Lenny did indeed lead Dora home, if that's what it was. She was so confused and torn about what was happening to her that she couldn't quite decide. They walked along quaint streets, and she noticed that some of the houses were decorated for Halloween with the craziest number of skeletons she'd ever seen. Many were almost as tall as the houses themselves. She paused outside a house that was lit up with pink and purple windows, gazing in awe. It was such a beautiful sight – there were so many pumpkins she couldn't count them all. Despite everything that had happened, somehow, she felt at peace in Salem. Strange as all of this was, she thought she might be able to call it home. It felt like what she had been longing for back in London: her real home.

Lenny didn't speak, as lost in her own thoughts as Dora was. They turned a corner onto a tree-lined street and Dora realised they were back at Sephy's house. A loud squawk and flapping of wings above their heads made her look up in wonder as she watched Hades swoop over them and straight to an upstairs windowsill, the one he'd been perched on when they'd arrived earlier. Lenny tutted.

'That bird is too nosy for his own good, he's been following us since we left the house.'

'He has, birds do that?'

'Normal birds don't, familiars have an annoying habit of it.'

Dora smiled up at him. She liked the thought of her crow following her, it was comforting. She wished she could remember him from her time before she arrived here. As Lenny pushed open the gate to the cottage she heard his high-pitched voice as he chattered to himself, 'Dora's home, Dora's home.'

Lenny opened the front door and turned to her. 'I will take you up to see Lucine and let the pair of you spend some time together. Try not to ask her too many questions, she is already tired.'

'What's wrong with her, Lenny?'

The warm light in the hall shone across her aunt's glistening eyes, unshed tears pooling in the corners.

'Cancer. Every single lifetime she gets it and dies before the rest of us. There is something else you should know too, Dora, seeing as how this has been a tell-it-how-it-is reunion. This curse means that you also die young. You always die before your thirty-fifth birthday.'

Dora's mouth fell open. 'I die? I'm thirty-three. How will I die... and why?' Lenny shrugged. 'I can't begin to take all of this in, is there no way for you to cure my mother? There are all kinds of treatments and the ones over here are far more advanced than in the UK. And can't you stop me from dying too? I'm far too young, I haven't lived, Christ I don't even have a boyfriend.' Dora's voice was getting higher with the panic that was rising inside of her.

Lenny held up her hand. 'Dora, I've tried. Why do you think I trained in medicine? I've tried everything, over many lifetimes, to no avail. And that's exactly why we kept you from Salem and from Lucine this time. We wanted to do something different – we've never, ever kept you away from your mother before. But we wondered if it might keep you safe.' Dora looked downcast and Lenny reached over and stroked her face. She held Dora's chin in her hand and Dora looked up at her. 'I'm sorry it didn't work. We didn't know what else to try.'

Dora felt Lenny's desperation. Somehow, she did understand. She couldn't remember all those other lifetimes, but she believed Lenny's heart. She must have done it for Dora's own good.

She thought of Lucine upstairs. She found it hard to be sad for someone she didn't know, who had never been a part of her life, and the shock of her looming mortality didn't help either. This woman hadn't taken her to school, picked her up, watched her terrible school plays, attended her parents' evenings, arranged birthday parties, taught her all her life skills. If anything, Dora was annoyed that her own mother had been willing to give her up so easily. If it had been the other way around Dora would have fought with everything she had to protect her child and keep her close. What kind of woman sent her kid to the opposite side of the world and never spoke to her ever again?

Her aunt sighed. 'The kind of woman who knows that to keep her only child safe she must sacrifice all of that.' Dora's suspicion was confirmed. Lenny could read her mind. 'You don't think your mother missed you, grieved over her loss of you, wanted to hug and kiss you good night? Lucine isn't a monster, she is a woman who gave up the one true thing she loved to keep her safe, and every lifetime it kills her that little bit more. Give her a chance. I know things are different this time and you're struggling to remember but please be kind to her, that's all I ask.'

Dora felt the heat rising up her cheeks. How many times had Lenny read her mind?

'I don't make a habit of it, for one thing it's rude to go

probing inside someone else's thoughts and I have enough problems of my own without worrying about everyone and their
dogs. But sometimes the loudest thoughts break through, and
you, Dora, practically screamed those words at me. Now go,
that damn bird will have already told her you're on your way to
see her.'

'What are you going to do? Lenny, I don't want to die.'

'Drink vodka. Sephy and I have been working on a plan.'
Lenny began muttering to herself. 'Maybe see if I can conjure
up a finders' spell so you will remember where you hid that
damn book back in 1692. I honestly thought that by keeping
you in London it wouldn't get to this, that Corwin wouldn't find
you. I should have known he would never give up that easily.
Do you remember the book?'

Dora shrugged and Lenny turned and walked straight down
to the kitchen, leaving Dora standing there staring after her,
head spinning and stomach churning. She pushed the thought
of her own predicament to the back of her mind; she would deal
with that later.

She looked up the stairs and began to slowly climb them,
her feet hesitant to get to the top. Before she knew it she was on
the landing, walking towards the door she'd seen her aunts come
out of earlier. Her heart was thumping so loud in her chest and
there was a lump inside her throat. Suddenly she wasn't angry,
she was afraid. What if Lucine didn't like her or was horrible to
her, she wouldn't know what to do.

Before she could knock, a voice that sounded just like
Sephy's called out, 'Come in.'

Dora pursed her lips, blowing out the breath she'd been
holding as she turned the handle and opened the door. This
room was bigger than hers, it was huge, and in the middle of it
was a massive bed, with a frail-looking woman who was the
double of Lenny sitting propped up on a mountain of pillows.
She smiled at Dora and opened her arms wide and every

thought that had been rushing around inside her mind stopped and she saw them as little paper tickets twirling around in the wind that suddenly dropped and all of the papers fell to the floor at the same time. She was aware of Hades sitting inside the window watching the two women and, before she knew it, she was sitting on the bed with Lucine's frail arms wrapped tightly around her. Tenderly pulling the woman close, Dora inhaled deeply. She smelled of jasmine and vanilla, but there was the scent of decay and illness lingering underneath the sweetness and she knew then that whatever her reason for sending her away, Dora would not question it too harshly. She wanted to make the most of the time that Lucine had left and get to know her. She felt the soft sobs against her chest and rubbed her back gently. She looked up to see fear in her mother's eyes, and with a trembling voice Lucine whispered. 'I'm so sorry to tell you this, but my life is in danger, and now so is yours.'

Dora stared at Lucine, fear making it hard to breathe, unable to speak as Lucine took a deep breath then continued to talk as if she hadn't just scared the life out of her.

'I've waited so long to see you, Dora, and you look beautiful. You turned into quite the stunning young lady.'

Dora glanced up at the wall opposite them to try and calm herself down ignoring Lucine's ominous words, it was covered in picture frames. In every picture was a photograph of Dora, from when she was a baby, and her toddler years, through to her teenage years where she was a full-on Goth, to recent photos of her with her black hair now chopped into a shoulder-length bob with a fringe, the delicate ring she wore through her nose and the tattoos on her arms. Not quite shedding her love of all things dark and punky. She pulled away from Lucine who was blotting her tears with the corner of a cotton handkerchief.

'I don't know what to say,' Dora started. She took a deep breath. 'I'm sorry, but this has all come as a bit of a shock.'

'Yes, I can imagine it has. One moment there is just you and

Lenny against the world, then she brings you here to introduce you to a whole new one with a talking pet crow, a curse on all of our lives and a failing mother you knew nothing about.'

Dora opened her mouth and Lucine gently touched her arm.

'I am not some cold-hearted monster. I need you to know that I did what I had to in order to attempt to break the curse. If I had my time again and my strength then I wouldn't have done that, you have no idea how much it pained me to say goodbye to you. A mother will give up everything for her child, even the child themselves if it means they get to be safe and live a happy life. I could not and would not let you stay here and endanger yourself, Dora. I love you far more than life itself and that will never change. We should have fought Corwin on home ground, but we didn't, we ran and hid, scared of what he could do to us, but no more. Sephy has a plan, something about binding him which I think is nuts, but we have to give it a go to keep our future selves safe if not ourselves in this lifetime.'

Dora stared into her mother's emerald-green eyes, mesmerised by the beauty of them. The colour was so pure, with the tiniest fleck of yellow running through each iris. They reminded her of cats' eyes, and they sparkled in the candlelight.

'Why is he hunting us all, what did we ever do to him?'

'I know that he lusted after Lenny back in the day and she wasn't interested in him. She was quite the talk of those petty villagers, with her striking green eyes, wild black hair and a figure to die for underneath all those meddlesome petticoats, and he followed her around like a besotted puppy dog. She doesn't talk about it, but I think that maybe because we were young and naïve – after all, that was our very first lifetime – she probably teased him a little, might have even broken his heart when she went out with his friend Jonas instead of him. Talk about not being able to accept rejection. I think Corwin also knew about the book your father left with me, he heard the rumours and knew it could change everything. He is the true monster. He turned on the women of the village and rounded them up, calling them witches, knowing fine well they were to be tortured and hanged for nothing more than being the object of a group of teenage girls' hysteria. He saved us English girls until last. I often wonder what would have happened if he hadn't been so obsessed with Lenny. Would it have changed all our lives and saved many others?'

Dora was listening to her mother enraptured, her jaw slack, her eyes wide as she imagined their lives back then.

'When was this?' she asked but she already knew fine well when it was. She'd studied the Salem Witch Trials back in college and had written an essay on them, having no idea of her own family connection to them. But she needed to hear this from the woman sitting in front of her. Her head was spinning, there was so much information to take in and try to make sense of.

'It began in the bleak, cold winter months of 1692. Corwin had become bitter, more distant, but by February he had given up his heart, his mortal feelings, and had turned into a hunter. Oh, he'd always been a hunter, but this was different. He no longer preyed on wild animals, it was innocent women, and his fire was lit by those girls who were more than happy to point the fingers and call women and some men out as being witches. His first victim was Bridget Bishop, she was sixty and no more a witch than she was a white rabbit. Poor Bridget's only crime was being a little outspoken and dressing rather flamboyantly for those miserable bastards. As more and more accusations were made and more women were rounded up, we begged Lenny to go and speak to him, but he was too far gone and too embroiled in his good fight to take any notice of her. Poor Lenny, we were the last women he came for. We didn't know back then the extent of the evil that lived inside of his sick and twisted mind until he had his men take us all from the captain's house on the edge of the common to the foul, damp jail while he went after you.'

Lucine closed her eyes, her entire body jerked as she shuddered. A rush of fear filled Dora's heart that she was making her already terminally ill mother relive the most terrible time of her life.

'It's okay, I'm sorry, you don't have to say any more.'

Lucine squeezed her eyes shut then opened them.

'Thank you. You are far more beautiful than I remember, Dora. It was a dreadful time. Ambrose heard them talking in the meeting house and he came to save you. The pair of you ran into the forest and you took the book with you, hiding it but no one knows where.'

'Why can't I remember any of this?'

'Some things are best forgotten, sweet child; it will come back to you, we need you to try and remember now that you know, it was the worst of times. You reached the place you hid the book before they set off on their witch hunt with the hounds and an angry mob of Puritan idiots who didn't have a single brain between them, led by Corwin. Ambrose risked his own life to save yours and for that I am eternally grateful. They took old Giles Corey and as they pressed his wretched soul to death, he cursed them all, but especially George Corwin who I was told smiled at every single stone and rock used to crush the man, and so set in motion this passage of time that spans centuries of our lifelong births and deaths.'

Dora felt confused. There was so much information to take in. But the name Ambrose caught her in her heart and this time at the mention of it she felt a warmth spread across her chest. She also felt overwhelmed and tired. Lenny must have felt her pain from somewhere in the house because there was a gentle knock on the door as Lenny pushed it open. She stopped Lucine mid-conversation.

'Come, Dora, that's quite enough for one evening.'

Dora stood up, then turned and kissed Lucine on her cheek. 'I'm glad I'm home.'

Lucine closed her eyes, a beautiful smile on her lips. 'Me too, sweetheart, me too.'

Dora followed Lenny out of her mum's bedroom, her mind a conflicted confusion of swirling thoughts threatening to make her head explode from the inside out.

Lenny lifted a hand. 'I know, this is difficult. Too many questions and so little time. The curse of the English women is that there is never enough time to figure all of this out before tragedy strikes.'

'I just don't know how or where to even begin to make sense of it,' said Dora.

She felt as if the weight of the world was pressing down on her shoulders and had an overwhelming urge to throw herself onto her bed and hope that she would wake up in the morning to find this was all a strange and unusual dream. She yawned loudly and Lenny pointed to her guest room.

'Perhaps you should sleep now, your system is still full of the anti-homesickness tea that Sephy overdosed you on earlier. You will feel better in the morning, I promise, then we can make a start on trying to figure out this mess and how to bring you back to yourself.'

She nodded. Her body ached for the soft mattress and cool cotton sheets to soothe her skin, which felt as if it was burning.

'Good night, Lenny, and thank you.'

'For what?'

'For everything, for taking care of me when you didn't have to and then bringing me home where I belong.'

Lenny reached out and patted Dora's arm. 'You're welcome, good night.'

Dora slipped into the room that was now hers, closing the door softly behind her. She felt as if the bed was calling her and she tugged off her boots and collapsed onto it, not even bothering to undress. Before she could even say good night to Hades, who was now sitting on her window ledge, she felt her eyes closing and wondered if he would stay there all night watching her or whether he would go to Lucine. Hades preened himself while watching Dora and gently cawed, 'Dora's home, Dora's home.'

19
LONDON, PRESENT DAY

Hi lovely,

    Please can you check on the shop today when you get a minute and let me know if Katie is managing okay, she's too stubborn to say she isn't. Salem is amazing and have I got a lot to tell you. Honestly, you won't believe it but if I said that my life has turned into an episode of Long-Lost Families *that will give you some idea. I hope you're okay, Mabel.*

    Love Dora Xx

Mabel read the text message from Dora several times. She had got up early because her hip ached if she lay in her bed for too long. The sound of the rain as it lashed against the window of the flat was both comforting and the source of the pain in her hip. It always hurt when the weather was cold and damp, lately it seemed that London had turned into the soggiest city in the world.

    Mabel didn't want to go down the steep stairs yet, at least not until her pain meds had kicked in. She loved this flat; it was so cosy and beautifully decorated, with cream walls and well-loved antiques she had picked up from stalls on the Portobello

Road, but she also didn't know how long she was going to be able to cope with that long, narrow staircase to get up here. If she told Dora she'd probably arrange to get a stair lift fitted, which wouldn't be a bad thing, but then she'd be admitting defeat and her age.

She went into the kitchen where she made herself some hot buttered toast with a teaspoon of homemade jam before she took the ever-growing assortment of pills the doctor had prescribed on her last visit. Two cups of tea, a quick watch of the news and she would be good for the day or as good as could be expected. As she swallowed the pills, she gazed out of the window that looked down onto the cobbled alley where the front of the shop was. The rain was heavy and the odd person rushing past had their heads bent against the weather or an umbrella above them. She couldn't see the lights of the shop downstairs reflected in the empty shop opposite like usual. Katie was lovely, but she suspected the girl wouldn't be as punctual as Dora. After all, it wasn't her shop, or her livelihood, if she was running the shop to Dora as a favour, she could keep what hours she wanted. Still, there was a little twinge of something inside Mabel's heart that she tried to ignore, but knew it was some kind of warning that there may be a problem with the shop.

Thirty minutes later she was dressed and as pain free as she was going to get, and took the spare key for the shop door that she kept on the hook behind her own front door. Wrapped in her warmest jumper and winter coat, she was cautious, taking one step at a time, holding on to the grab rail, and pausing at the bottom to catch her breath. She wondered what Dora's exciting news was going to be, she loved the girl as if she was her own granddaughter, not that she had any. She had never married or fallen in love with anyone she considered worthy of having children with, but she imagined if she'd had grandchildren then they would have been just as loving, kind and considerate as

Dora. Stepping out of the front door into the driving rain, she screwed up her face, bent her head and walked the ten paces to the pink shop door. Inserting her key and turning it, she pushed the door open and was hit with a smell so bad it made her wrinkle her nose in disgust. What was that, had Dora forgotten to put the bins out before she left? It was then she realised the shop was in darkness and so cold inside she could see her breath fog out as she exhaled.

'Katie, are you here, love?'

Mabel knew she wasn't, the shop was small and obviously empty. Sighing, she reached for the row of switches by the door and flicked them down, bright lights illuminating the space filled with buckets of fresh flowers and greenery. The sweet fragrance was overtaken by the bitter smell of something gone very bad and for a moment she was almost too afraid to go any further into the shop. Looking around, she saw the broken glass of the countertop and gasped. Had someone broken in?

She hurried towards the small box that she knew Dora used to keep her cash in. Expecting it to be missing, she saw it sitting under the counter, the key still in the lock. Mabel knew she should phone the police – something was wrong, and she might be putting her clumsy feet and hands all over a crime scene – but she slipped her fingers underneath the sleeve of her jumper and turned the key. She opened the cash box and saw there was money still inside, a lot of money. Closing it, she wondered if Katie had maybe dropped something and had an accident, which would explain the mess. Walking towards the tiny kitchen area at the back of the shop where the toilet was, she stopped dead in her tracks. There were smears of dark liquid all over the floor, a lot of smears that looked an awful lot like drag marks, and the white walls were covered in splotches of... *dear God, it's blood.*

A chill settled over Mabel, and she felt a fear deep down inside the pit of her stomach. She hadn't brought her phone with her but saw the landline on the wall and hurried towards it, dialling 999. It took her several moments to realise there was no dial tone. Whoever had been inside the shop had hurt Katie and it was then Mabel saw that the wire to the phone had been snipped in half, probably with the pair of secateurs lying open on the broken countertop directly below it with what looked like splashes of blood on the blades.

Fear made her dash towards the door as fast as she could, and she pulled it shut behind her, too scared to take the time to lock it. Her hands were shaking so much she struggled to open her own front door. Once inside the dark hallway she bolted the door and hobbled up the stairs to the safety of her flat. She grabbed her phone off the kitchen counter and for the first time in her life dialled 999. She had no idea how long it would take for the police to arrive; she had never had a reason to phone them before. Her voice quivered as she told the man on the end of the line the reason she needed them, he was lovely and so calm, talking to her the whole time. He didn't end the call until he told her the police were outside her flat door and she was safe to open it, bless him. There were three knocks on her front door, so loud it had shaken in its frame. When she opened it, she felt better to see the two policemen standing in front of her, their van parked half on the pavement. Another van pulled up behind it, flashing lights and sirens, and a policewoman got out and joined her colleagues.

'I'm sorry, the flower shop.' Mabel pointed towards the shop door with a trembling finger.

'It's okay, love, we're here now. What's the problem?'

'There's broken glass and I think it's blood on the floor too; it smells awful.'

The woman nodded, she was already tugging on a pair of bright blue gloves, then she pushed open the door. One of the men did the same and followed her inside, the bigger of the two men smiling at her.

'Should we go inside your flat, do you live above the shop?'
Mabel nodded.

'Come on then, let's wait upstairs to see what's happening, get you out of the cold.'

She was thankful for his kindness. The pain deep inside her hip joint had returned on a mission, making her struggle with the stairs for the second time. He never said a word as she tried to get back up to her safe haven, patiently waiting for her. She was shaking and in agony, those painkillers hadn't been able to handle the rushing up and down the steep stairs.

'Why don't you sit down, and I'll make us both a nice cup of tea. You look as if you need to take the weight off for a bit.'

'Thank you. My hip, it's worse in the rain.'

'I should imagine these stairs won't help either. I'm Eric, by the way, and you must be Mabel?'

She smiled at him. He had a kind face, and she knew from his smile that she could trust him.

'So, what do you think has happened in the shop? Is the owner not here? We're going to need to talk to her.'

'Poor Dora, she's going to be beside herself.'

'Who's Dora?'

'The owner, she went on a last-minute holiday with her aunt to the States. Her friend Katie is keeping the shop open for her while she's away.'

Eric busied himself boiling the kettle and rinsing out the tea pot on the side. Within a few minutes he'd poured the boiling water onto some fresh tea bags and let it brew, then he took a seat next to her, pulling out what looked like a mobile phone but much bigger.

'Now, can you give me Dora's contact number and I'm going to need Katie's if you have it. How well do you know them?'

'Dora is my friend; she has been since she took over the shop a few years ago. Such a lovely girl, we go to the bingo and eat lots of cake. I know Katie but not very well. I can give you Dora's phone number but not Katie's. Do you think she's okay? That looked like a lot of blood and someone cut the phone wire.'

Eric raised his eyebrows at her, then began using a stylus to write on the phone screen.

'I don't know what's going on, Mabel, but my colleagues will take care of it.'

'Thank you.'

She took hold of her phone and scrolled through to find Dora's number which she then repeated to him. He stood up, poured out two mugs of tea and carried them to the coffee table. Mabel didn't have the heart to tell him she'd rather have a double shot of Jack Daniel's to steady her nerves and instead picked up the mug and sipped at the too hot, too sugary tea. He took a few sips of his then set it back down.

'Did you hear or see anything, Mabel? Hear any loud noises from the shop below?'

'No, I didn't. I have the television on a little too loud and then I sleep very well, I always have done. My mother used to tell me that a bomb could go off outside my bedroom door and it wouldn't wake me.'

Eric smiled at her, and she smiled back. 'I'm very worried about Katie.'

He reached out and patted her arm. 'I know you are, let me go down and speak to my colleagues. I'll come back to update you shortly.'

He stood up. He was so tall his head almost knocked the light shade off its pendant, and it swayed from side to side, the light casting dark shadows on the antique cream walls that Mabel was too afraid to stare at.

'Thank you.'

He left her there, her hands shaking, her hip aching and her heart racing as she sipped the hot, sweet tea because she literally had no idea what else to do.

20

SALEM, PRESENT DAY

Sephy was busy in the kitchen. She had a cloth spread over the kitchen table with an assortment of dried eggshells, some lumps of charcoal that hadn't burned in the grill out back last time she'd used it, a giant bag of sea salt and her trusty mortar and pestle.

Lenny walked in and took one look at it. 'Black salt, really? You think that's going to work against Corwin, did it work in the past?'

'Good morning to you too, Lenny, and yes, it always works to a certain degree. Must you always be so dismissive, the old ways are the best, you know that.'

Lenny took the pot of coffee from the stove and poured herself a mugful.

'I guess living so far away from you in London where I rarely got to use my magic has kind of wiped all of that whimsical charm right out of me.'

'Well, if we are to stand the slightest chance of defeating Corwin for good you better make an effort to bring it back. We won't have any power if you're in denial and Dora can't remember a single thing.'

Sephy continued grinding the eggshells into a fine dust with her mortar and pestle then tipped them into a large, clear glass mixing bowl. Next, she began to grind the charcoal, which was much harder.

Lenny sat down opposite her. 'Would you like a hand?'

Sephy, who had a fine film of perspiration on her brow, nodded, then pointed to a cupboard. Lenny took a glug of her coffee then opened the cupboard to take out another mortar and pestle. There were eight of them all lined up in various sizes, and she chose the largest and carried to the table.

'Let me do the charcoal, get some of my early morning angst out of my system.'

Sephy looked at her sister and laughed. 'I hate to tell you this but it's not just early morning, you seem to hold on to it all day and night too.'

Lenny gave her the finger. 'Did we ever live an uncompli-cated life? One where we weren't always running from a psychotic witch hunter, or trying to rein Dora in? I feel as if they've all merged into one long nightmare.'

'You know that we did, we just didn't appreciate how simple and special it was at the time.'

'Oh, spare me, are you going to tell me that living in that draughty old cabin, with no heating and lumpy straw for a bed, was the most perfect of them all? Because I would not look back fondly on the sixteen hundreds.'

'Then I won't say it. Don't you remember how it was back then, seriously?'

Lenny was crushing the charcoal to a fine dust in the bowl in front of her. She shook her head.

'Okay, it was basic, and we lived rough, but there was nothing other than our love for each other and living our daily lives the best way we could and helping those that needed our help.'

'What did it get us though, that helping out the needy?'

'Well, if you hadn't teased that man, it might not have ended the way it did.'

Lenny looked at her sister with her mouth open, her green eyes sparkling with fury.

'Teased that man? I did no such thing, he followed me everywhere and I disliked him back then although nothing compared to how much I hate him now. What would you have me do, go back in time and marry him, live a miserable life as his wife? It wouldn't have stopped him, Sephy, he would have still hunted them down, tortured and hanged them because that's the sort of man he was and still is. I can't believe you said that. Is that what you and Lucine think, I should have shacked up with that misogynistic maniac to save our own necks?'

Sephy rushed over to Lenny and wrapped her arms around her.

'No, of course not. I'm sorry, I didn't mean that to come out how it did, and you're right, he would have still done it regardless. I guess some people are born evil, time and time again, just like some of us are born good every lifetime.'

They both looked up to see Dora standing there, her hair mussed and rubbing at her eyes.

'Morning, is it morning or is it afternoon? I have no idea, and I had the weirdest dreams.'

Sephy straightened up. 'We weren't arguing.' She glanced at Lenny unsure of how much Dora had heard.

'What, oh I wasn't listening, I just came down to get a drink. My mouth is so dry, I feel as if I spent all night at a bottomless prosecco party.'

'Oh, I'm sorry, that's my fault, I got carried away with the valerian root. Apart from a sleep hangover, how's your sickness?'

'I haven't got any, I feel great, sort of – or at least I will when I get a drink.'

'Help yourself. There's a jug of freshly squeezed grapefruit, pineapple, pear and mint in the cooler. It will revitalise you and give you a spring in your step. You should have a glass too, Lenny, might be better for you than pure caffeine.'

Dora poured herself a glass of the ice-cold juice and took a seat at the table. She looked at the charcoal and salt.

'What are you doing?'

'Making some black salt, dear, it's wonderful for protection and you're going to need it. I was thinking that maybe if you had a wander around town on your own you might get a feel of the place. See if it brings back your memories. Perhaps pop into the apothecary – I have an assistant at the shop who can help you collect a few things for me.'

Dora smiled at her aunt. 'I'd love that, of course I will.' She finished her juice and rinsed her glass under the tap, placing it on the draining board. 'Do you not want me to help you make the salt?'

'Maybe you could help me with some protection jars when you get back, I need this to be powerful so I'm infusing it with mine and Lenny's magic. And then I'll work on this finders' spell. When you've had some fresh air, we could work on your memory a little too.'

'I'd like that. Of course I will anything I can do to help.'

But Sephy had another reason to send Dora out into Salem on her own. She hoped that the first memory that came back to Dora this time would be the location of the journal they needed so badly. Might she be drawn to it if she wandered around looking for memories? Sephy hoped so. She could create this finders' spell, but she knew Dora was their best hope of securing it.

She took a notepad and began to write down what she wanted from the apothecary. She wondered if Dora might find Ambrose in town, it was Margo her other assistant's turn to open the shop today. He had been waiting for her for much longer in this lifetime than he'd ever waited before. Ambrose would surely help Dora and perhaps together the pair of them could find where she hid that blasted book. She clasped her hands and said a silent prayer to Hecate, asking her for her help.

'How's Lucine this morning?'

Sephy dropped the pestle into the bowl, a look of pure panic on her face.

'Oh my, I forgot to take her breakfast up, I was so busy making salt. She'll be starving.'

Lenny stood up. 'Let me, I have some catching up to do and when I popped my head in, she was fast asleep.'

Sephy nodded, the worry that was etched across her face smoothed itself out and her shoulders relaxed. She smiled at her sister and niece, so glad to have them home even if the happiness would be short-lived. None of them knew when Corwin would make his move and come back to Salem, but she hoped this was the lifetime where they'd break the curse.

21

Dora stared at her reflection in the bathroom mirror and saw the tiniest glint of silver running through the front of her hair. Carefully parting it, she took hold of the strands and looked at them in the light. Had they been there before she came here or had they appeared since she'd arrived? It was hard to say. She didn't think there had been any silver strands when she got ready for the airport, her aunts had the most beautiful silver hair, so she didn't mind if hers eventually turned the same colour, but surely not yet. Although if they were right she only had two years of living left to do so what did it matter? She pushed those thoughts away. She needed to focus on the here and now. Stopping Corwin. There was so much that she didn't understand, but if her aunts told her she needed her memories back, then she knew she had to focus on that. She hoped the streets of Salem would help. And she felt a strange pull to be out there. To that name: Ambrose. Applying her eyeliner and a hint of the palest pink lipstick, she backcombed her hair a little to give it some life and got dressed.

When she'd finished lacing up her boots she glanced in the

mirror and smiled. She had been this way since she could remember. Always wore black, no matter what the weather. Had she known somewhere deep inside of her witchy connections or was she just a born Goth? Either way it didn't matter. Or did it? There was something niggling at the back of her mind. It was if there was a tiny box tucked away inside a corner of her head and inside it contained all her past memories. If her aunts were telling the truth this wasn't the first time Dora had lived, she had been around for hundreds of years, yet all this information was locked away and she had no idea where the key was to open it and let it out. She could only recall little snippets: her love of flowers, the memory of bathing in an icy-cold forest stream. If her aunts could remember each life, why couldn't she?

Hades was nowhere to be seen this morning and she realised that she missed the bird. Who would have thought it? In London she was terrified of the pigeons that swooped low looking for scraps of food and yet he was much bigger than any pigeon and talked too. He was also very good company. A talking bird... maybe she was going as crazy as her aunts.

She heard Lenny talking to Lucine and slipped out the room. She was so conflicted about how she felt that she needed a little more time to get her head around this whole long-lost family scenario. A walk around Salem on her own might help her to clear her thoughts and get out of her own mind. As she reached the garden gate, she heard a cawing sound and turned to see Hades preening himself on Lucine's windowsill. She blew him a kiss then walked along the quiet street, turning left at the corner onto Summer Street. She could see the striking black-painted house everyone referred to as 'the Witch House'. A couple of women were taking photos of each other, both wearing black pointed witch hats and smiling. She felt a coldness spread down the entire length of her body, but her feet kept walking towards it; the house was drawing her in. She stared up the three gables mesmerised, something was happening inside her mind, and she couldn't do anything.

'Excuse me, sweetie, could you take a photo of us both, then we can take one of you.'

Dora turned to see the woman holding her phone towards her with a big smile on her face.

'Oh, sorry, of course.' She took the phone from the woman and pointed it at the grinning couple who had a whole routine of poses they were working their way through. When they finished Dora handed the phone back.

'Your turn, let me take one of you. Isn't this the most glorious of houses. It's so iconic, we've been wanting to visit for a long time.'

Dora nodded; the house was something. Maybe it was iconic, but it scared her on some deeper level than she had known existed.

'Oh, my phone's at home, I haven't got it.'

'No problem, I'll take some on mine and mail them to you. What's your address?'

Dora gave her the shop email address and thanked her. Then she stood in front of the woman with her phone, her back to the house, trying her best to smile. A few shots later the woman smiled.

'Are you okay? You look kind of scared.'

'I'm fine. Sorry, a bit jet-lagged and finding my bearings. Thank you.'

'No, thank you, honey, you're a pretty good photographer. We almost look presentable.'

The other woman laughed, then linked her arm through her partner's.

'Have an amazing day, witch, blessed be.'

They turned and walked away without a second glance, leaving Dora standing there staring at the hay bales and mounds of pumpkins surrounding them. The old wooden sign next to her said 'Closed' and she was glad that it was. She didn't know if she wanted to go inside there and had an awful feeling that her feet would force her around to the entrance at the back door if it was unlocked. It struck her then that the women in the pointed felt hats had addressed her as 'witch'. She looked down, expecting to see a long grey linen dress with black pointed boots on her feet and a crocheted shawl around her shoulders, but she was still wearing her Docs and ripped black jeans. Stepping carefully off the broken paved path onto the grass – she didn't like standing on those grey, jagged stones – she heard a child's voice whisper in her ear.

'*Step on a crack you'll break your mother's back, step on a stone you'll end up all alone.*'

Dora spun around to see who had spoken and saw no one. She was alone. Hurrying across the road to get to the opposite side of Essex Street, she never looked back. She was going straight to the apothecary and getting whatever it was that Sephy had written on the list.

When she reached the door it was to find the shop empty. She realised why – it was closed. Dora cupped her hands across her eyebrows and peered through the glass, hoping to see some sign of life.

A woman's voice behind her asked, 'Can I help you?'

She jumped, then turned to see an older woman with a head full of tight curls and huge hooped earrings swaying in time to the chomping of her jaw as she chewed gum.

'Hi, yes I hope so. Do you know what time the shop opens?'

'Ten minutes ago, I'm late.'

The woman fished around in her handbag and pulled out a set of keys, inserting the biggest into the lock and turning it. 'Give me a minute, hon, while I turn on the lights then you can come inside. You're keen, trying to beat the damn crowds. Can't say I blame you, another hour and downtown turns into bedlam.'

Dora smiled at her and waited for the lights to turn on, which moments later flickered into life.

'So, how can I help you, lady, is there anything in particular that you're after?'

'Actually, my aunt sent me.'

The woman tilted her head, nodding at the same time. 'Who would your aunt be?'

'Sephy English.'

At the mention of Sephy's name the woman's eyes widened.

'Sephy has a niece, a nice-speaking, British niece? Well, I never, that old girl can keep a secret or two. I'm Margo by the way, come on in.'

Dora smiled. 'Thank you.' Margo went through the black curtain into a room out the back, and Dora realised she should probably take a look at the list Sephy had given her. She unfolded it.

Raw amethyst chunks
Raw obsidian
Silver wire
Cinnamon sticks
Fresh pine needles

She looked around for the items but all she could see were vials of different liquids, tarot cards, coloured glass balls hanging from the ceiling and a small table with baskets of tumbled crystals inside them, all smooth and shiny. Margo walked through the curtains with a glass of water in her hand.

'Can I grab these things for Sephy?' Dora asked, passing her the list. Margo put the glass down and studied it.

'She has all of this at home,' Margo replied. She looked

quizzically at Dora. 'I've been told about you before.' Margo smiled.

'By my aunt? But you just said she kept me a secret?' Dora looked at her, puzzled. Why had Sephy sent her here if she had all of these ingredients at home?

'Beautiful alabaster skin, he always says,' Margo replied dreamily. 'And the most perfect eyes, like jewels.'

Ambrose... Dora thought to herself. Was 'he' the man from 1692 that her mother had mentioned? She hadn't been able to get him out of her head ever since Lucine had mentioned him. Was he cursed too? Was he here? She felt drawn to him.

'The man who talks about me, is he here?'

'He's down at the Ugly Mug.' Margo picked up her phone and was instantly connected to whoever she had called. 'She's coming to you. Get her to eat something, will you, she looks like she needs some carbs and caffeine inside her to bring her back to life. Either that or a quick zap of a heart-start machine.'

Dora didn't know whether she should be insulted or grateful that Margo cared enough about her. Margo came back into the shop and smiled at her.

'Sorry, I get a bit carried away sometimes. I can't help it, I'm always a sucker for a lost cause, they get to me, you know. You should see how many stray cats I feed every evening; those greedy suckers drive me mad. I think they go around telling all their cat pals to come on by to Margo's house where the food is free, and the kitty toilet is her front flower bed.'

Dora laughed. 'Am I a lost cause?'

Margo shrugged. 'Ambrose certainly is. He's been my friend for years. He's been pining after you for as long as I've known him. I don't know what you did to him when you last saw him, but he's quite smitten. The Ugly Mug is a diner down on Washington Street. You get to the corner of this block and turn left; you can't miss it. It's painted black and white with a picture of an ugly mug in the window. Food's pretty good, or at least it must be because Ambrose goes there every day.'

'Thank you.'

'You're welcome. Don't be a stranger and say hi to Sephy for me. I haven't seen her in a while, she's been busy looking after her sister.'

Dora nodded then, clutching the paper, she left the shop and headed towards the corner and the diner.

22

The Ugly Mug was a little hard to spot, even though there was a big black-and-white-striped sign in the window and a Pride flag next to a picture of an ugly mug in the other. Dora stepped inside and smiled at the sunshine-yellow-painted walls with huge skillets attached to them, inside which were knitted eggs and bacon. Dora smiled. She felt a sudden rush of nervous energy but at least she didn't have to worry too much about finding Ambrose. There was only one man sitting in the corner by the window with his back to her, the rest of the tables were full of couples and families. She realised her hands were trembling; she was nervous, which wasn't like her.

He was staring down into a really horrible, huge, black-speckled mug of coffee, stirring it slowly with a spoon. Suddenly Dora felt a rush of something so warm and inviting it made her whole body tingle just looking at the back of his head, with his collar-length brown hair. As if sensing her staring, he turned around to look and a smile broke out on his face.

'Dora.'

His face was tanned, and his aquamarine eyes sparkled with joy. He had to brush back the fringe of his floppy hair. He reminded her a little of Hugh Grant in her favourite romcom, *Notting Hill*, and she felt as if she'd known him her entire life, yet this was the first time she had ever set eyes on him. He stood up and pointed to the chair opposite him. And she soon found herself sitting on the chair, unable to speak.

'It's so good to see you again. How was Margo with you, did she say anything?'

'Erm, Margo, was fine and say anything about what?' Dora replied.

'Ah.' He nodded his head. 'Well, I hope she didn't offend you, she's a little bit wild at times, not to mention outspoken, but her heart is in the right place. To be honest I'm a little scared of Margo so I tend to always do what she tells me.'

Dora laughed. 'You do? Are you a little scared of all women?'

He shook his head, and his voice was much deeper when he spoke. 'Of course not, there are only two women in this world who scare me, and who I will never, ever, cross.'

'Who's the other one?'

'Your Aunt Lenny, I find her terrifying.'

A teenage boy ambled over with a tray bearing pancakes and another horrible mug of coffee, placing it on the table. Ambrose pushed the plate in front of Dora.

'Get you guys anything else?'

Ambrose shook his head. 'Nope, we're good for now thanks.'

He waited until the boy was behind the counter again, but it was Dora who spoke.

'You know my Aunt Lenny even though we've lived in London for as long as I can remember?'

He lowered his eyes, then, lifting his mug, he took a sip of his coffee as if trying to find the right words.

'I guess this is all a bit of a shock to you this time, Sephy told me that you were struggling to remember. It's weird, right? I mean, who knows why some of us just keep living again and again while others don't.'

Dora felt a sharp pain in the side of her temple as it began to throb and she lifted two fingers to massage it.

'Do you not have any memories?' He looked confused. Dora shook her head 'Wow. You don't remember, say, long walks in the forests picking wild strawberries with me on the Fourth of July?' Dora shook her head. 'The ring I gave you last time, with the black crystals around the sides? The first time I saw you at the wharf and I had to pay some kid to take me to your house on the common?'

Dora found the sound of Ambrose's voice mesmerising; she could listen to him talk all day. But she was sad to have forgotten such things. She felt jealous that he remembered her, and the many lives they'd spent together. She felt suddenly sad. If what her aunts and mother had said was to be believed, they would never grow old together.

'And to top it off, as far as I know my entire life has been one big lie. I'm a florist, I own a flower shop that sells beautiful bouquets for birthdays and anniversaries. I'm no witch, as far as I know I didn't drown in a pond or get burned at the stake. I didn't have to flee for my life across muddy fields and through dense forests where brambles tore at my flesh.' She laughed lightly.

His eyes locked with Dora's. 'None of them were burned at the stake over here or dunked then drowned in a pond. The Europeans were far more brutal than the Puritans, who were plain crazy. Over here victims were tortured and hanged – apart from poor Giles who was pressed to death. That was horrific, but he never gave in, he wouldn't confess and give them what they wanted, all he kept saying was, "More weight." I don't know how he found the strength, but he did. And are you absolutely sure about that?'

Ambrose pointed to the tangle of tiny scars on her wrists

and forearms peeking from below the long sleeves of her sweater. They had always been there, so old they were barely visible, tiny threads of silver running through her soft pale skin like minute rivers.

'How did you get those?'

She looked down, tugging down the sleeves of her sweater, and shrugged.

'I don't know, probably when I was a kid playing in places I shouldn't have been. I was always trying to pick pretty flowers to take home for Lenny. They've just always been there, I've never really thought about how they got there.'

He nodded and leaned closer to her. She could smell his cologne, it was subtle, a hint of citrus and jasmine, as he whispered, 'I was there when you got those. I bathed your torn, bleeding arms with salt water once we were in the safety of the boat out in the bay. We huddled together in the darkness, listening to the hounds as they trailed after us through the woods.'

Dora pulled away from him and stared. 'I don't believe you. How could you have been in my past life that I have no knowledge about?'

She pushed her chair back and stood up fast. As she walked past him, he reached out for her arm and a jolt of electricity so intense ran up her arm she thought he'd Tasered her. Ambrose jerked his hand back, letting go, clearly feeling the shock too.

'I'm sorry Dora, I would never—'

She didn't listen to him, and as she walked away the smell of burning tinged the air and her skin tingled where his fingers had touched her.

23

Dora decided to walk back to the house. She was feeling more confused and alone than ever. She realised that she needed a phone and hers was out of bounds, she had to call Katie to see how things were, so she wandered back to the bustling, pedestrianised part of Essex Street, and saw the red-brick building of Witch City Mall. There were a group of little kids splashing in the water feature out the front, their teacher looking as if he was having a nervous breakdown. She gave him a smile of commiseration and went inside to see if there was a phone shop she could buy a basic model from until she got back home. There was a small shop in the corner with an assortment of phone cases in the window, lots of glittery ones, most of them with silhouetted black witches on. Dora sighed; she had just about had enough of flipping witches, they were everywhere. She glanced down at her arm where Ambrose had touched her to see what looked like small red burns where his fingertips had brushed her skin. Inside the shop there was a huge guy squeezed behind the too-small counter, looking down at a phone.

'Hey, what's up?'

She wondered if that was the official Salem greeting.

'Hey, I need a basic phone to use until I go home. Do you have any cheap ones for sale?'

'You're from the UK, smashed your cell?'

'Something like that.' As nice as the guy seemed she didn't want to go into any details with him as to why she wasn't supposed to be using her own phone.

'Don't look so sad, it's only a broken cell. I can fix you up with something that will put you on until you get home. Arnie's my name and phones are my game.' He was grinning at her, revealing a set of the whitest teeth she'd ever seen, and she realised that she liked Arnie, he seemed like a fun kind of guy.

'Thank you, anything will do.'

He leaned down and picked out a phone from behind the glass counter, passing it to her.

'It's not pretty but it will do the job, you know what I mean.'

Dora turned the gold Motorola flip phone over. 'I didn't think they still made these?'

'They don't, she's special. I've been saving her for the perfect woman.'

'Really?'

He laughed. 'Boy, that sounded awful. Sorry, not trying to pick you up but you kind of look like the kind of gal who'd look cool with an old flip phone. It sort of meets your needs and matches your look, which is vintage and pretty cool, am I right?'

She smiled. 'I have no idea, but I need a phone so as long as this works, I'll take it.'

'Oh, it works okay. Let me set you up with a prepaid SIM card and you'll be on your way.'

Five minutes later she was the owner of the antique flip phone. As she thanked Arnie he grinned.

'Be sure to tell your friends where to come if they need any help getting connected, won't you?'

'I certainly will.'

'Cool, 'cause Arnie loves helping those accused witch gals

out, it's the least he can do, you get me. We owe you something for the way they treated you back in the day. There was just no need for it.'

Dora paused. Did everyone think she was a witch because she was wearing all black or did they know much more about her history than she knew about herself? Too flustered to even ask him what he meant, she smiled at him and left.

Once outside, she typed in Katie's number and waited for her to answer but it went straight to her voicemail. Next, she tried the shop but the phone didn't even connect, there was just a series of high-pitched beeps. Dora began to get a bad feeling about all of this. Why wasn't Katie answering and why was the shop phone cut off? Her last resort was Mabel and she hated to bother her but what choice did she have? She'd already texted her earlier and hadn't heard back from her either. She felt a terrible sinking in her stomach. Why had Katie not contacted her as she said she would?

Panic filled Dora's lungs, making it hard to breathe. She needed an internet café, maybe she could get hold of Katie online – this phone could make calls and take basic photos but that was about it. Hurrying towards her Aunt Sephy's house, she wondered if she had a laptop she could use. She hadn't noticed any computers, but it didn't mean she didn't own one. She dialled Mabel's number – hers, Katie's, the shop and Lenny's were the only four numbers she knew by heart. It took a few moments to connect to the phone and then she heard the familiar sound of Mabel's voice.

'Hello.'

'It's Dora, is everything okay?'

'Hang on, Dora. Somebody needs to speak to you.'

There was a slight pause before a male voice spoke. 'Dora English?'

'Yes, speaking. Who is this and why isn't Mabel talking to me, is she okay?'

'Yes, she's okay, just had a bit of a shock. There's been an incident in your shop, we can't locate the woman who Mabel said was running it while you're away.'

'What kind of incident?' A little further up the street there was a small wooden bench in front of a shop, The Coven's Cottage, and she sat down, her heart beating in double time at what she was about to be told.

'Mabel said you asked her to check the shop, which she did. Inside she found some damage and quite a large amount of blood. We have officers out looking for Ms Ryan and checking the hospitals. Do you know of anywhere she could be?'

Dora couldn't find her voice; her mind was spinning, and she felt as if she might pass out it was so hard to breathe.

'Ms English, are you there?'

'Yes, sorry, it's a bit of a shock, that's all.' *Was it though, Dora?* a voice inside her head asked.

'I'll give you her parents' address, as far as I know she's in between boyfriends at the minute. There was one guy though, he kept coming to the shop and was a bit strange. Katie liked him and went out for supper with him a few days ago.'

'If we can't locate Ms Ryan, we might need to speak to you in person and get a statement, you probably want to take a look at your shop too.'

'Of course, I'll get a flight home as soon as I can.'

'That's probably wise under the circumstances, could you please give me the name of the guy, where they went for dinner, Katie's parents' address and any other information you think is relevant.'

Dora began to list everything the policeman needed, her stomach churning the whole time. This was her fault, all her fault. If George Corwin was actually a witch hunter he was looking for Dora and she'd thrown Katie to him and ran away, leaving her friend as bait. The policeman on the other end thanked her, gave her his direct number and hung up.

'Hey, are you okay?'

She looked up to see Ambrose walking towards her, holding two take-out lattes in his hands, concern etched across his face. Dora wanted to cry. This was too much; she didn't know what to do.

'Not really.'

'Sorry, I shouldn't have been so forward with you. It's just...' He looked down at the floor, his cheeks redder than last night's sunset. 'I've missed you, like you wouldn't believe.'

Dora stood up. He was so handsome, and she knew deep down he was the kindest man she had probably ever known, but right now she didn't know him or remember him and her friend was her priority.

'I'm sorry, Ambrose, I wish I could remember you, but I can't, and now something has happened to my friend back home and I need to get back as soon as possible.'

'What's happened to her?'

'I don't know, the police are looking for her. My shop is full of blood and there's no sign of Katie. I feel terrible, this is all my fault.'

She walked away, she needed to get back to Sephy's house and book a flight or at least get her passport and head for the airport. She heard Ambrose's voice call after her.

'You can't go back, it's too dangerous especially when you can't remember who you are or what you need in order to save yourself.'

She didn't turn around, instead she kept walking, forcing one foot in front of the other. She felt as if she was going insane and despite how much she'd fallen in love with Salem, her Aunt Sephy and now meeting her mum who was dying, she knew that she had to leave it all behind. Katie had gone missing because of her and she had to figure out how to get her back.

24

Dora ran down Chestnut Street as fast as she could, but she wasn't a runner and as far as she knew never had been. She felt a black shadow in the sky above her and looked up to see Hades flying overhead. As she pushed the gate open and ran down the path, he swooped down to land on her shoulder, rubbing his beak against her ear.

She paused and pressed her head against him, then whispered, 'What am I supposed to do, Hades?' For once he didn't answer.

When she opened the front door and walked inside, the house was silent. The radio had been playing when she'd left, she was sure of it. She walked down the hallway to the kitchen where both Sephy and Lenny were sitting at the battered old pine table, jars of freshly ground black salt in front of them and solemn expressions on their faces.

'I can't do this. All of this.' Dora waved her hand around, pointing at the jars on the dresser stocked with teas and potions. 'You know that, right? I must go home, something has happened to Katie, there's blood in my shop and the police are with Mabel.'

Dora spoke quietly but there was no mistaking the fury in her voice, it was also tinged with fear.

Lenny stood up. 'What do you mean, there is blood in your shop? Where is Katie?'

'I don't know, if I knew that I wouldn't be panicking, would I.'

Sephy walked to Dora and wrapped her arm around her.

'Come sit down and we can talk this through, dear. I'm sorry for sending you on a wild goose chase but you needed to meet Ambrose and I couldn't think of a better way, sometimes we all need a little push in the right direction. Did you find him?'

Dora let her aunt guide her to a chair. Hades hopped down onto the table and Lenny shooed him away. 'Bird, you know the table is out of bounds, scat.'

Hades hopped across it and then glided to the windowsill. Sephy smiled at him. 'Thank you, Hades. Now Dora, explain how you know all of this please.'

As she talked Lenny looked horrified. 'You didn't take your phone, did you, please tell me you haven't used it, Dora?'

'No, I went and got an ancient one from some guy in the mall called Arnie.'

'Oh, that's okay. We would have struggled to keep you safe if you had.'

'Keep me safe? What about everyone else? George whoever he is Corwin has hurt and taken Katie, I'm sure of that, and unless I go home God knows what he will do to her. I won't stay here and hide like a coward; you must understand that. I'd never live with myself if I didn't go back. I'm not afraid of him, whatever he is.'

Sephy's eyes shone with tears, and she dabbed at the corners with a cotton handkerchief.

'Oh dear, this is most troubling.'

Lenny rolled her eyes at Dora. 'Excuse her, she always was

an emotional wreck. How do you know all of this, who told you?'

'I phoned the shop and Katie with no reply so then I tried Mabel, and a policeman told me.'

'Did you get his name and rank?'

'No, I didn't think to ask. I was too shocked at what he was telling me.'

Lenny looked at Sephy this time. 'How did you know he was a policeman?'

Dora let out a small gasp and lifted her hand to her mouth. 'Oh no, Mabel, what if he wasn't?'

'He could be keeping both her and Katie hostage to get you to go home, Dora, to get to you.'

She stood up. 'Then I have no choice. I'm going back and once I've found out what's happening, I'll come back here.'

'Oh, you can't, dear, it might be a trap and you'd be walking straight into it. Without us or your own knowledge of your power you'd be helpless to defend yourself.' Sephy was wringing her hands.

'Look, I'm sorry, both of you, but for all I know the pair of you are as crazy as a box of frogs. I love you both dearly, but I need to go home and find Katie, make sure Mabel is safe. Surely you both understand that?'

Lenny nodded. 'You're a grown woman, Dora, maybe it's time to let all of this go, what will be will be.'

This time it was Sephy who gasped. 'Lenny, we can't, we just can't.'

'What else are we to do, tie her up and keep her captive, for Christ's sake? Sephy, she doesn't remember so what does it matter? This time around we failed, maybe we were meant to, and she is to take a different direction in life. Next time might be different. Are you not tired of this same, centuries-old bullshit? Why do we bother trying to break this curse?'

Sephy straightened up. 'No, Lenny, I am not; this is not

bullshit. This is our life, our history, our heritage. We might finally be able to stop that maniac but not if Dora goes back to London, we can't agree on anything and Lucine dies her slow, pointless death again. I love my life, I love helping women that need a little push in the right direction, I love brewing potions and casting spells. I love you and Dora, I love Lucine and Ambrose as if he were my own son. We are not going to let Corwin win again, we need to stop him. Dora is destined for something more than this.'

Lenny nodded her head. 'That was some speech.'

'It's how I feel. Dora, I can't stop you from leaving, but I'm begging you to please consider the danger you could be putting yourself in, all of us in. What if Lenny went instead and then you and Ambrose could try to figure out what you did with Lucine's spell book, where you hid it because I'm certain that is the key to this whole mess?'

Dora's head felt as if it was going to explode. She had never imagined that the quiet, gentle-natured woman in front of her would be so passionate about standing up and fighting some evil force that Dora didn't understand and wasn't sure if she ever would.

Lenny was staring at Sephy, who was still dabbing at her eyes. Standing up, she swiped a bottle of the salt off the table and handed it to her. 'I'm sorry, Lenny, we can't let her go back alone, it's far too dangerous... But you could go and find out what's happening. We could keep Dora here; you know him, you will spot the signs and be able to keep yourself safe.

'Take this with you, it's not much, but enough for you to get away. If you have any left, throw it in his eyes and blind him. Come on, I'll drive you to the airport.'

Dora stared at the jar of salt and felt hot tears prick at the corners of her own eyes. She didn't want to let Lenny go back and face Corwin, it was her mess, her responsibility, but she knew something had to be done.

Lenny was shaking her head but left them there and went upstairs to grab her passport. She didn't bother packing her stuff back into the case, it could stay here. All she needed was her purse and documents.

She walked down to Lucine's bedroom and knocked on the door.

'Come in, sweetheart.'

Lenny walked into the room, the smell of lavender tinged with the underlying, cloying smell of decay in the air. Lucine looked frailer today than she had yesterday, and a sudden rush of guilt filled Lenny's head.

Lucine patted the bed. 'Come, don't be afraid. You're leaving already.'

Lenny sat on the edge of the bed. 'How did you know? I'm sorry, Dora's friends are in danger.'

Lucine nodded. 'What good will it do you leaving?'

Lenny shrugged. 'I wish I knew, sister; I love you and I'm sorry that this time I didn't spend time with you like I should have. We should have known that he'd find us, that he wouldn't forget. All that time apart from you both, living in a different country, and for what, for nothing.'

Lenny bowed her head, her shoulders quivering a little, and Lucine pulled her close. They lay and sobbed together, knowing it might be the last moment they ever spent together.

25

Dora watched from the door as Lenny and Sephy walked along the garden path. Hades was on one of the thick branches of the twisted hazel tree, pacing up and down.

Dora stared up at him. 'I know, I feel the same, I feel terrible.'

He kept on hopping up and down and didn't answer. She felt truly awful. There was a chance she was letting Lenny go face Corwin all alone and, judging by what her aunts had told her, that wasn't a wise decision. Lenny didn't even turn to wave when she left, which stung Dora even more than she expected. Her aunt was mad and she didn't blame her but she hadn't wanted her to go, she had wanted to go herself and was just as mad at the pair of them.

Lenny hugged Sephy and took the van keys from her, pushing Sephy back in the direction of the house.

Dora went back inside and rushed up the stairs to knock on Lucine's door. A faint voice called out, 'Come in, my dear girl.'

Dora stepped into the room where the smell of death lingered in the air and she knew it was bad.

Lucine patted the mattress. 'Come, child, tell me what worries you so.'

She rushed to sit on the bed next to the beautiful woman who was her mum, a mum she'd never known existed, and felt a rush of emotions – love, sadness and anger – all rolled into one giant ball that lodged itself inside her chest.

'I feel so bad about everything, that I don't remember the past, that I've let Lenny go back to London to face that evil man when it should be me.'

Lucine took hold of Dora's hand, her grip much stronger than she expected. 'I know how conflicted you are, and I know a lot of things, it's just the way I am. You are honourable, brave and courageous, Dora, the way you always have been. Of course you feel as if you needed to be the one to go to London, but none of this is your fault, you always were a complete innocent in all of this. Life was never meant to be this hard and the choice is yours whether you decide to carry on with the suffering or enjoy every precious minute. The hanging times were horrific, and no one knows that better than us English women, but they are over to a certain degree. Time has moved on thankfully or at least it has for everyone except Corwin.

'You need to make a choice and live for the moment, stop burying the torch of pain deep inside your heart for I fear it's this that is keeping your memories blocked. I think once you open up and accept who you really are then all of this uneasiness, the confusion and amnesia will leave and, in their place, you will see your true self and the woman you are. I am so proud of you; I always have been and always will be. Maybe this lifetime you are not meant to remember who you really are and there could be a very good reason for that.

'I love you more than life itself, Dora, and I am always by your side. You only have to close your eyes and think of me. I will be there, in the beauty of a summer's sunset, the sweet smell of a rose as you pass one by, the cool air on your skin, the fire in your heart, all of them will keep me in your mind as they keep you in mine. All I ask is that you be kind to your aunts and accepting of their quirky ways, that you give Ambrose a chance and that you tell Corwin if you have to face him that he will never defeat us, ever. This is where you belong. It's where we all belong, no matter what destiny throws in our way; we were born in Salem, and we are supposed to live all of our lives here. This place is magical, made even more so by the fact that those foolish Puritans tried to wipe it away before it even began, which instead only made it far stronger.

'You have to find my book, Dora. I know you did a brave thing when you and Ambrose hid it, but we've never been able to find it. If you really want to try and help put a stop to this blasted curse, I know the answer is in there. I never told Lenny or Sephy this, but I fell in love with your father the moment I saw him riding his horse through the village. It was like an invisible electric force that jolted us both out of our heads, and I have never known anything like it. He followed me home; I had been leaving the meeting house and he asked if he could walk me back.'

Lucine smiled to herself. 'He was magnificent, Dora. He was dressed in brightly coloured clothes, he had the greenest eyes and the most impudent of smiles, my heart didn't stand a chance. Every woman in the village square watched as he bowed to me and introduced himself. He was a sight to behold, and I knew that he had taken my heart and there was no getting it back. He stayed for a week before he was chased out of town by those Putnam's. That John Putnam was one of the angriest men I have ever met, who sent word to Sheriff Corwin that he needed to do something about him.

'We had the most glorious time, Dora, he talked about magic as if it was real, and nothing to be scared of. He showed me things that could have got him hanged if it had been anyone else. He could turn toads into rabbits, could make a wizened, dead bush bloom again – which is where your love of flowers comes from. He could tell the future, but he said he would do no such thing around the Puritans for he knew that they would cast him out and call him the devil. John Putnam told everyone he had bewitched me, and I suppose in a way he did, but I was in love and he was a good man, he was born far too in advance of the times we lived in.'

'Does he never live again, like we do?'

Lucine shook her head. 'Maybe he does, I don't know, but on that day he was cast out of the village and told never to return he warned me what was going to happen. He said that the girls in the village were up to something and that we were all in grave danger. He asked me to leave with him and even though I only lay with him the once he must have known I was pregnant with you, before even I did. I refused, I couldn't leave my sisters, and so he gave me the book. It was so old, so heavy, and it felt as if it held every secret in the world. He told me that I would need it one day to save my soul and that he would come back to me when he could so we could be together. He never did.

'I looked inside the book and was terrified by what was inside of it. I knew that if the Reverend Parris or any of those damn Putnams ever set eyes on it, we would hang for it so I put it out of sight. I used to tell you stories about a magical book when you were little but I never showed it to you. Then one day I found you lying on the floor with the book, and you were tracing your finger along the pages, tiny blue crackles of light bouncing off your fingertips. I was terrified and I hid it away and made you promise not to touch it ever again. That night when they had already arrested us and Ambrose came to save you, the only thing you chose to save was the book. I think that deep down you knew that one day we would need it. That day has come, Dora, we do need it and you and Ambrose must try and remember where you hid it. It might just save all of our lives and send Corwin to hell where he belongs.'

'Why did my dad never come back for you if he loved you so much?'

'I think that day he was chased out of town by Corwin he didn't get any farther than the outskirts of the village. It was an angry mob of men, riled up on ale from Ingersoll's Ordinary and fear that he had corrupted one of their own. I don't think he stood a chance; I know he came to some terrible harm that day, Corwin has always hinted at it but never come out and admitted it, but I know that in my heart the only thing that would have kept us apart was death. I'm tired now, my darling, talking takes its toll. I'm going to rest. Please go and speak to Ambrose, try to locate that book. It's the only thing that might save us and keep this with you.'

She passed a small, linen pouch to Dora.

'What's inside it?'

'Some of Sephy's famous black salt and crystals for protection, you need all the help you can get my sweet girl.'

Tears fell down Dora's cheek as she kissed Lucine.

'I love you, Momma.'

Lucine squeezed her hand, then let go as she rested her head on the pillows, her eyes closed and a smile on her face.

'I love you more, Dora. Now go find Ambrose before I get the damn cat and the bird to stop you from leaving this room. It's hard to let you out of my sight now that I have you here again.'

Dora swiped at the tears with her sleeve and stood up. She felt a wave of grief for the woman in the bed, but she also felt a strong sense of duty that she was doing the right thing. She might still not know much about herself, but she knew one thing: she would find Lucine's book and have her day with Corwin to put a stop to all of this for good.

26

Ambrose knew something was wrong, just like he'd known it the first time around and every other time that followed. His heart sank. For once it would have been nice to live a life that was simple. He had hoped that Dora would remember him, at least some tiny spark, but there had been nothing and it pained him a lot more than he'd imagined it would.

He walked to the apothecary. Margo was serving a woman with the reddest hair he had ever seen and piercing blue eyes. He smiled at her and walked through the curtain to the back room of the shop. He knew she was watching him, he could feel the heat from her eyes boring into the back of his skull, but he didn't turn around. Some witches knew he was different, some even guessed his secret, but he wasn't bothered about any of that. He would have to keep out of the way until she left, he wasn't interested in any woman except Dora. He'd spent life-time after lifetime waiting for her to come back to him, but something was wrong this time, she was far more distant than she'd been in any other life and he was worried. He placed the coffees he'd bought on the way here on the small table and wondered if he should go and speak to Lenny. If Dora was home, then Lenny must have brought her and maybe she knew what was going on.

'Jeez, you went for breakfast almost two hours ago. I'm parched and it's almost time for you to go to lunch now.'

He smiled at Margo. 'Sorry.'

'What's with the long face?'

'It's Dora.'

'What about her, did she not fall for your devilish charms this time?'

Margo cackled. She picked up the pumpkin spice latte and she began to sip it, not taking her eyes off him the whole time.

'No, she didn't remember me or anything else.'

'She didn't?'

He shook his head; Margo was the only person apart from the English sisters who knew his life story. She had come to him years ago and taken him under her wing, fussing around him like a mother would. She had no kids and had run away from her abusive husband to come live in Salem and start a new life. She had ended up in the apothecary one cold, dreary December day with a black eye and a suitcase. Ambrose had offered her a couch to surf on there and then, and she'd accepted because she had nowhere else to go, he was sure of that. The pair of them had become best friends. She told him all her darkest secrets and he told her all of his. If he was certifiable, he adored her.

'Well, whatcha gonna do about that, kid? Seems a bit off to me if she can't remember anything.'

'I don't know, maybe I should go and see the aunts. They might know what to do.'

She was nodding. 'I think you need to do something; you can't leave it like that. You know it's terrible when your one and only true love can't remember that's who she is. It's kind of like a fairy tale but in reverse, you need to either step up your game or go find yourself a white steed and suit of armour to go rescue the damsel in distress.'

Ambrose smiled at her. 'Dora could probably rescue me to be fair. Times have changed a lot; women no longer need a man to do that kind of thing.'

She shrugged. 'Maybe we don't, some of us don't and would smack you over the head if you offered. Then again, some of us do appreciate a real, kind, caring guy and you tick all those boxes. You saved me when I had nowhere to go and you didn't want anything in return. Hey, if you go to fight this evil guy that's stalking Dora and you die, can I have your apartment?'

'Margo, it's yours. I've already taken care of that. But thanks for the vote of no confidence. Who said I'm going to die? Maybe I'll beat his sorry ass so bad he'll never set foot in Salem again.'

She smiled at him. 'I think you could if you had to. I'm team Ambrose, I'll get some pompoms and cheer you on when it comes to it. However, why can't you all team up to whup his ass? There's strength and safety in numbers. It could be like some big showdown good versus evil for the last time – hey, we could sell tickets, it would be a knockout, the tourists would go crazy for it, the witches and witch hunter battle it out at dawn on the common. It would be the highlight of the Salem year.'

Ambrose smiled but it didn't reach his eyes. He wanted nothing more than to whup his Uncle George Corwin's ass but all these lifetimes it had never worked. He finished his coffee and grabbed one of the hand-etched leather journals from the counter, hoping Dora would love the moon phases on the front of it embossed in silver. He wondered if she was as in love with the moon and her phases this time around. The Doras of the past had always lived their lives and made their decisions by the waxing or the waning of the moon cycle. Or had she forgot all about that too? Margo watched him and he realised he was leaving her alone again.

'Shoo kid, I have nothing better to do and at least someone is getting a bit of excitement, which is more than can be said for me.' She looked down at the journal clutched in his fingertips.

'Who said romance was dead?' she added, winking at him. He grinned at her, then turned and pecked her on the cheek. She lifted her hand to touch where his soft lips had kissed her skin.

'Be still, my beating heart.'

Ambrose grinned at her then pushed his way through a family all wearing black felt witch hats, who were bickering over the price of a happiness spell kit. He jogged through the crowds now congregating on the pedestrian part of Essex Street, turned onto Summer Street and ran all the way to Chestnut where Sephy's house was. As he opened the gate and walked down the path, he saw a shadow circling above his head and looked up to see Hades flying around.

'She's gone; she's gone.'

Ambrose felt his heart sink. 'Hey, where's she gone, Hades?' But the bird didn't answer. Ambrose knocked on the front door and it was opened moments later by a red-eyed Sephy.

'Ms English, what's the matter, is Dora here?'

She beckoned him inside. 'I haven't seen her for a few hours.'

'Damn, I'll see if I can find her. Are you okay?'

Sephy shook her head. 'Not really, it's a mess and Lenny has gone back to London so we're not even together.'

Ambrose felt a kind of relief that it was Lenny who the bird was talking about. 'Why?'

'Dora's friend is missing, and her flower shop has been broken into. There is blood in there apparently and the police told her they needed her help, but we couldn't let her go. So Lenny has gone in her place, but it all feels wrong and off kilter.'

As Sephy led him down to the kitchen, they passed the cat sitting on the bottom step who reached out one paw to claw at his leg, but it was only a feeble attempt. Ambrose absentmindedly bent down and scratched her on her favourite spot behind her ears for a few seconds then followed Sephy into the kitchen where the table had rows of black salt on top of it.

'I'll find Dora…'

Ambrose reached out and hugged Sephy, who smelled like the sweetest vanilla essence with a tiny bit of lemon thrown into the mix. She held onto him for a few moments, then let him go. She picked up one of the jars of salt and handed it to him. There were dishes containing crystals on the dresser and from them she grabbed tiger's eye, selenite and large chunk of jet, wrapped them in a tissue and gave them to him.

'Keep those in your pocket to protect you and the salt might be enough to help keep him a safe distance away if you find him or he finds you. I gave the exact same ones to Dora.'

He pushed them into his pocket. 'Thank you.' He didn't want to find his Uncle George but he would be ready if he did.

Then he turned and found himself running this time. He thought of his old bookstore. The one that had vanished all those lives ago. Was she there? Had she finally found it? He'd loved Dora for all of his lifetimes and always would. Dracula may have crossed oceans of time to find his love, but Ambrose had lived through centuries of lives to find his true love and that was and always would be Isadora English.

27

Lenny drove to Boston in record time, the highways were clear and before long the signs for Logan airport were directing her to the departure terminal. Dora hadn't spoken much before she left, and she knew she was worried for her friends, Lenny got that although she herself tried not to make friends and get too close to people. They either left, died or turned into huge disappointments. Family was what mattered and Ambrose, too – that poor kid had got dragged into this a long time ago and all he'd done was help Dora. Lenny supposed none of them had expected this to happen, but it had and here they were. She'd long given up trying to understand how they could be born again and again with the same memories, they didn't always look quite the same except for their black hair that turned silver by the time they had to prepare to battle Cowrin and emerald-green eyes, those were the two constants every lifetime.

She needed a drink and walked into the departure terminal where she spotted a cocktail bar.

Lenny was seething with anger. She'd done her best, had given up her family, her life to keep Dora safe and for what? Here they were, Dora had a head full of mixed emotions after meeting her aunt and her dying mom, she was in mortal danger and had been about to rush headfirst to the very person Lenny had spent the last quarter of a century keeping her safe from. She sat at the bar and ordered a double bourbon on the rocks. She took her drink to a small table tucked away in the corner, a part of her hoping that there were no flights today, she didn't want to go back to London so soon.

Her phone rang and she answered, hearing Dora's voice. 'Are you angry with me?'

Lenny shrugged. 'I don't know what I am, Dora. Tired is probably a good enough word to describe how I'm feeling, weary is another.'

'What am I supposed to do, Lenny? I can't ignore that my best friend in the world is missing and Mabel my other friend might be being held hostage in her own flat.'

'I wouldn't expect you to.'

'Good because I can't.'

Lenny took a large sip of her drink. 'I'm sorry about your friends, I really am, but me rushing off to London is putting everyone in danger, I need you to be aware of that. I'm not saying I won't go because I will, but you need to know that this is serious.'

'I do know that and I'm very grateful to you for going, but I'd rather go myself. I can get an Uber and come there now.'

'No, Sephy would kill me if I let you go. She may look all sweetness and light, but she has a wicked temper. You need to find the missing book.'

'I know, I'm looking for Ambrose now to see if he can help me.'

'Thank you. I should have given you some of this information before, some little life hacks to help with the day-to-day stuff. But I didn't so here they are: when you get back be sure to pop a rose quartz in your bra, always keep tiger's eye in your pocket and some citrine in your purse. If you have no citrine a condom will suffice.'

'What?'

'It's simple magic, Dora, the simplest any fool can use. Rose quartz encourages self-love and other kinds of love, it will keep your heart open and warm, you need that; tiger's eye provides protection, which you almost certainly need, to be fair you need a chunk the size of the Eiffel Tower but you'd never be able to fit it in your pocket; and citrine attracts abundance. A condom will save you against expensive life choices so it's basically the same.'

'Are you being serious?'

'I never joke about love, wealth or protection, Dora. Inside that pouch Lucine gave you earlier are some of the strongest protection crystals along with the black salt. They should help if for some ungodly reason Corwin finds you before we're ready. Don't be afraid to use them, they could just save your life.' She stared into space over the top of the heavy crystal bourbon glass.

Dora didn't bother asking her aunt how she knew about the pouch, Lenny always knew everything. 'Are you insane?'

Lenny laughed, tipped her head back and swallowed the amber liquid then clicked her fingers at the barman for another. She continued, her voice no longer a whisper.

'You have to believe what you will. When you're finally up for an intellectual discussion on the basic principles of magic then come and see me when I get back.'

'Why are you being so loud?'

'Because no one cares. And why are you still in denial about who you are? After the last twenty-four hours and what we've tried to show and tell about your heritage, you still think we're talking a load of crap.'

Lenny leaned back as the waiter approached carrying a tray with another drink. He couldn't tear his eyes away from Lenny who looked as though she had just devoured him with hers.

A voice shouted, 'Hey Mike, order's up.'

Finally looking away from Lenny he walked away.

'What's happening?' Dora asked.

'Nothing. Obviously you don't really believe in any of this witching or bewitching stuff so don't worry about it.'

'I have a headache.'

Lenny waved her hand dismissively in the air. 'Not sure all this confusion is helping you, Dora.'

She swirled ice cubes around in the glass and Dora must have heard the clinking. 'Are you drinking?'

'I'm not going to be flying for a few hours, there's no availability until later. I have a date.'

Dora sounded shocked. 'You do?'

Lenny was smiling at Mike. 'The bar man can't take his eyes off me; this old bird still has life in her, you know.'

'You are incorrigible.'

'I know, but you love me, right. I love you, Dora, don't ever forget that. As do Sephy and your mom.'

Dora's voice was a whisper. 'I wish I remembered them, the good times.'

'They weren't always good, to be fair a lot of them were tragically dismal and downright terrifying, but we've always had each other.'

'Can I not go back to London with you?'

'I think that maybe it's time to let you live a little on your own steam and right now there is no safer place on earth than Salem. It might be what you need to jerk your memories out of whatever place it is you've locked them away in. And as I told you, when Mike gets off, we're going to have a good time before my flight.'

Dora laughed. 'I love you, be safe; I can't believe I'm saying that to my old aunt. Please will you ring when you know what's going on?'

'Less of the old, I'm young at heart.'

Lenny smiled. She loved her niece more than anything, but

she had a feeling that this lifetime for the English sisters was hurtling to its climax and was about to have the most spectacular ending of them all. If that was so she was going to enjoy herself, maybe lose herself for a couple of hours in Mike's company where she could forget all her past and present witch wounds, and for the first time in a very long time maybe live a little and have pure, hot, wild sex.

28

Lenny had spent the most glorious two hours in Mike's company. He lived in a small apartment close to the airport and had not even flinched about asking her to go back there with him. She'd known he was a player and must hit on lots of single women in the bar. She had been pleasantly surprised by how neat his apartment was, she'd expected it to be a typical bachelor pad, all empty take-away cartons and six-packs of Bud. Not that she'd spent much time admiring his cleanliness. It had been so long since she'd felt this way about a man, she had almost forgot how it felt to be with someone who made every part of your body tingle.

He was snoring now and she was pleased that she'd managed to exhaust him. Extracting herself from under his arm and leg she crept around the bedroom, picking up her clothes. Slipping out of his room, she washed up in the bathroom and dressed. She would go home to her apartment in London for a long soak in the bath, but she had been missing for far too long already. She knew Sephy would be going out of her mind and sent her a quick text saying she'd met an old friend at the airport while waiting for her flight. But she knew her sister was a proper worrier and wouldn't settle until she was home.

She let out a sigh and hoped that Dora was okay. At least Mike had helped to take her mind off the impending doom heading the English sisters' way for a short while. She left his apartment and began the walk back to pick up Sephy's van, which in all probability had been towed away. Damn it, she should have moved it.

The early evening traffic whizzed past her, and she wondered if she was going to have to pay for a cab back to Salem when she came home or if the van would be there. As she reached the pedestrian footpath, she passed the pick-up point for arriving passengers and felt a chill rattle her entire body.

She stopped in her tracks and slowly turned around. He was here or close by, he had to be. She had the same reaction every time she was within a certain distance of George Corwin.

A tall man had just got into a cab. Slamming the door shut, the driver set off just as his passenger slowly turned to stare at Lenny through the window of the back seat, his eyes locking with hers. He looked nothing like the Corwin she knew from the 1600s but her inbuilt sensor didn't steer her wrong.

Panic filled her chest and she found herself back in 1692. She could smell the mud and the horses as she was bundled into the cart to be taken on her last journey before they hanged her.

George Corwin had always been a vile man, he absolutely thrived off causing pain and being cruel. She had witnessed his atrocious behaviour several times on her trips into Salem town. She wished that they had never set eyes on each other, but he had found her outside Ingersoll's, attending to Goodwife Ingersoll who had gone into an early labour. He had helped her get her into the ordinary, now it would have been a bar but back then everything was more complicated, and upstairs to her bedchamber, but had been unable to draw his gaze away from Lenny, much to her embarrassment. She had to chase him out of the room, asking him, if he wanted to be of some use, to go and fetch her sisters from the cabin to bring what herbs they needed to make a tincture. She had even given him directions. Lenny shook her head. She had led that animal straight to their door and he had been like a dog with a bone, he had kept coming back again and again.

At first, he'd been charming, and Lenny had almost fallen for him, giving in to his constant requests to join him for walks, if only to stop him following her around. In today's world she would have reported George Corwin to the police as a stalker, and he would have been served papers to leave her alone at the very least, but back then men ruled the world and women were nothing more than entertainment. Lenny shuddered.

She had promised to go to London for Dora. But time was running out.

29

Dora was walking through the streets of Salem, her feet leading the way until she found herself at the witch trials memorial sandwiched between Liberty and Charter Streets. It was shaded by trees and, despite the time of day, very peaceful. She stared at the stones with each victim's name and date of death carved into them. On the other side of the wall was The Old Burying Point Cemetery and inside of it were the gravestones of many of Salem's notable figures including the notable hanging judge Hathorne. Ambrose's father, and owner of the historic Witch House, was Judge Jonathan Corwin and he was buried in Broad Street cemetery, not this one. She paused. How had she known that?

She stepped closer to the first stone and saw Bridget Bishop's name. A wave of sadness washed over her and she kissed her fingertips, pressing them onto the stone. Everyone knew Bridget's name. Her only crime was being a little outspoken, not one person had anything good to say about her, yet Dora had been fond of the woman who had not deserved to die like that. How cruel that the judges and accusers all had graves with headstones in cemeteries and the victims had been tossed into a ravine, their bodies left to rot with the elements and animals with no proper burial.

She shivered. It was cold in here and reminded her a little of those dark, dank cellars in the jail where Lenny, Sephy and Lucine had been held. She caught herself – *the courthouse's dark cellars where her aunts had been kept as prisoners for being nothing but kind, helpful healers.* There was a sharp pain in the side of Dora's temple, it was so severe she had to squeeze her eyes shut and put both hands to the sides of her head to try and rub it away. The stones and trees swam in and out of focus, going blacker and blacker until she couldn't see anything, and then there was an explosion inside her mind so loud it sounded as if a huge firework had gone off in her skull and she stumbled to lean against the wall.

Dora thought that she was having a stroke or maybe an embolism of some kind, that this was how it was going to end this time. She hadn't even made it to the age of thirty-five. She felt as if she was being sucked through some great black void and her mind was falling in on itself. As she leaned there, holding her head and rocking backwards and forwards to ease the pain, a bright white light filled her mind, so piercingly brilliant that she couldn't see through this either, and then there was the loudest pop that she had ever heard, followed by a whooshing sound.

At some point someone must have called for paramedics when they saw her flailing around as she fell to the floor because the next time she had a conscious thought that seemed to belong to her she was lying flat on her back on a hospital bed in a cubicle in the ER at Salem Hospital. She felt the top of her arm tighten as the blood pressure cuff cinched the flesh on her bicep and heard a voice say:

'Well hello Dora, how are you feeling?'

She blinked a few times and stared at the nurse, who had

the most amazing lilac and pink dreadlocks fashioned in a top-knot.

'I, erm. I don't know, what happened? I remember being at the witch trials memorial.'

'According to that very nice policeman that brought you here you were having some kind of seizure. Do you suffer from epilepsy?'

'No, at least I don't think I do in this lifetime.'

The nurse arched one eyebrow at her. 'This lifetime? What a curious thing to say, how many lifetimes have you lived?'

She started to laugh, and Dora realised she should probably be careful what she told the hospital staff, or she might end up back in an asylum like Lenny had said she had once before.

'Sorry, I feel a bit confused but I'm okay. Did I have a stroke or something?'

'Not that we can tell, all your vital signs are good. Have you been feeling a bit off? Sometimes when we get run-down and are working too hard our bodies find strange ways to tell us to slow it down a little bit. I'm Estella, by the way.'

'Not working too hard but I did fly to Boston from London yesterday.'

'Do you drink a lot of alcohol, Dora?'

'No, God I'd like to but an occasional cocktail or glass of wine once a month if I'm lucky.' She didn't mention the anti-homesickness tea that Sephy had overdosed her on.

The curtain opened and in walked a tired-looking doctor in washed-out green scrubs. He picked up her chart and began to study it. The nurse removed the cuff and started taking her pulse.

'How is everything?' asked the doctor.

'Good, her stats are looking great.'

'Dora, I'm Ash. Can you tell me what happened?'

'I felt something pop inside my head and everything went blank. The next thing I know I woke up here.'

'How are you feeling now, headache, nausea, dizziness?'

Dora moved her head from side to side and was pleased to find there was no pain or sickness.

'No, I feel fine.'

He shone a torch in her eyes and told her to follow his finger, which she did. When he'd completed his tests and was satisfied, he took hold of her hand.

'I think you are good to go, Dora, I can find no reason to keep you here. Your blood pressure is a little high but that's to be expected. I think it will decrease when you leave here. I have no concerns except maybe you should take it easy for a couple of days. I overheard you telling Estella that you've recently flown to Boston. Do you travel much?'

'No, that's the first time I've been on a plane.'

'Do you have any pains, worries or concerns that I need to know about?'

Dora wondered what he would say if she told him that her brain had exploded with many lifetimes of memories, but decided to just smile at him. Maybe Sephy's anti-homesickness tea had caused this, but she wasn't about to tell him that in case he made her stay in, thinking she'd been poisoned, and got Sephy arrested.

'No, I feel fine now. I also feel like a fraud. I'm so sorry for wasting your time.'

He smiled at her and waved his hand. 'That is what we are here for, Ms English. Are you happy to be released?'

'Yes, absolutely. Thank you.'

He nodded and left her with Estella who was busy writing everything up on her chart.

'I can go then?'

'Yes, if you feel okay then you can go. Just make sure you sign the forms. Any repeat of those symptoms and you get yourself straight to the nearest hospital to get them checked out.'

'I will, I'm sure it was just a moment. Thank you.'

'You're welcome, take care.'

Estella pushed the curtain open and rushed to help a colleague who was struggling to get an elderly man out of his wheelchair and onto a bed. Dora stood up, grabbing her backpack and jacket from the chair before making her way out of the busy unit and out into the waiting area, which was rammed full of an assortment of people who looked far more in need of medical help than she was.

After signing the release forms, she made her way to the exit. Pushing the button to open the double doors, she stepped out into the cold, damp air and shivered. She needed to find Ambrose if that was at all possible. Just then, a bright orange cab with a black witch silhouetted on the side pulled up and a drunken couple staggered out of it. She waved at the driver and jumped in the back.

He set the meter running and drove her away. She was trying to stay focused on the roads and nothing else because inside her mind were a thousand memories threatening to come forwards and take over.

30

Sephy had spoonfed Lucine some of her favourite broth and she was now fast asleep. Sephy sat in the rocking chair next to the window so exhausted that she kept feeling herself dozing off. If it hadn't been for Hades hopping in and out, she would probably have fallen into a deep sleep. She felt helpless, Lucine was getting weaker by the day, Dora was out looking for the book and she had a sneaky feeling that Lenny had gone to some bar whilst waiting at the airport and picked up a bit of stuff – when the stress was high her way of dealing with it was by sleeping with a handsome young man half her age. Sephy sighed, a long, drawn-out sigh that she felt carried the weight of the world in it. She spotted a squidgy black spider in the corner of the window spinning a web of intricate gossamer threads and watched her. The spider moved deftly, weaving away until Hades hopped back inside the open window and opened his beak. She waved a finger in his direction.

'We don't eat or kill spiders in this house, Hades, mind your manners.'

The spider, who had sensed the bird and was now frozen,

waiting to be swallowed up, seemed to be staring straight at Sephy. She shook her head and whispered to it:

'You are quite safe here, dear. My friend will not pose a threat to you, he knows better than that.'

She reached out and petted Hades' head, stroking his soft feathers. He let out a low caw and rubbed himself against Sephy's arm. He glanced over at the bed where Lucine was tucked in and gently snoring then hopped out of the window and took off. Wearily, Sephy stood up. This time it was taking its toll on all of them, today they were a little more drained than yesterday. She desperately wanted to hear Dora's voice; now that she'd come back into their lives, even only for a few hours, she found that she didn't want to let her go and hoped that the little bit of protection she had given her had been enough. Tugging her shawl around her, she tiptoed out of the bedroom to go downstairs and see if she had any missed calls or updates from either member of her AWOL family.

The front door opened and in walked Lenny, a black cloud around her blotting out her aura. Sephy shook her head.

'Why aren't you on a plane to London? What did you do?'

'Nothing.'

'Your aura tells me different, Lenny. Have you heard from Dora?'

She sighed. 'No, I haven't heard from Dora, well not for a couple of hours. I thought you were keeping tabs on her? In any case, I have some very bad news for you.'

Sephy turned her back on her, walking away to the kitchen, her safe place, the heart of her home where she cooked up spells and made her magic, always for the good of others.

'Do I want to know this bad news?'

'No, but I'm going to have to tell you regardless. I saw him.'

Sephy turned to face her. 'You saw who?'

'Don't be coy with me, you know exactly who I saw.

Corwin. He looks different this time, but I guess we all do. He walked right past me at the airport and got into a cab.'

Sephy was wringing her hands. 'Oh my, oh my, what are we going to do? I'm not ready yet, we're not prepared.'

'I followed him.'

'You did what?'

'I drove your van and followed him.'

'Why? Are you mad Lenny, are you trying to get yourself killed without even trying?'

She laughed at this. 'No, but I've been thinking. Perhaps keeping Dora from Salem has worked this time. We've never seen him panic like this – chasing us across continents. I think we might be able to slow him down with our own spells. Maybe we can buy Dora a little more time to find the book.'

Lenny put her arm around her sister and pulled her close.

'Remember those freezing-cold winters the first time we lived and how if we hadn't hunted to eat, we would have starved?'

'Yes, but I hated it. I hated hurting those animals and how we ate them I will never understand.'

'We did it because it was survival. If we hadn't, we would have died without their skins to keep us warm and no, I didn't like it either, but we never even questioned it. We had to do it; we didn't think about it. This is the same. We've never wanted to hurt anyone, not even him. But we have to this time.'

Sephy sighed. 'How did we end up with such complicated lives?'

Lenny shrugged. 'I wish I knew; I think the day Giles Corey cursed Corwin was the catalyst and, God knows, who could blame him, being slowly crushed to death like that. We've always had the power; we just haven't used it to its full capacity. Oh, the irony, they tortured and hanged us and all those poor souls for being witches when we've never hurt anyone – not even Corwin.'

Sephy left the room, heading upstairs, and Lenny knew she was going to the attic where she kept her own book of spells, curses and hexes. Their second lifetime had been one filled with powerful magic; had written the spells themselves, all three of them. The binding, curses and hexes were so pure that they worked every time, but also scared the shit out of them. They had hoped they'd never have to use them. But the timing was right.

Corwin had wanted Lenny, even asked her to marry him but because she had said no, he had turned on them. A tear fell from the corner of her eye as she wondered yet again how their lives would have turned out if she'd said yes, how much heartache it would have saved, how much pain they could have avoided if she'd traded her own freedom for that of others.

A loud thwack as Sephy dropped their ancient book of spells onto the table, sending tiny dust motes into the air, snapped her out of the darkness inside her mind.

'Are you blaming yourself again?'

Lenny looked up at her. 'Yes, I always deny it but you and I both know that I will forever blame myself. This could have been prevented if I hadn't been so selfish. I realise that now, this is and always has been my fault.'

'It most certainly isn't, I know I hinted it was earlier and I'm sorry that was stupid of me. You didn't ask him to become obsessed over you, he was like some stalker from hell only we didn't know what a stalker was back then. He wouldn't leave you alone, watching you, following you, he was downright creepy. Who in their right mind would want to marry a man who behaves that way?'

'Are you telling me now that you don't blame me one little bit, that I shouldn't have been so wild and instead should have tamed myself to be a good Puritan woman who accepted an offer of marriage from the nephew of one of the most highly respected men in Salem town?'

'Jonathan was no better than his nephew George. It amuses me to see that it's him who was made out to be the monster of the witch trials – just because his bloody house managed to survive, so did his name. You have no idea how much I want to write a book on it all, the true account of the Salem Witch Trials written by Seraphina English who lived and breathed every awful moment of them.'

Lenny laughed. 'You should, it would be a *New York Times* bestseller, that's for sure.'

Sephy smiled at her. 'It would, but then people would think I'm even crazier than they already do, and we all know what happens when an English woman is accused of being crazy.' She winked at Lenny.

'So, what are we going to do?'

'We are going to gather everything we need to do the dark night binding spell and then we are going to call Dora back. Once Dora is back here, and hopefully with Lucine's lost book of magic, we are going to teach her everything she has forgotten. She is our last defence and our biggest hope but, in the meantime, we are going to equip ourselves with the power to stand up to him. It's time the English women ruled their own destiny and feared no man, especially not Corwin. We are going to take away his power and bring back our own.'

Lenny stood next to Sephy, and they both placed their hands on the ancient, cracked, black leather book with its fine gilt edges, full of many lifetimes of spells. They were tried and tested, they worked well, from finding lost things to making a lover true; maybe the spells weren't as powerful as the original ones in the missing spell book but it was a start. Both placed their right hands on the front of the book and closed their eyes, and the air around them fizzed, crackled and popped with tiny blue and gold bolts of electricity.

Hades had hopped through the open kitchen window and was perched on the sill next to Ophelia, not moving as they watched the two women intently. They had never bore witness to this before but the pair of them seemed to know that something magical and powerful was about to happen. Upstairs Lucine murmured in her sleep, too weak to get up and stand with her sisters, but she could sense what they were doing, and she joined them in spirit. Placing her right hand on the book in the middle of theirs, the power of three was the strongest magic of them all and it was about time that they reclaimed it.

31

Dora was tired and felt washed-out, but she had to find her mum's journal. She got out of the cab and hurried across Essex Street. Ambrose stepped out of the side door of his small condo above Sephy's apothecary. He looked pale and just as tired as her, but when he spotted her he smiled with relief.

'Dora.'

'Ambrose, I don't know what to say to you.'

He looked hurt and she felt awful that she kept on being like this to him, but what else was she supposed to do? She didn't remember him, even though he'd never forgotten about her.

'I've been looking for you everywhere. Can we talk?'

She nodded, unable to refuse him. Memories of his soft skin and warm hands had flooded her mind in the cab. She followed him up a small staircase to his apartment where he pointed to the couch and she sat down, relieved to be somewhere safe.

'My memories are coming back fast and furious,' she said as soon as her back hit the leather. She closed her eyes. 'I remember the randomest things, like washing in freezing-cold forest streams, I know that the Salem Witch Trials were held in

1692, I know that we were hanged, all of us, and that you tried to help me in some way. Sephy said that you saved my life once, thank you.'

'I know this is weird, Dora, but I feel pulled towards you.' This made her sad, her heart felt as if it was tearing in two. His big blue eyes were so full of kindness that she wanted to hug him and tell him it was okay. And maybe it was. Because she was starting to remember so much more with every passing hour.

'You need something to release the blockage, the memories are there inside your mind.'

She thought back to the witch trials memorial, the loud popping sound inside her head and waking up in hospital, but she didn't tell him about that in case he worried too much and wouldn't let her do what she needed to.

'If I was a witch, did I have a costume: a pointy hat, a magic wand, a broomstick?'

He laughed, but not in an unkind way. 'This isn't *Hocus Pocus*, Dora; you don't keep young by sucking the life out of the kids of Salem.'

'Phew, I'm glad to know that at least. You know what I mean though, did I have anything that was important to me?'

'You had Hades, who never left your side. You had your dark grey linen dress with lace cuffs that Sephy sewed for you, by hand. You said that you loved it, that you felt powerful whenever you wore it. I don't know what happened to that, but I can tell you one thing. You don't need a magic wand or a witch costume, your magic is deep inside of you, and it always has been. Whether you choose to believe that or not.'

'Do you think I still have the dress or that Lenny has it somewhere?'

She closed her eyes and saw herself standing at the edge of a forest, wearing a grey dress with a shawl wrapped around her shoulders. Her long black hair was blowing in the late summer breeze and her boots were speckled with mud from walking too close to the shore. She was young, sixteen at most if she had to guess. Hades was sitting on one shoulder, and she was watching the cottage she had once called home burning to the ground. She blinked and shook her head.

'Did our home burn the first time?'

He nodded. 'It did, after they took your mom and then your aunts, they didn't burn anyone. Instead they hanged them from the thick branch of a tree. They came back for you, but we'd escaped, we made it to the forest and hid. They couldn't find you, so they burned down the house and we left then. I had a small boat in the cove, and I hid you under a blanket and rowed away. I left my family behind, I left everything.'

'For me?'

He nodded. 'For you, and I'd do it again in a heartbeat, Dora.'

'Thank you, I'm lucky to have you as a friend, Ambrose.'

She reached out and stroked his cheek. Where her fingers touched his skin, she felt a tiny fizz of electricity in the tips and wondered if he could feel it too.

32

'You look a little pale, Dora, have you eaten?' Ambrose asked.

She shook her head.

'Why don't you get cosy and I'll make you something. We can't go out hunting for a book on an empty stomach.'

Dora nodded and lay back, not sleepy in the least but afraid of talking to Ambrose for much longer. As she closed her eyes, she felt the room begin to swim a little as if the sofa had been tipped to one side, like being in a bunk on a boat, the way the swell of the ocean made it rock from side to side, and then she was there on a huge sailing ship, not a cruise ship but one that looked like the *Marie Celeste*, which was the only sailing boat she could name. There weren't many other passengers, just the crew, herself and two young children. She called out to them, but they disappeared before her very eyes and the next moment she was walking along a dirt track through a forest, then running as if someone was chasing her. She reached the end of a cliff and threw herself down into the sea, a silent scream on her lips. She didn't hit the water though; in the blink of an eye, she was scurrying down an alley carrying a velvet box in one hand.

She could see the Empire State Building in the distance and

realised she was in New York. Her mind took her from one place to another, in all of them there was the same woman, yet slightly different, and she realised it was her. In New York she was smiling and flirting with a floppy-haired young man who she knew was Ambrose although his eyes were darker, and his skin tanned as they sipped cocktails in a bar on Fifth Avenue. The captain on the boat turned to smile at her; it was Ambrose's smile, there was no mistaking it even though he had a rough beard and a hat pulled tight on top of his head. She turned onto her side. She needed to find the book and hopefully it would loosen the rest of the memories to fill the blanks in.

She saw herself in Salem. Recognising the main street and the common, she walked arm in arm with Sephy and Lucine. They were smiling and laughing at something, all three of them dressed in gowns that would have been fashionable in the 1700s. This was really happening, for some strange reason Dora and her aunts were living life after life, and some of them looked fun, others not so much. At some point her mind must have shut down and her eyes closed, letting her fall asleep, because when the phone began to ring, she took a moment to wake up and find her bearings.

'Hello.'

Dora's voice was rough, tired and she was getting a cold.

'Ms English, this is Officer Eric McKinley, did I wake you up?'

She looked at the light that was filtering through the curtains and sat up.

'I'm sorry, not really. I've just had a bit of a day.'

'It's late, but I thought you would want to know as soon as possible.'

A lead ball settled in the pit of her stomach, and she wanted to end the call. If she didn't hear him say it then it wouldn't be true. Katie wasn't dead, she couldn't be, it wasn't supposed to end this way for either of them.

'How are you by the way?'

'I'm okay, thanks.'

'Good, I'm glad. We found your friend Katie.'

Dora sucked in her breath and held it.

'She was found in an empty shop, unconscious and badly beaten by a homeless guy looking for somewhere to shelter for the night.'

The breath Dora had been holding escaped with a loud sob. 'Oh my God.'

'She's not dead, she's in a coma and currently in the intensive care unit at St Thomas' Hospital.'

'She's alive, oh thank you. Thank you.'

'Her parents have been notified, and I believe they are travelling up to be with her. I thought it only right that someone let you know.'

'I can't thank you enough. How is Mabel?'

'Mabel is fine, she's a tough woman and after two cups of tea she shooed me out of her flat. I'm still going to need you to go through some mugshots and give me a detailed description about the man you thought might have done this. Is it possible to email them to you?'

'Of course.' Dora didn't know what this meant but at least Katie was in a safe place for the time being and Mabel was okay too. Officer McKinley was who he'd said he was and the relief was tangible. He wished her well and ended the call. She raced into the kitchen where Ambrose was putting the finishing touches to a bagel.

'I have great news, the police have found my friend Katie. She's in hospital unconscious but she's alive.'

He jumped in the air and yelled, 'Yes,' making her smile. He looked unashamedly handsome in the kind of understated way that a man can when he doesn't actually love himself more than anyone else.

'Thank you for this, Ambrose,' Dora said. 'For being so nice and kind, I really appreciate it.'

His cheeks flushed a deep red and she leaned across and kissed his lips, a soft, tender kiss that made her heart flutter wildly like a flapping bird's wings. Shocked, he paused and then kissed her back almost as softly. And then she remembered. The small wooden cabin. The tree outside. The rows and rows of books. The store as it vanished into the woods just like she'd wished it would back in the boat.

33

Sephy glanced at Lenny.

'It's not enough,' Lenny said. 'We have the binding spell, but we don't have the power to make it work when we're all fractured this way. And Lucine is failing fast, she will be lucky to last another twenty-four hours.'

Sephy blinked back a tear and nodded. 'I know and it never gets any easier. I just wish it was different.'

Lenny reached out and took hold of her sister's hands. 'I know, it's getting harder each time.'

Sephy clenched her hand tight. 'We should begin our preparations; I've gathered most of the things we need over the last six months, but Dora is the main ingredient. I wonder if she's found the journal yet.' She stopped for a moment. 'Are you ready for this to be your last life?' she asked thoughtfully.

Lenny shrugged. 'Would that be such a bad thing? Are you not a little jaded with the whole live a life, die, then come back and live another life with the same ending? I know I'm finding it a little repetitive. It wouldn't be so bad if we didn't live in fear most of the time and just got to enjoy our time together as a family, like we did so many moons ago.'

'I don't know, I find it kind of comforting knowing that when I die it's not final. That I'll be back, and we will all be reunited with each other.'

Lenny reached out and stroked Sephy's cheek. 'You always were a soppy soul.'

'And you never used to be so tough.'

'We've been through a lot. Things change but I'm glad that you're always the same Seraphina English every time we reunite, I wouldn't have you any other way. But we need to do this for Dora. For her to finally live, love, have children. What if in reliving, we're denying our family from carrying on?'

Sephy reached out and squeezed her sister's hand. She knew deep down inside her heart that the time was finally here.

34

'We need to piece together what happened that night. Up to now I remember you hammering on the cabin door, I remember you telling me I would die if I didn't run but where did we run to? Do you remember a library? A bookstore? A hideout?'

Ambrose was nodding. Dora had told him about the memory. He was squeezing his eyes shut, deep frown lines appearing on his forehead.

Dora reached out and took hold of his hand. 'Maybe if we sit together and try to remember, close our eyes. What were the woods called, are they still the same now?' He kept a tight hold of her hand and she realised that she didn't want him to let go.

'I don't know what they were called back then.' He jumped up. 'But the store vanished. It was my own hiding place, somewhere I stashed books that weren't allowed in town. I've never been able to find it. You mentioned a tree. Hang on, I can get some yellow pamphlets written by a historian Marilynne K Roach, she did like this *Time Traveller's Map of Salem Witchcraft Trials.*'

He left her and she heard his footsteps thundering down the narrow wooden steps. Moments later he burst through the door, waving two yellow booklets at her. He passed her one and they both began to study the hand-drawn maps of the area. It was handy living above Sephy's shop, Dora thought.

'Your cabin was in the fields near to what's called Pine Street,' Ambrose said. 'We ran through the woods which have been mostly cleared for luxury houses since then, we were heading to the cove to what's now called Singing Beach.'

Dora looked at him, then back down at the maps. 'That was a long way, how did I manage that?'

He chuckled. 'Not very well. You complained and moaned the entire time until you heard the dogs chasing us and then you realised that I was being serious. But this tree – if it was a large cedar, we have to go into the woods and see if it's still there.'

'What if they built houses on it? We can't go into someone's house and ask them if we can dig the cellars up.'

He was shaking his head. 'No, the woods that border the immediate area surrounding the beach are a conservation area, they've never been touched. We just need to figure out where in the woods it was, it's been some time since we were last there.'

He was giddy with excitement, and it was catching, suddenly Dora was raring to go. Every bit of exhaustion and brain fog had lifted at the thought of finally finding Lucine's book and taking it back where it belonged.

'Do you have a car, how long will it take to get there? Can we walk it?'

Ambrose held up his hands. 'Whoa, slow down a moment. I have no car and it's too far to walk from here.'

'Have you got the Uber app?'

'Yes.' He took his phone out and opened the app, typing in their destination, then double clicked to pay and smiling at her. 'Four minutes to meet us on Washington Street. Come on, we better get moving. Do we need anything?'

'A bag to put the book in, maybe a spade?'

He rolled his eyes. 'Oh, damn. Hang on, let me go speak to my friend and see if they can help out with the spade.'

They went back down into the shop and found Margo, who stared at the pair of them. 'Geez, you two have ants in your pants, you can't keep still for more than ten minutes.'

Dora smiled at her as Ambrose grabbed her hand and dragged her out of the shop down the road to a shop on Essex Street called The Magic Parlour where the owner was busy chatting. He took one look at Ambrose and nodded. 'What's up, dude?'

'Have you got a spade I could use?'

The guy looked confused but nodded. 'Be a minute, watch the shop.' Then he went out into the back and returned with a spade in his hand. 'I have no idea what you need that for, but as long as you're not about to start digging Essex Street up looking for buried treasure I don't care.'

Ambrose smiled at him, and Dora wondered if he was a little psychic. If they found Lucine's book it would be better than any treasure chest full of gold sovereigns.

The Uber driver dropped them on a street nearest to where Ambrose had worked out had been the path through the woods they would have taken. A lot of the land had been cleared and there were the most beautiful mansions standing on it. They got out of the car, Ambrose with his spade and backpack.

Dora looked at him. 'You know, we look like a couple of criminals about to break into someone's house. How long before the cops get called?'

He shrugged. 'We better not waste any time then. Can you tap into any of your powers to try and remember where the hell it was?'

Dora wished that she could, wished she could do something because time was running out. What was her power? Sephy had said she spoke the language of flowers. Did that include trees, she wondered. There were lots of them around still and Dora walked over to the biggest, oldest tree and placed her hands on the trunk. She closed her eyes and whispered, 'Do you know where I need to go?' She felt stupid, Ambrose was watching her along with probably at least ten home surveillance cameras.

But underneath her fingertips she could feel the slightest vibration. She pressed harder and although she didn't hear a voice telling her she felt something shift inside her and closed her eyes. Placing her ear against the trunk, she waited, listening. Her mind began to spin, and she saw the land as it was before the woodlands had been cleared to make way for the houses. There was an overgrown path they needed to follow a little further down the road.

'Hey, is she okay? Do you need help?'

Dora jumped and opened her eyes; an older man was standing behind the gates of the beautiful mansion they had been dropped outside of.

Ambrose smiled at him. 'No, she's fine, she's a tree hugger, always been a bit weird. Sorry, we're going now.'

Dora's mouth dropped open and she had to stifle the laughter threatening to burst out of it. Ambrose grabbed her hand and waved at the guy. 'Have a good one.' Then he was dragging her away, hissing, 'We better keep moving before he calls the cops. Did you get anything?'

She nodded. 'I know where there's a path.'

He stared at her in wonder. 'You still have it, who'd have thought.'

She knew he was referring to her ability to communicate with flowers. Now she could add trees to that list.

Half a mile down the road there was the tiniest of paths leading between the trees, so overgrown she almost missed it, but she heard a voice inside her mind telling her to stop and she did, so abruptly that Ambrose walked straight into the back of her.

'This is it; we need to go down there. I'll go first, although I don't know what exactly I'm looking for.'

She looked around to see if anyone was watching her, there was nobody, and she pushed her way through the low evergreen branches of white pine which filled the air with the scent of Christmas. There were lots of brambles, too, that kept catching on their clothes. After what felt like forever the path opened into a small, wooded area but none of this looked familiar to either of them. Dora didn't want to sound pessimistic but she felt it. A large flat rock jutted out of the ground, and she sat down on it, and Ambrose did the same.

'It's so different. I have this clear image in my mind of where it was, but this doesn't feel at all familiar. I'm sorry, Ambrose, I thought that I would have no problem finding it.'

He reached out and clasped hold of her fingers. 'Don't give up just yet, Dora, we're close, I can feel it.'

She closed her eyes to stop the tears from falling and to give into the exhaustion she felt. The burden of knowing she was being chased by an evil hunter who wanted to kill her was making it hard to think of anything else, that and Lucine. Her beautiful, dying mum who she wasn't going to spend much time with. She heard whispering and opened her eyes.

'Can you hear that?'

'What?'

'Shh.'

Dora stood up, where was it coming from? It was like a swoony, sing-song sound of kids singing nursery rhymes. She let her feet move in the direction of the voices and hoped that this wasn't some kind of trap.

35

There was a patch of brambles so thick that Dora doubted even rabbits could get through it, but that was where the strange singing was coming from, and she found herself standing in front of it. She turned to look at Ambrose.

'It's through there, I can hear them calling to me.'

He looked at the thick branches, their sharp thorns, and whistled. 'We didn't need a spade; we need a machete, maybe even a chainsaw to get through that.'

Dora lifted her fingers in front of her face, staring at the chipped black nail varnish and her silver rings, wondering if it was worth a try. Then she realised that she had no option. They had managed to come this far, if they left without even trying to get to the cabin, they might never find it again. She closed her eyes and pointed at the clump of thorny branches, criss-crossed to stop anyone passing through them.

'Vines so thick and brambles sharp, grant me the way deep into your heart, lead me to find the books I need, to save my life and honour thee.'

A tiny crackle of static electricity shot out of the end of her finger and the vines and brambles began to slither back. She watched, eyes open wide in awe, and whispered, 'It's like something out of a fairy tale.' Then: 'Thank you, thank you, thank you, you did a great job of keeping Lucine's book safe, she will be so thankful to you for protecting it all this time.

Ambrose was laughing and clapping. 'You did it, Dora you did this.'

Dora was watching in amazement, and a tiny voice whispered, 'You did this, you really can speak the language of flowers.'

She clapped her hands and smiled. 'This is wonderful, I don't know where those words came from, but they worked.' She held out her hand and Ambrose took hold of it. Together they stepped forward, walking along the narrow winding path until they saw the small wooden door that looked as new as the day Ambrose had built it, protected by the canopy of the ancient cedar tree.

Dora grinned at him and rushed towards it. She placed her fingers against the wood and jolted as a rush of memories flooded her mind: Ambrose was dragging her through the woods, she had a stitch and was moaning at him, the sound of the dogs searching for them making her blood turn to ice. She had Lucine's heavy book clutched in one arm, Ambrose pulling a loose board away so she could hide the book. She remembered the gentle sway of the boat on the water, the first kiss they shared, so tenderly, how he declared his love for her and how she knew he loved her deeply. Dora turned to Ambrose and kissed him; he pulled her close and she didn't want it to end but when she did draw away from him he stared at her.

'What was that for?'

'For always being my saviour, for loving me across centuries of time and for saving me that night. I'm sorry I couldn't save myself for you, but I will try this time, I promise I will stop this, for once and all.'

He stared into her green eyes. 'I've loved you forever, Izzy.'

She nods. 'I know you have and I'm grateful you never let me go. I'm sorry that I left you that night, after all you did to save me. It wasn't enough, and I couldn't save myself, but things have changed. Times have changed and it's my turn to do what I was powerless to do all those years ago. It's time to end this curse and stop Corwin for good. I know with the book's help I can do it and if I don't...'

Ambrose had tears falling from his eyes. 'If you don't then I lose you again for who knows how many lifetimes. I cannot bear it, Izzy, we were meant to be together. I could help you; do you know how much I've wanted to kill him, time and time again I've dreamed of hurting him the way he hurt you all.'

She trailed her fingers across his cheek. 'I imagine a lot, but it wouldn't stop him if you killed him and that's not who you are. It would change you as a person and I'm in love with this Ambrose, the kind, gentle, honourable one. If you did, it wouldn't make a difference because, like us, he'll be back, and we'll be in the same position. I need to be the one to stop him – it's the only way.'

'But he hurt you all so much.'

It was all coming back to Dora. She remembered the muggy warmth of that New England day as the rope was roughly placed around her neck, she watched that rickety old cart as it came through Salem town up Essex Street with her family on it and she remembered the looks of grief and shock on her mum, Lenny and Sephy's faces when they saw her already balanced on the back of an equally rickety old horse-drawn cart. Did she ever explain to them that she'd tried to save them, but failed miserably?

'He did. He took our lives one by one that day out on the ledge, but he never took our souls. Hades did that, he took us somewhere we were safe until it was our time to be born again. He never let your uncle win and Corwin was furious about it.

He has carried that anger over into many lifetimes, he really needs to let it go.'

Ambrose laughed and she grinned at him. 'Now, let's find Lucine's book and keep it safe.'

They stepped inside the ramshackle wooden cabin that had stood the test of all this time. The ceiling was low, and it was dark in there, but it smelled gloriously of old books. Dora used her phone torch to light up the small space, letting out a small gasp of delight to see the leather-bound books that Ambrose had bartered for centuries ago sitting on the shelves as good as new, no mildew or mould.

She picked up each one and kissed it, flicking through the pages. 'I never thanked you for this either. You changed the course of our lives by giving us stories to read when we thought the bible and God were all that there was out there. These books took us on so many adventures; I'm pretty sure it was these books that gave me the courage to go back that night and face your uncle, foolish as it was.'

She clutched a copy of *Romeo and Juliet* to her chest. 'They may have been star-crossed lovers, but our story is far greater than theirs ever was. You should write about this one day, Ambrose, it is a story worth telling. Our love has spanned centuries, not mere days.'

He laughed. 'I might just do that. But you know what all great stories need, don't you?'

'Likeable characters, great plots, a villain everyone hates?'

He shook his head. 'Well, those are important too, and we definitely have all of those ingredients. But a really good story has to have a happy ending, Izzy. I can't write our story until we have our happy ever after.'

Dora smiled. 'Then it's time that we did. It's time to give it to ourselves, don't you agree?'

Ambrose pulled her to him, the heat radiating from his body making hers melt into him, and they kissed harder, faster and with more passion than the pair of them had ever known existed. The air inside the cabin was fraught with tension as they began to fumble with each other's clothes. Dora knew that this had never felt so good, they had never got this far to loving each other in the past. Falling to the floor, they landed on the earthen ground on a bed of leaves, cloaked in darkness, surrounded by the books and the magic that held them in a warm embrace.

After, Dora laid her head on Ambrose's chest and sighed. 'Why did we wait so long?'

His fingers stroked her hair. 'Perhaps we had to wait.'

She smiled. 'I love you, Ambrose Corwin, even if you do have the shittiest family on earth.'

At that he laughed so loud it echoed around the cabin. 'I'm sorry, I truly do.'

Dora sat up, hurriedly dressing. 'Come on, we have to find the book and return to my family.'

She closed her eyes, slowly turned in a small circle then let her feet lead her to the place they had hidden it that terrible night in 1692. She bent and pulled at the loose board by her feet and saw the corner of the heavy leather book. Bending down, she picked it up and clutched it to her chest, tears of joy in her eyes and a newfound belief that this time really was going to be different, this time she would fight Corwin face to face and, with the help of the spells in the book, put an end to his reign of terror, end this curse and get their happy ever after.

36

Ambrose left Dora to go back to the apothecary and relieve Margo, soon Dora heard the familiar flapping of wings above her head and felt the cool breeze as Hades croaked, 'Dora's home, Dora's home.'

She looked up at him and smiled. 'Yes, I'm home and for good this time.'

He nodded his head at her, flew a couple of loops then swooped and landed on her shoulder where he began to preen at the hair above her ear.

She giggled. 'Stop that, it tickles.' He did, but instead rubbed his head against the side of hers and she lifted a hand to stroke his soft feathers. 'I had no idea I even had a pet crow, but I've missed you, bird.'

She walked to the front gate. Anyone watching would have stopped and stared at the beautiful young woman with hair as black as the crow on her shoulder and skin as white as snow, with a huge leather book tucked under one arm. They made a formidable pair and Dora realised that this was where she had always belonged as she walked down the path to Sephy's pink front door. This was her home, and she wasn't leaving again until everything the English sisters had spent their lives fearing had been stopped for all of eternity.

The front door opened, and she saw her aunts standing there.

'Lenny, I thought you would still be on your way to London.'

Lenny lifted a finger to her lips. 'Shush child, I'm back, I'm okay, and boy am I happy to see you too.'

Dora grabbed hold of her aunt and held her close, and it felt good. Then she let go of her and pulled Sephy close. When she released her, she smiled at them.

'I'm still a bit woozy on the finer details but I remember the first lifetime and what happened and...' She thrust Lucine's book at them. 'I'm ready to learn everything I need to break this curse. Will you show me how?'

Lenny let out a loud whoop and punched the air as Sephy began to cry. 'You did it, Dora, you found the book. Well done, sweet girl, I knew you could. And yes, dear, of course we will. We're so happy to hear you say this but remember, no matter how much we can teach, you are a blood witch, and your power is deep inside of you. All you need to do is to connect with the things you love and let it unlock itself.' She patted her heart.

Dora nodded. 'I am, or at least I'm trying to, I used the language of flowers to get to the cabin and it was so magical. The bookstore where the book was hidden revealed itself to me. It had vanished – Ambrose had struggled to find it for all of these lifetimes – but a clear path came to me in the woods, and there it was. Tucked behind a cedar tree. It was the most magical, incredible sight to behold. A store of happy endings, of stories and instructions.'

Sephy and Lenny looked at each other in amazement.

'A vanishing bookstore? Is it still there?' Sephy asked.

'I'm not sure. Perhaps it only revealed itself long enough to let me find the book.'

Sephy looked thoughtful, but she and Lenny smiled, relieved. 'It's been a long couple of days for you, how do you feel? Any sickness this time?'

She shook her head. 'I feel great, no nausea, and even if there was, I'd rather not sip that anti-homesickness tea. No offence, Sephy, but it's time to teach me everything I need to know to put an end to all of this and I don't think teas are the way to go.'

'No, unless you throw it at him and scald him, then I guess it isn't.' Lenny laughed.

Dora grinned. 'Who'd have thought it, the English women finally reunited and ready to rock and roll one last time.'

Sephy smiled at her, then turned to Dora. 'We have some sad news for you, dear. Lucine is failing fast. Would you please go and sit with her for a little while and tell her that you're ready to end this. It would be nice for her to pass knowing this.'

Dora felt a crushing wave of grief wash over her shoulders so strong that her knees almost buckled.

'Why can't we stop her from dying? If we possess magical powers can't we put a stop to it?'

'We can't interfere with the life cycle, dear, it's not possible unless you practise dark magic, and we don't do that. It doesn't work anyway – if you were to use it to bring someone back who has passed on you wouldn't be bringing the same person back. They come back flawed, like a shell of their past selves, and it's far too much heartache.'

'How do you know if you haven't tried?'

Lenny nodded at Sephy. 'We tried it once and it was terrible. Your mother was not herself, she was cruel and mean, she thrived off wickedness and it was the worst mistake we ever made. To bring a loving soul back as a sick and twisted half version of themselves is worse than death itself.'

'But can't we just break the curse? Live another lifetime so I can spend time with my mother? Break the curse next time?'

Dora's aunts looked at one another with sadness.

'We think this is our only chance. I know you haven't spent time with her now, but you've spent many lifetimes with her. This is about you finally living past thirty-five – with Ambrose. Getting a chance at having your own family. That's what Lucine wants.'

Dora nodded, wishing she could do or say something. Instead, she turned and ran up the stairs to Lucine's bedroom. Opening the door, the first thing she smelled was the medicinal, clinical smell of illness. Lucine was even frailer than she had been the day before, her head had shrunk into the pillows and she looked so tiny. Her eyes fluttered as Dora drew closer to the bed, sitting carefully next to her, they finally opened.

She looked at her and whispered, 'Dora.'

Dora couldn't stop the tears this time, they fell down her cheeks and she gently took hold of Lucine's hand. 'Mum.'

Lucine lifted her left hand and stroked Dora's cheek. 'You came back.'

'I found your book and I'm home now. I'm never leaving again, I promise you.'

Lucine smiled at her. 'I'm so happy, I knew you would. Do you remember everything?'

She nodded. 'I do.'

'Good, then you know that Corwin is not to be trusted and how dangerous he is.'

'Yes, I do. I'm going to stop him this time, I promise I will.'

'I want you to be careful. He's as mean as a hungry moose but you're able to take care of yourself and him. I'm sorry I can't be here to help you; this lifetime is almost up, and it makes me so sad that we didn't get to be together longer.'

Dora was trying not to cry but it was hard to get air into her lungs because her breath kept hitching.

'I don't want you to go, you can't leave me when I've only just found you.'

Lucine smiled at her. 'I will always be with you, my sweet child.' She tapped her chest, just like Sephy had, then tapped Dora's heart. 'Whenever you need me, I'll be in your heart. You will always carry a piece of me around with you, just as I always carry a piece of you within me.'

A dark shadow appeared at the window and Dora watched as Hades hopped inside and flew to the bedside table next to Lucine.

She turned her eyes to stare at him. 'Is it time to go, my old friend?'

Hades buried his head into Lucine's neck, and she gave him a gentle smile then closed her eyes, her grip on Dora's hand loosening as she took her last breaths. Time stood still. Dora watched as a glowing white light rose from Lucine's frail body, so bright she had to shield her eyes. Hades flew to the window, the light following him, and he took off into the sky, soaring so high that all Dora could make out was a small black dot followed by a glowing ball of brilliant white light. She heard a loud sob and realised that Sephy and Lenny were standing in the doorway.

'What was that?'

'Hades is guiding Lucine's soul to the light where she belongs. He is such a wonderful watcher, he will take care of her now just like he always does.'

Dora looked at her mum's frail body lying on the bed, she did look like a shell of the woman from yesterday.

Lenny stepped in and sat next to Dora, wrapping her arms around her.

'It's been a tough few days, eh kid? But Lucine is in a kinder, better place, where there is no pain, and she can be free to enjoy herself until it's time to come back. Hades will make sure she's safe, while we take care of this mortal body.'

Dora sobbed; she didn't know what else to do, there was nothing to say. Sephy came in and bent down to kiss her sister's head. 'It never gets any easier, does it? We live our lives and watch her die, only to come back and do it all over again.'

She took a deep breath. 'I need to phone the funeral home, Richard is waiting on our call and he will take good care of Lucine. He's a good man, a kind man, despite his rather morbid job, but someone has to take care of the dead and he's the finest there is at it.'

Sephy left Dora and Lenny, Dora still had hold of Lucine's hand. Lenny touched Dora's shoulder.

'Take your time. I'm sorry you didn't get to be together for very long. We thought we were doing the right thing, but we weren't as usual. We screwed up spectacularly and now we're in the same mess as always.'

Dora looked at her aunt. 'You tried to save me from my destiny, and I get that, all of you did what you thought was the right thing to do. I don't hate you for it, I love you. I'm just sad that our time together was so limited. I can tell you one thing though, when I get to go head to head with that bastard, he's going to pay for all of this, for all of our lost lifetimes. For betraying the English women the way that he did. If it's the last thing I do, I'm going to send him to hell or wherever he deserves to be.'

37

Dora waited downstairs while Lenny and Sephy washed Lucine and changed her into a pair of soft, cosy PJs that she'd requested to be cremated in. There was a knock at the door and she answered it to see a tall man all dressed in black with a beard wearing an AC/DC T-shirt underneath his suit jacket. He held out his hand to Dora.

'I'm so sorry for your loss. I'm Richard Thorne, funeral director.'

She nodded. 'Thank you, I, erm... they're upstairs. My aunts, I mean, and Lucine. Should I show you?'

He shook his head. 'I'm quite familiar with this house, thank you. I was good friends with Lucine. Such a terrible loss, she was such a wonderful woman.'

Dora smiled at him. He seemed genuinely upset, which was nice considering he must be used to dealing with death every single day. She stepped to one side to let him in, and he made his way upstairs to where Sephy was waiting for him.

She opened her arms. 'Richard, thank you for coming so soon.'

He stepped forwards and hugged her, pulling her close. 'I'm sorry, Sephy, I know how hard this must be for you all.'

They stood that way, holding on to each other for a few moments. It was Sephy who let go first and it was then that Dora realised Richard was more than just a funeral director, he must have known Lucine on a personal level which must have made this so hard for him. Sephy pointed to the open doorway, and he walked in. Dora could hear hushed voices as he talked to Lenny, then he came back down, his eyes red and swollen. He went outside and beckoned the younger man sitting in the passenger seat of the minivan with blacked-out windows. The guy got out and walked towards the house, his earbuds in, his head nodding to whatever he was listening to. Richard glared at him, and he tugged the earphones out, tucking them into his trouser pocket.

'Where's the gurney?'

'Sorry, dude, I'll go get it.'

Richard looked at Dora, an expression of exasperation etched across his already grief-stricken face.

'You just can't get the staff; he drives me insane at times.'

The guy unloaded the gurney with a clean body bag on top from the back of the van and wheeled it down the path towards the front porch. He jammed the wheels into one of the uneven paving slabs, throwing the body bag onto the ground. Richard groaned and the guy looked up at him, an expression of horror on his face.

'Sorry, Uncle Richard.'

'Guy, just get inside without breaking everything in sight, will you.'

Dora smiled; the guy was actually called Guy, who'd have guessed that one. As he came up the steps, he looked at Dora and grinned.

'I'm Guy and you are?' He held out his hand towards her.

She didn't take it. 'The deceased's daughter.'

'Oh, jeez. I'm sorry, it's just you're hot, you know. I like a woman with tattoos and piercings.'

Richard's face had turned from a whiter shade of pale to tomato red.

'Guy, I swear to God if you open your mouth once more, I'm going to sack you right now in front of these good people.'

Guy held up his hands. 'Chill, dude, compliments where a compliment is due. I'm truly sorry for your loss.'

Dora didn't know whether to laugh or cry. She opted for nodding and heading down to the kitchen, the heart of Sephy's home, where she began to tidy around the many jars that were lined up on the side. She didn't want to see Lucine being wheeled out of her home in a body bag, she also didn't want Guy to get himself into any more trouble than he already was. He seemed like a nice enough person, maybe a little too chilled for an undertaker – or maybe that was a good thing in that profession.

Hades had been gone a couple of hours now and she wondered how far he had taken Lucine on her next journey. Dora was sad, but she felt better knowing that there was something more than the finality of death and how privileged she was to have witnessed the beauty of it. After a lot of hushed talking and some clanging around, Dora breathed a sigh of relief to hear the van doors slam shut and the engine start. The front door closed softly, and she didn't need any magical powers to know that both Sephy and Lenny were standing at the kitchen door watching her. She turned around to look at their grief-stricken faces. Lenny looked tired and for the first time in her life Dora felt worried about her formidable aunt; no matter their lineage and bloodline, they were still mortal beings. It was their souls that were immortal, and she didn't know how to feel about that.

'I'm so sorry.'

Sephy shook her head. 'No, we are the ones who are sorry.

We should have brought you home sooner, you barely got to see her before...' She stopped and pulled out a chair, sitting down.

Lenny joined her. 'Are you okay, Dora? You've never had to deal with death this time around.'

Dora took a seat opposite her aunts. 'I'm sad beyond belief, but I also feel better knowing that Hades is taking care of her.'

'Hades is a good bird; he's always been there to keep our souls safe and he's been around as long as we have. He will take good care of Lucine, he always does, then he will come home and take care of you, Dora, if you let him. If you don't, he will go his own way for a little while, but he always comes back. Try not to chase him away, he's like our little good luck talisman and I couldn't bear to lose them both in one day.'

'I would never chase him away, I love him.'

Lenny nodded. 'Good, that's good. I'm glad you're over that fear of birds you had in London.'

'I never knew birds could be so beautiful or clever. Those pigeons scared me, all they did was swoop at your head for food. So, what's next?'

'What do you mean, dear?' Sephy asked.

'What's the plan, how am I going to fight Corwin, is he human like us, can he be killed?'

'It seems to me that he will know that Lucine has died soon enough and know that we are all at our most vulnerable. If he is the monster that I think he is, he won't wait around, he will come for us when we're least expecting him and unfortunately not, Dora, he is what we call an in between, both worlds part human, part immortal.'

Lenny nodded. 'She's right. He's here in Boston, which is why I couldn't leave for London, I had to come home. We need to focus on what we can teach Dora to make this work.'

'But Lucine?' Sephy said.

'She would tell us to get to work and not mope around. What would you want us to do if it was you?'

'Weep forever, throw yourselves on top of my grave and never stop loving me.'

'Sephy, darling. I love you more than life itself and yes, I would weep forever, but I would not throw myself on top of your grave for love nor money. What would you really want us to do?'

'Beat that brute at his own game, end this madness forever.'

'And how exactly do we do this?'

'We teach Dora everything she needs to know.'

Lenny shrugged. 'Of course, we're grieving and always will be, but we have no time to lose. I'm ready to do this, are you, sister?' She held out her hand and Sephy took hold of it, clenching it firmly.

Sephy nodded. 'Let's do it.'

Then she stood and rushed into the small conservatory attached to the side of the kitchen where there was a huge pine dresser filled with plants, herbs, bottles and candles. Opening the bottom drawer, she pulled out the huge black book Dora had brought back. She slammed it onto the pine kitchen table and looked up at Lenny. The book was striking to look at and Dora felt a quiet determination building inside her. They were giving her strength, and she would take everything they could give her.

'The old ways always were the best,' Sephy said. 'We've tried all the modern stuff, and yes it works to some degree, but we need strength, we need to reignite our power that we buried long ago and bring it all back into force.'

'Lucine's book... your father's book.' Lenny looked at it with trepidation.

Dora watched her aunts. 'I thought that Sephy was the most powerful out of you all, she has the shop, she gives out the spells, makes the tea and potions?'

Sephy smiled at her. 'I'm good, but I was never as good as your mother.'

Dora's mouth was agape.

'But I thought you'd all been hanged for being witches when you weren't in the first place?'

Sephy sat back down at the table. 'We were healers, Dora, at one with nature and good-hearted enough that we would not watch another soul suffer when we could help them. We can turn on the lights without touching a switch, stir our coffee without touching a spoon, we can shut doors, open them, cloak ourselves so people don't see us, anything not too strenuous. But when it comes to the real stuff out of fairy tales... we never used proper magic. Your father gave your mother this book of real magic.'

'Then why didn't she put a stop to Corwin herself?'

'We think it was always meant for you.'

Dora let all of this new information settle in.

'You need to strip him of his powers and bind him to this earthly plane where he will no longer be able to travel through time and space to hunt women like us. We've always had an inkling that there are lots of us dotted around the world. In every country there are immortal women and some men like Ambrose. But that's a story for a different time.'

Dora opened the heavy book. Despite their age, the pages felt like the softest velvet against her fingertips, and she marvelled at the words, the spells to bring back a loved one, the soul of someone dearly departed, eternal youth. There was a small note tucked into the spine that she pulled loose.

I love you dearly, Lucine, I promise we will be together again.
Never lose faith and keep this book safe for inside these pages is
the key to my heart.

Tears pricked at Dora's eyes. To think her father had written this centuries ago, declaring his love for her mother, was beautiful.

She nodded. 'I'm ready.' A loud squawk from outside the kitchen window made all three of them jump, and they turned to see Hades watching them from the windowsill. Dora stood up and opened the window to let him in.

'You came back, darling, thank you for taking care of Lucine.' She stroked his feathers, and Hades bowed his head.

'Lucine is home, Dora is home.'

Sephy let out a sob and Lenny also bowed her head. Dora held out her arm for Hades to jump onto.

'Yes, thank you. I'm home and so are you; we have work to do, are you ready?'

He jumped up and down.

'I'll take that as a yes. Will you help me, Hades?'

The bird puffed out his chest and stared at Dora with his small, sparkling black eyes.

'Hades is here.'

'Good, then we have everything we need – or almost everything. Do either of you know where my grey linen dress is, the one Sephy made for my sixteenth birthday?'

Sephy stood up. 'I do, but we can't get it back, dear. It's in the conservation department of the Peabody Essex Museum.'

'Why is it there?'

'We left it behind a couple of lifetimes ago and they found it, it's on display.'

'I want it back. It's my dress and I think that when I last wore it, I felt powerful and I want to feel that way again. I think it will tie me to my past lives and give me more strength, which is a good thing, right?'

Lenny looked at Sephy. 'I told you we should have sorted that out when we first realised they had it.'

'How was I supposed to know she would want the dress, Lenny?'

Lenny rolled her eyes. 'Are you forgetting how stubborn Dora is?'

'I wish you wouldn't talk about me as if I'm not here, it's rude.'

Sephy nodded. 'Sorry, dear, but you know it's been a while since you've even thought about that dress. I could make you another.'

Dora shook her head. 'I want that one, it's mine.'

Lenny answered her. 'Well then, we're going to have to steal it back. Unless Ambrose can speak to the girls in the department and charm them into giving it back.'

'Do you think they're going to give out an authentic linen dress from the sixteen hundreds that was worn by the daughter of an English woman before they were hanged at Proctor's Ledge? It's steeped in more history than that spell book and if we tell them it's our property, which technically it is, it will blow their minds and it won't be long before Corwin hears about it. We can't afford to give him the slightest advantage.'

'But they don't know about the spell book, do they, or that we're still alive. We can only try.'

Lenny pursed her lips. 'Dora, do you positively need that dress?'

Dora thought about it for a few moments then nodded. 'Yes, I'm sorry but I think it's the key to unlocking everything. I can remember how much I loved it, how I felt when I wore it. I've never felt that way about anything else I've ever owned.'

'Then we're going to have to steal it back, it's the only way.' Lenny stood up. 'Sephy, get the spells and stuff ready for when we get back.'

'Where are you going?'

'To get Dora the damn dress back. Come on, Dora, we might need to enlist Ambrose's help. He's always maintained a good relationship with the people down at the museum, he can distract them while we take it.'

Dora felt bad; Sephy was breathing so fast she looked as if she was having a panic attack.

'I'll take the blame if we get caught, don't worry, Sephy. Hades, you better stay here, I don't want you to get in any trouble.'

Hades was busy drinking water from the tap and didn't pay Dora the slightest bit of attention. Lenny pulled on her coat, and Dora did the same then followed her outside.

'I can do this myself; you don't need to come.'

'No, you can't. We're going to have to cause a distraction and you can't do both. Ambrose will go and chat to the staff while I pretend to pass out or something. When they come to help me, you grab the dress and walk out of there. I'll use my power to shield you the best that I can so they don't notice you.'

They headed to find Ambrose, and Dora wondered what she was getting them all into. But she needed that dress. All she could see when she closed her eyes was her younger self wearing it and feeling as if she could conquer the world. She needed to harvest all the energy she could and if a simple dress was the key to understanding everything then she had to have it back.

38

Ambrose was talking to a customer when Dora and Lenny walked into the apothecary, but he stopped when he saw them. Excusing himself, he called Margo over to take over and hurried to where they were standing.

'Is everything okay?'

Lenny didn't speak, leaving it to Dora.

'Lucine is dead, and I need a favour from you.'

His hand cupped his mouth. 'I'm so sorry for your loss.' His eyes filled with tears and Dora felt a little piece of her heart breaking away and moving towards him.

'Thank you. I know you are, but we didn't come to tell you that. I really do need a favour.'

'Anything at all, just ask.'

Lenny shook her head. 'Not so sure you'll agree to this one, kid.'

Dora ignored her aunt. 'I need my dress back. It's in the Peabody Essex Museum and I need you to go and distract the staff while Lenny fakes passing out so I can take it back.'

Ambrose arched an eyebrow. 'You want to steal your dress from the museum with our help?'

'Yes, please. I need it, don't ask me how or why I do, I just know that I do.'

He glanced at Lenny. 'You're all right with this?'

'I haven't got much choice; she will go get it herself if we don't help her, and I think she stands more of a chance if we at least do our part to distract the staff.'

'They're going to notice an empty display cabinet. Have you not got something to replace it with? There are dresses in the shop across the road that are replicas of the style the Puritan women wore.'

'This wasn't exactly an authentic dress, although if we could get one a similar colour it might just do.'

Lenny left to go in search of an alternative dress, leaving Ambrose staring at Dora.

'Are you okay?' His fingers reached out to touch hers. 'I mean, stealing from a museum is a serious offence, Dora. This has all been a huge shock to you and now Lucine has gone and you're about to commit a federal crime.'

'Even if I'm stealing my own dress? It's not theirs, they stole it from me.'

'Who is ever going to believe that?'

'Well then, I'll just have to make sure I don't get caught.'

He smiled at her, which made her more determined than she had been moments ago and she pulled her hand away from him.

'I will do what I can to help,' he said. 'The staff are pretty nice. We could always ask them if you could have it back or say you need to borrow it for a while. That it belonged to your great-great-great-grandmother or something.'

'I haven't got the time and if they know I want it and say no, they will know who has taken it. Better to borrow it for a little while and replace it with a replica. Sephy said she could make another, I just don't know how long it will take her.'

'I'll grab my coat.'

Ambrose walked towards the counter where Margo was ringing up the sale for the customer and she looked at him.

'You leaving so soon?'

'Duty calls, I won't be long.'

'Jeez, you're a huge help around here, you know that, don't you?'

He laughed. 'You know I love you, Margo.'

'Yeah, I'm not so sure about that. You use me.'

He pecked her cheek and her cheeks flushed red.

'Get out of here.' She pushed him away, but Dora didn't miss the kindness in her smile. Margo had a real soft spot for Ambrose, which was sweet. Lenny walked back in clutching a brown paper bag. She opened it and Dora peeked inside at the grey cotton dress.

'It's nothing like it, but if you can swap them over it might just buy us some time. Hopefully the staff won't notice straight away. You know that stealing from a museum is a federal offence.'

'I do know that, Ambrose just told me before you came back.'

'Just checking, I don't want you to end up in the cells without knowing it's a possibility.'

'Thank you.'

'I will use my cloaking power as best as I can, but it's October and I can guarantee the place will be full of tourists. Look around, there's no room to manoeuvre, they're everywhere.'

'We might be able to use it to our advantage then.'

Lenny smiled. 'Always the optimist, just like Sephy.'

All three of them made their way along Essex Street, the Salem Trolley full of tourists rang the bell as it drove past and an old guy waved at them with a kind smile on his face. Dora waved back, it was taking the tourists on a guided tour of the town and she thought how nice it must be to be able to enjoy being in Salem without the fear of a life-or-death battle with a crazed witch hunter. They reached the enormous glass-and-metal entrance to the museum in a matter of minutes. They had a plan: Ambrose was to go in first, Dora a few minutes after and Lenny after her. Dora was to make her way to the conservation hall where she would find her cherished dress on display.

Lenny turned to her. 'Grab a lanyard on the way in or something. If you act as though you work at the museum, no one will bother you.'

Dora smiled. 'I think you've been down this route before.'

'Not for a dress. The last time I had to do this was to break you out of that god damn awful insane asylum you were locked up in. It was a very long time ago now, but I can still smell the urine and despair whenever I think about it. One day I'll remind you just how terrible it was so you can appreciate everything you have now.'

'You've got me out of a lot of scrapes over the years. Thank you, Lenny, for always being there for me. I love you more than you could ever know.'

'Don't get all soppy on me, Dora, I simply do what I have to in order to ensure you're safe. It's my duty as your aunt. Now get inside and do your god damn best not to get caught or we're all going to be suffering for it later.'

Dora knew that she meant Corwin, not the cops. Cops they could deal with; Corwin was much trickier. They waited a few minutes as Ambrose went in first, as Dora walked inside the entrance of the museum, a security guard nodded at her and she paid her admission fee; she looked around at the busy cafeteria and wished she had time to stop for a latte. She could do with a caffeine hit before she committed her first real felony. Dora wandered over to the help desk where a flustered man was trying to deal with a group of teenagers on a day trip with their teacher. He was facing the other way, his hands in the air, and she spied his lanyard on the desk.

'Could you all please just speak one at a time, I can't hear myself think,' he said.

The teacher was trying to get the kids to shut up when two boys began to push and shove each other, Ambrose and the guard rushed towards them to intervene. Dora, who had never stolen anything in her entire life, tripped forwards and, putting a hand on top of the lanyard to steady herself, she swiped it and walked briskly away. The ID badge clenched in her closed fist, she looked around then slipped the lanyard over her head. She followed the signs for the conservation hall, which had a barrier across it and a sign that read 'Temporary Closure'. She slipped around it and into the darkened hall, looking around at the display cases, then finally she caught sight of it.

It was a plain linen dress with lace cuffs, a high lace collar and a row of tiny buttons on the back. She felt a rush of memories so strong they threatened to send her to her knees as her legs weakened just thinking about them. There were images from so many lifetimes. She was sitting by a riverside having a picnic with a wavy-haired man wearing a big, floppy bow tie, he was telling her the story of an inquisitive girl called Alice who fell down a rabbit hole. Then she was screaming as she was dragged by two men down a dark corridor that reeked of stale urine and thrown into a dirt-stained, once-white padded cell in a hospital ward. She was running through thickets of brambles in the woods at the back of their small cottage on the outskirts of Salem village with Ambrose pulling her hand, the fear inside her so great that she was running for her life.

Dora shook her head to clear it. She had to get her damn dress back. She rushed towards the glass display case and prayed that it wasn't locked because she couldn't break the glass, it would set off an alarm or something. As she reached for the back of it, she tried to pull the glass door open, but it wouldn't budge. Closing her eyes, she pushed her index finger against the small chrome button and felt a fizzing, popping sensation and the door released.

Dora sucked in a breath of air through her teeth, taking a quick look around to make sure no one was running to see who had set off a silent alarm. Then she smiled to herself. What was the point of having magical powers if she didn't use them and although she couldn't use them to their full potential, they had helped her when she was in desperate need, imagine what she could do when she did know how to harness their strength? This thought both terrified and excited her at the same time.

When she was positive there was no alarm, she opened the door and reached inside, her fingertips brushing the soft, supple linen. She felt a burst of energy so powerful it ran down the whole length of her arm. She reached up on her tiptoes and began to undo the row of tiny buttons. Slipping the dress off the mannequin, she folded it and took out the one Lenny had bought in the gift shop, then pulled it down over the mannequin. She fastened the much larger buttons a lot quicker and pushed the glass door shut. It didn't look anything like her sacred dress, but it was similar enough to buy her a little time. Placing her dress into the bag, she hurried towards the barrier tape and ducked back under it. Dora tugged the lanyard off her neck and walked past the customer service desk where she kept her head down and placed it back where she'd taken it from.

Then she hurried towards the exit and never looked over her shoulder, instead practically jogging all the way back to Sephy's house. Lenny was loitering by the gift store, the group of students had provided a distraction so she hadn't needed to, her and Ambrose could make their own way, Dora had to get the dress home. As she clutched it to her chest, she wondered how she would feel stepping into it again after all this time and realised that she was both terrified and excited. It would be like stepping back through time as all of her lives finally awakened her long-dormant magic powers.

39

One at a time, the three of them had reconvened at Sephy's house, with Dora arriving first, followed by Lenny, then Ambrose. Sephy had greeted each one of them at the door and hugged them tight. Dora could see her aunts watching her and Ambrose intently and she wondered how it must feel to finally see them together.

Now they were all sitting around the old kitchen table, Dora clutched her dress in her lap and looked at Sephy.

'Now what?'

'How do you feel about your dress, Dora?'

'I'm not sure. Excited and scared of what will happen when I put it on.'

Lenny let out a groan. 'You made us all accomplices to your crime and you're not sure?'

'No, I want to wear it and of course I'm going to. I had so many flashbacks to so many different lives, it's kind of mind blowing.'

She looked down at the dress. 'How can something so inno-cent-looking hold so many memories?'

Sephy reached out and poured herself a cup of the tea she'd had steeping in the old, blackened, cast-iron tea pot. 'It's not the dress really, dear, it's a part of the key to unlocking your magic, like a joiner has a tool chest full of saws and hammers, different tools for different jobs. That dress is part of your toolkit.'

'What else did I have in my toolkit?'

Sephy pointed a finger at the cup and the hot, amber-coloured liquid began to swirl around inside like a minor hurricane. It began to churn so fast that it spilled over the edge onto the saucer.

'Oops, I'm a little out of sorts with everything today.'

Dora poured herself a cup of tea, then pointed her finger at the cup. Nothing happened. She swirled it around in the air, but still nothing happened.

'Why can't I do that? If my magic is so powerful, why won't it work? It did in the museum before.'

Lenny shrugged. 'You haven't used it properly this lifetime. There have been moments that you probably weren't aware of, or when you desperately needed it, when you have. That's when you fully believed in yourself. Look at your uncanny knack of knowing every scent and being able to describe them. The flowers, plants and seeds love you and anything you put your hands on grows into a beautiful specimen. That magic will come back if we can find the place you locked it in and set it free.'

'How could I lock it away if I didn't know it existed, Lenny?'

Sephy intervened. 'Real magic is the feeling deep inside of you when you realise that your veins are filled with moonlight and stardust. It's an instinct, a calling, when you can sit outside and hear the insects and birds chattering to you, when you notice the rainbows and the shooting stars, the moon's glorious phases, the changes in the weather, the trees whispering as you walk on by. Magic is all around us, yet few people choose to acknowledge it. For some of us, the lucky ones, we can soak it up, harness its power and use it for good things.'

Lenny tapped a finger to the side of her head. 'Our subconscious mind is a more powerful tool than any of us will ever understand. Maybe this time around, though, you needed protection from the power, after all you have lived some dreadful lives that always get cut short at such a young age.'

Dora nodded. 'I get that, I suppose after everything I've been through it might try to protect me from it all. But what about Corwin? We are talking about fighting him and binding him to this earthly plane, is that not dark magic?'

Sephy shrugged. 'Darling, if we don't stop him, he will once more annihilate the English women. Although I like to live my life as calmly and peacefully as I can, I cannot stand back and watch him do this again, I am well and truly done with it. Therefore, I would say that by taking the steps to stop and bind him here where he has no power, we are most certainly acting in the best interest of every single witch in the world. We owe it to ourselves and to them to end this mindless persecution of women. Look at your friend, did she deserve to be hurt so badly she could have died? She was nothing to him, just a pawn in his quest to find us and to find you so he could do the same.'

At the mention of Katie, Dora felt a sickness spread inside her stomach at the thought of her lying there letting a machine breathe for her.

Ambrose's phone began to vibrate in his pocket. He took it out, read the message then stood up.

'Dora, I have to go there's been an influx of customers at the shop and Margo needs a hand. Your aunts are the best teachers you could ever wish for. I would listen to them and learn what you can. I have a feeling that we don't have long before Corwin makes his move. And you're stronger with me a little farther back.'

He left them all staring after him and not one of them spoke until the front door was closed behind him.

'You could at least try the damn dress on, Dora. We went to a lot of effort and if it doesn't fit you, we need to know so Sephy can alter it.'

Dora stared at Lenny, straight-talking, say-it-as-it-is, tough-cookie Lenny. Her aunt was right though; she could sit here all day and what would it achieve? She stood up and took the dress into the downstairs bathroom where she held it up in front of the mirror. Undressing down to her underwear, she kicked off her boots to get her jeans off and tugged it over her head, lifting her arms into the linen material that had once been stiff and a little uncomfortable but after centuries now fit like a glove .

Dora stared back at the woman in the mirror. She didn't recognise her. She was so familiar yet a stranger. And then a bolt of electricity ran down her entire body, so shocking that she had to grip onto the sides of the small porcelain sink to keep herself upright. If she'd looked up, she would have seen a stream of fizzing white light splashed with touches of gold running straight through her body. She could smell smoke, wood smoke, she could see trees and a small wooden cottage with a well-tended herb and vegetable garden. Her fingers gripping the sides of the sink were crackling with unseen electricity and her hair had a static charge running through it, like when you rub a balloon on your head, making the strands stick up. She stared at her reflection in the mirror and could see tiny flecks of gold dancing in the irises of her eyes and feel the unharvested power deep inside her belly. She was no longer plain old Dora English, she was Isadora English, the daughter of an English sister, and she was ready to fight to save herself and her aunts from being attacked by George Corwin ever again. She could feel the power inside her like a glowing ball of light that pulsated and throbbed so strongly that she fell to her knees.

There was a knock on the door and Sephy's voice whispered, 'Are you okay in there, dear?'

'Fine, I'm fine. I'll be out in a moment.'

Dora sat on the cold tiled floor, her back against the toilet, and lifted her fingers in front of her face. They were trembling with vibrations and there were tiny blue and green sparks snapping from them into the air before disappearing. Looking for something, anything, she spied a toilet roll balanced on the corner of the sink. She pointed at it and her finger did the tiniest twitch, the tissue paper flying into the air as if it had been hit by a gun. It exploded into minuscule shreds of white paper that rained down all over Dora and the floor as if it was snowing. She held out the palm of her hand and caught some of it, staring in wonder, and then she began to laugh. *Well I never, a witch for centuries and I've just managed to blow up a loo roll. Way to go, Dora, what talent.* This made her laugh even louder and she got a case of the giggles.

She closed her eyes and could see both of her aunts standing outside the door, Lenny was leaning against it with one ear while Sephy was wringing her hands. Dora pulled herself up, smoothed down her dress and tried to tame her hair, which was now positively wild. She pointed at the brass doorknob with her finger and sent a bolt of electricity through it to the other side where Lenny was gripping it with her fingers. Sephy let out a scream and there was a loud crash. Dora pulled the door open to see her Aunt Lenny sprawled on the floor, looking dazed, with Sephy fussing over her.

Mortified, Dora bent down. 'Oh my God, Lenny, did I kill you?'

Lenny looked at her and began to laugh, a loud, hearty belly laugh that Sephy couldn't ignore and soon she was laughing too. Dora, who was terrified she'd hurt Lenny, stared at the two women, full of confusion. They were laughing so loud it almost deafened her and Ophelia came running down the stairs to see what all the fuss was about.

Lenny was struggling to speak. 'Dora, don't stroke the cat; you'll electrocute her and that would never do.'

This made her aunts laugh even louder. Dora sat on the bottom step and watched them both crying so hard they were wiping tears from their eyes. Eventually Sephy held out her hand for Lenny who took it, and she dragged her to her feet.

'What's so funny?' Dora asked. 'I don't get it. I nearly killed you, Lenny.'

Lenny opened her mouth and got another fit of the giggles. She shook her head, held up her hand then cleared her throat.

'I'm good, although my ass may be bruised for a while but that wouldn't be the first time.' She winked at Sephy who slapped Lenny's arm.

'You are incorrigible, Lenora English. Dora, don't look so alarmed, I'm sorry we got a little carried away but that was one hell of a shock. Lenny's face as she flew through the air was priceless.'

Lenny smiled at her. 'Dora, by that little display of untamed power, I'm assuming the dress worked.'

Sephy turned to Dora and sighed. 'You really are too beautiful; you look just like your mom when she was your age, only you have an air about you that she never did have.'

Dora had given up trying to understand what had just happened or the mystery that was her aunts. She had taken to staring at her fingers. They were no longer cracking and fizzing, they were just her usual fingers with her black nail enamel that was starting to chip.

Sephy patted her arm. 'Come, child, we have a lot to discuss. Let's start with a little black magic and take it from there.'

'Black magic?'

Lenny smiled and mimed lifting a glass to her lips.

'Oh, right. I see.' Dora nodded. 'You mean alcohol. Yes, I will take all the black magic you have because I think I'm losing my mind.'

Sephy began to dance towards the kitchen, and Lenny followed behind her, the pair of them swishing their hips and moving their shoulders to some music that Dora couldn't hear.

40

At the exact same time as the stream of light came shooting through Dora's head whilst inside Sephy's bathroom and unleashed her full magical powers, George Corwin opened his eyes and stared out of the Boston hotel room window into the fast-approaching darkness. It was as if someone had turned on a beacon in the distance and he was drawn to it.

He sat up and looked around. The room was filled with shadows, but they didn't scare him. He was made of darkness. He crossed to the window. He could no longer see the faint white light that had for the briefest of moments filled the early evening sky, but he knew what it meant. Somewhere, someone – and that someone was most likely to be a witch – had found their powers or had used them and they were in the general vicinity of Salem. This gave him great cause for concern because as far as he knew the only witch who didn't know she was a witch in that area was Isadora English.

He pressed his hands to the glass, staring over the lights of the city out into the darkness, a smile curling his lips and whispered, 'Let the games begin.'

He knew he was on borrowed time; if he left those women

unsupervised, they would try to break the curse. But he wasn't too worried. He knew that they had tried and failed throughout all their lives and he always overcame them. He thought of that fool Corey. Despite the fact he'd used his cane to push the man's tongue back into his mouth, Corey's curse had managed to awaken something deep inside George that had scared him a little and then fascinated him. He found he himself had strange and unusual powers that could not be explained. They had been weak at first and he had ignored them, but at the time of Corey's last mortal breath he had inhaled his soul – for want of a better word – and felt that small grain of power grow stronger. His uncle, the overzealous fool, had been so caught up in the witch trials and accusations the afflicted girls had made, he had unwittingly brought George new victims without realising it. Every time Jonathan Corwin had ordered an innocent person to be hanged for the crime of witchcraft, George was there, in the shadows, waiting to come forth and steal their souls. He didn't care that they had been tortured enough and should have been sent on their way to heaven to be welcomed into the arms of God. Instead, he interrupted that journey and took them inside him. Eventually he had been so overcome by the power he had harnessed that it had caused him to die a rather sudden and untimely death.

He had fallen in love with Lenora English the moment he had set eyes on her in her too tight petticoats.

He had tried so hard to make her fall in love with him, but she'd turned him down and walked away, leaving him so furious and full of hatred that he'd decided if he couldn't have her for himself, he would take not just her soul, but the souls of those she loved so dearly – her sisters, even the girl. They would all hang and he would be there to take away their essence at the last moment. Only it hadn't gone to plan.

Of all the innocents accused of witchcraft in Salem, he thought that the only true witches were the English women.

They were good people, they harmed no one and helped everyone who needed it, and he admired that trait in them. They always worked hard and provided for themselves, taking care of each other, and he was more than a little envious of that. If Lenora had not spurned his advances each time they met, he would never have started the rumours about them. But she had and little did he know that hanging them would only be the beginning of their lives. He had discovered that turning lust into hate was a pretty good use of the wasted emotion and because of that he had been able to track them down in every lifetime they lived.

If he was honest with himself, he was getting a little weary of it. They made it too easy. Seraphina never left Salem, which amused him because the townsfolk had tortured and killed her. He had tried to take her soul, but it was not his to take. Neither hers, Lucine's now Lenora's, which at first had puzzled him greatly. He had been there, watching from the sidelines as they kicked and gasped their last breaths, yet, unlike the others, nothing released his way. They had clung onto theirs and for each sister's hanging a black crow had been nearby, soaring away at their moment of death. Of course, there were always crows around on the trees near Gallows Hill when a hanging was about to commence, waiting to peck the eyes out of the unfortunate victim.

This crow was different though; George had studied it with great interest and there had been something about its eyes that was more human than birdlike. The other crows were waiting for the chance to peck at the bodies, eat the eyes and get their fill of soft, warm flesh. Not this one though, it never came back to scavenge like the rest of them.

When they took the English women that night after luring them to the captain's house, that idiot cousin of his had helped the girl Dora to escape, but for some reason she had come back to fight him. She was brave, he'd give her that, foolish too, and he'd overpowered her, giving Lenora one last surprise before she hanged. When they had been loaded onto the cart and taken up to the ledge in the shadow of Gallows Hill, their beloved Dora was already there with a noose around her neck. Oh, how he'd savoured the anger that radiated from Lenora. He'd found her exhilarating that day.

It had pained him to watch the woman who could have led a comfortable life as his wife swinging from the branch of the old tree, but it was her own doing. Ambrose had fought him, but he was a boy and no match for a man like him. He had given the lad a beating that had left him bedridden for days and his uncle could not say anything about it. Ambrose had turned traitor, he should have hanged him too. George thought about that crow, and it occurred to him then that the crow might be the key to the English sisters and their immortality. He suspected that it was some kind of guardian sent to watch over them. But nothing could stop him now, not even the damn book that Ambrose had been so keen to search for his last few lifetimes. It was entertaining to see them searching for it, but there was no book on earth that could stop him.

41

The jug of black magic was empty except for a few drops in the bottom. All three women sat around Sephy's ancient pine table with flushed cheeks and a sparkle in their eyes. Hades was watching them from the kitchen window and each time Dora looked at him she could swear he was smiling. Did birds smile, could they smile? She had no idea, but he was looking at them with such love she wondered at how little the world knew about birds. She held out her arm and he flew towards it, landing on it with grace. She pressed her head against his small chest and he let her.

'Did you know that crows have the largest brain-to-body ratio of any bird? Seven times bigger than a human and they are also one of only four species able to make their own tools, as well as being pranksters and very cheeky.'

Dora lifted her head to look at Lenny. 'I didn't know that. I don't know anything about birds full stop.'

'Except how to love them. Of all living animals you always did love the birds more than anything.' Sephy's voice was light and dreamy. 'Maybe you could call on the birds to help when it comes to end that brute for good.'

'I think I shall, I will take all the help I can get and if a flock of crows—'

'Murder.'

'What?'

Lenny smiled. 'A group of crows is called a murder, not a flock.'

Sephy laughed. 'Your Aunt Lenny is great for useless facts on just about everything.'

Dora stroked Hades' feathers along his back and he made some small cawing noises that were obviously pure delight. 'You're such a clever boy, aren't you. I love you, Hades, and I'm sorry I didn't remember you this time around. Can you ever forgive me?'

He began to peck at her hair and Sephy clapped. 'You're forgiven, he's preening you to make you look a little more presentable.'

Lenny stood up, pointed to the huge black book on the table, then slammed the palms of her hands onto it.

'It's time to get to work, witches.'

Dora began to laugh, and Lenny grinned at her. 'See what I did there? Witches are far more powerful than bitches.'

Sephy leaned forwards and took hold of Lenny and Dora's hands in each of hers.

'Just look at us, back together, the power of three. It's time to work our magic.'

Lenny laughed. 'Oh Lord, she's off. Would you look at her, she's the opposite of Winifred Sanderson, aren't you, dear. Before you know it there will be pink smoke rising from the chimney and all the children of Salem will be drawn here to eat cake and candy.'

Dora asked Sephy, 'You know *Hocus Pocus*?'

Sephy laughed. 'Of course I do, dear, the whole town thrives off that movie. To be honest, I think Bette Midler modelled herself on Lenny, whereas I'm more a *Practical Magic* fan. I would quite happily drink midnight margaritas every time the clock strikes twelve, but my own black magic is a happy substitute.'

Dora smiled. 'It's my favourite film.'

'Well then, how lucky are you that you've just been blessed with a life far more magical than either of those movies. Although George Corwin is an ugly thorn in our side and would fit in quite well with the Sanderson Sisters and their soul-sucking.'

'Is that what he does?'

Lenny nodded. 'Yes, I believe so. Somehow, when the victims of the witch trials were being executed, he came to understand that ingesting a soul at the time of death would give him power and immortality. It took us a long time to figure this out.'

'But he's never done that to us?'

'No. He kills us, of course. But he's never got to taste our souls because Hades is always there to guide them before he can get his grubby hands on them, aren't you, Hades?' The crow looked at Lenny and nodded his head just the once, a quick, sharp nod of agreement. 'God help us if that happened. We wouldn't be reborn, but we'd also live in pain eternally, along with all those poor victims he's done that to.'

'But how, how did Hades come to find you?'

'Does it completely blow your mind?'

Dora nodded.

Sephy looked at her. 'We find it easier not to think of the schematics behind it all, too much to get our pretty little heads around. It happened and that's the way it is, or at least it is for us. We accept that we are blessed with the most magical, wonderful lives but for every good thing there is also a bad and Corwin is ours. Which is why we are going to put a stop to him forever this time. Now, enough of the questions, we have work to do. I think we should start with a simple spell to warm up your magic and take it from there.'

Sephy flicked the pages of Lucine's book until it rested open on one with a heading that said:

To Harness Your Power
Ingredients

White or purple candle
Crushed dried nettles
Dried lavender
Dried juniper
Anoint the candle with the herbs and a little oil then light it and
chant three times
I call my power to return to me
Find its way and let me be
Power my life through day and night
To help me fight another's plight

She turned to Dora. 'This is relatively simple; we need to work on making all your power work for you.' She went to the dresser and ran her finger along the rows of small glass jars filled with everything. Then she took hold of one and opened a drawer, pulling out a small, purple, beeswax candle and placing it in an old brass candle holder before giving it to Dora along with the jars.

'You need to anoint the candle. There is little point in me doing it, I am quite aware of my power. There is some rosemary oil which will help to clear your mind and strengthen it.'

Dora picked up the bottle Sephy was pointing to. She nodded her head.

'Now, tip out some of the herbs.' She passed her a wooden cutting board. 'It won't sting. Pour a little of the oil onto your finger and rub it from the top to the middle downwards all around. Then from the bottom up to the middle upwards and roll it in the herbs.'

Dora did as she was instructed, the smell of lavender and rosemary soothing her soul. They were such familiar fragrances and instantly conjured memories of happy times throughout her lives. When she had finished, she placed it into the candle holder and Lenny interrupted.

'While you're at it, try and light it with your finger. Simple candle magic is a good way to start.'

'What, how?'

Lenny turned to one of the huge pillar candles on the dresser and flicked her finger towards it. A small flame appeared and Dora clapped.

'You are such a dark horse. Brazen one-night stands with younger men and a closet witch, I couldn't love it any more.'

Dora closed her eyes and pointed in the direction of the candle. Nothing happened.

Sephy tapped her on the arm. 'It really would be best if you looked at it, dear, you might set your Aunt Lenny alight or the cat.'

Dora giggled and shook her head; this time she kept her eyes open and aimed her finger at the candle. Still nothing happened. She tried again and again.

'Where is all that electricity that was shooting out of them before?'

She didn't miss the look Lenny gave to Sephy, who put her arm around her.

'It's complicated at times; it doesn't always go to plan. Magic can be a little unruly until you learn to use it the correct way.'

Dora stared at her. 'Unruly? How the hell am I going to use it to fight Corwin if it only turns up when it feels like it and not when I need it?'

Lenny tossed her a box of matches. 'It takes time, unfortunately time is something we don't have a lot of. Don't be disheartened, it worked when you needed it to find the book and at the museum. You don't learn to ride a bike the first time you take the stabilisers off. You wobble, you fall off, you get up and keep trying. It's kind of like that sometimes, but the biggest thing you need is self-belief. You have to believe that you can work your magic, you must feel it deep inside of you, feel all the wonders of the universe like a billion stars inside your soul, lighting the way. Take a deep breath and count to four, tell yourself you are made of magic, release it and aim for the candle.'

Dora did as she was told and whispered, 'I am made of magic,' then pointed at the candle. There was the slightest crackle of blue light that erupted from her index finger, but it fizzled out before it could reach the wick.

Sephy began to clap and jump up and down. 'See, you can do it. You need to practise, that's all, you're just a little rusty. Use the matches for now and incant the spell.'

Dora flicked a match against the rough sandpaper of the small box and watched with fascination as the tiny flame appeared. She held it to the wick and it began to flicker.

She inhaled and then said out loud. 'I call my power to return to me, find its way and let me be, power my life through day and night, to help me fight another's plight. I call my power to return to me, find its way and let me be, power my life through day and night, to help me fight another's plight. I call my power to return to me, find its way and let me be, power my life through day and night, to help me fight another's plight.'

As she spoke the words the candle flame began to dance, growing taller and glowing almost pure white. She watched it, fascinated; both her aunts were watching too with smiles on their faces. Dora felt the fizzing in her stomach, the ball of energy growing inside her, and she imagined it was a brilliant white light, even brighter than the candle flame. She could feel it running through her veins as if her whole body was charged with static electricity. She looked to find another candle and spied one on the windowsill not too far away from where Hades was watching the three of them with growing interest.

Dora lifted her finger and aimed it at the candle. A stream of blue and gold light hit the candle and the flame burst to life then it hit the windowpane and shot off in Hades' direction. The bird, who had already been keeping a wary eye on them, exploded in a puff of feathers and loud squawks as he took off out the window, the smell of singed feathers hanging heavily in the air.

'Oh my God, I'm sorry, Hades. Are you okay?'

Dora yelled after him as she raced to the back door and threw it open; she ran outside and frantically searched the old oak tree that grew in Sephy's garden to see if he was there. She saw him perched on the highest branch, a look of shock in his glittering black eyes.

'Sorry, Hades. I didn't mean that, please tell me you're okay?'

He ignored her and began to preen his singed feathers. Lenny walked out of the door, tears rolling down her cheeks and laughter so loud coming out of her mouth Dora thought she would deafen her. She stared up at the tree.

'You okay up there, bird? You still have enough feathers to fly then?'

Sephy rushed out. 'Lenny, stop that. You'll upset him. Dear me, Dora, we need to work on that a little. This is my fault, I should have warned you about reflective surfaces.'

'What about them?'

'Well, for a start, they're reflective. They can send your energy straight back to you, which can be dangerous.'

Lenny was still laughing. 'Not as dangerous as it was for the bird.'

Both Dora and Sephy turned to her and said in unison, 'Shut up.'

Hades took off in the air, circled around them once, then disappeared.

Lenny waved her hand. 'He's okay, you gave him a shock, that's all. He'll be back when he's finished sulking.'

She turned and went back inside the kitchen, they followed her. Dora stopped to pick up the trail of feathers that had fallen off Hades' tail. She tucked them into her pocket and Lenny winked at her. 'Once a witch, always a witch. Before you know it, you'll have a cupboard full of empty glass jars and a crystal collection bigger than you could ever imagine.'

'Are you going to be of any use to us, Lenny, because if not I would like you to go and open the shop for an hour for me.'

Lenny stared at Sephy with a look of confusion. 'Why?'

'I have a very important customer calling and I can't not be there, Margo and Ambrose will have finished for the day, I forgot to ask if one of them could stay a little later. Everything she needs is out the back packaged up. All you must do is give it to her, it's already paid for. I can't leave Dora like this.'

Lenny shrugged. 'Why do I get all the best jobs? You know how much I dislike the people who come into the shop.'

'Stop being a grouch, you do not. You just don't like seeing people relying on our magic to improve their lives or the tourists. But she needs me, and the herbs in that package. Just because we're focusing on the curse doesn't mean I'm going to abandon my other witchy duties.'

Sephy took the key from her pocket and tossed it in Lenny's direction. She caught it deftly and nodded. 'Only if we can have take-out for dinner.'

'We can have whatever you want if you go fetch it.'

Lenny left them to it and Sephy smiled at Dora.

'That was a very good attempt, I think the power incantation worked. Maybe we could try something a little less dangerous though. I have a basket of peas that need shelling. Should we see if you can use it to do that?'

Dora smiled at her aunt, feeling so much love for the woman standing in front of her.

'How is that going to help me fight Corwin. Am I going to distract him with my pea shelling?'

It was Sephy's turn to laugh. 'Don't be silly, dear, we just want you to be able to focus on using your power and aiming it in the right direction. I'm afraid we're going to need a lot more than a basket of peas to stop him, but I suppose we've never tried that particular one before so never say never. Once you've mastered that we'll move on to the next thing, we don't have much time so I'm going to keep at you until I'm happy you know what you're doing and have some semblance of control over your magic.'

She went into the pantry and came back with a seagrass basket full of freshly picked peas, placing it onto the table in front of Dora, who looked up at her and smiled. She didn't ask if Sephy wanted to use them for supper because she had a feeling, by the time she'd finished, they would be nothing but a charcoaled mess.

42

Lenny strode the short distance to the shop with an anxious smile on her face and the aroma of caramel apples, popcorn and hot dogs surrounding her. There was a street market in full swing going on along Essex Street and the tourists were every-where. It wasn't that she hated them, it was more a case of disliking the crowds, the sheer volume of them and the noise. It sounded too much like execution day when the crowds of villagers had been jostling and baying for blood, caught up in the frenzy and not really thinking about the absurd behaviour the afflicted girls had displayed, or listening to the accused as they pled their innocence. It made her blood run cold just thinking about it and the fact that Corwin was probably onto them, which meant their time was short, they needed Dora to pull it together before he figured out where they were and came looking for them.

She passed the Witch House and frowned; it hadn't looked anything like that when that pig Corwin lived there. Now it looked all dark and spooky and had people forever taking photographs outside. She understood the need to own the town's history, it kind of also made her glad that the house no longer represented Corwin, but it had become a beacon for all witches, who flocked to see it. *I hope you are turning in your grave, Jonathan Corwin, it's the only kind of immortality you deserve.*

Oh, how it tickled her. She would have loved to see his face at the irony of it all. It made her sad that they would never be able to tell of how it really was. They'd tried over their lifetimes to get the history books right, but they would never be able to tell the world the true story of the English women. Unless they wrote it as a fiction story, that was always a possibility. If she didn't go back to London and her career as a surgeon she could retire here and live with Sephy, write their stories and watch Dora flourish.

A wave of grief washed over her; they had only bid goodbye to Lucine a few hours ago yet it felt like years. Would Dora want to stay here? Anyway, Lenny was getting away with herself, they had one major problem to contend with before any of them could live happily ever after. Corwin, he had to be stopped this time for good. Neither she nor Sephy had told Dora that they'd tried and failed so many times in the past. Maybe this time it would be different, though. Dora had finally found the lost spell book and discovered the vanished bookstore.

Standing outside Sephy's shop, Lenny took the key out of her pocket. As she leaned against the door it clicked open and she stared at the lock. She hadn't even inserted the key, had Margo forgot to lock up last time she left? That was always a possibility, Sephy had mentioned the woman could be quite the forgetful one at times, very much like Sephy too. Lucine used to say that she had a head full of cotton candy some days, which was a pretty good description of Sephy's mind, Lenny didn't know Margo but if she was anything like her sister it was possible.

Lenny stepped inside the shop; the stench of decay filled her nostrils along with a sense of pure dread. Corwin was here or had been recently. Most people couldn't smell it, he disguised it with expensive aftershave, but Lenny knew that he was like a piece of rotting meat underneath the sharp suits and good looks. Her brain screamed at her to turn around and leave, get out of there and warn her sisters. Yet there was this tiny part of her that wondered if she would need to take this chance to slow him down. Dora wasn't ready to fight him yet.

Lenny flicked on the light switch by the door and the shop burst into life. All the black shadows dispersed and there was no obvious sign Corwin was here apart from the foul smell. Maybe she'd got lucky, and they'd narrowly missed each other by minutes. If that was the case, she needed to warn Sephy. The phone was out the back of the shop, which was hidden behind the curtain. Lenny cast around for something to defend herself with and spied nothing of any use except for a large chunk of jet-black obsidian. She looked around for something to put it in and her eyes fell on a small cotton bag. She slipped the stone inside the bag and pushed it as far as it would go into her coat pocket. She began to hum 'Eye of the Tiger' to herself; she'd loved watching *Rocky III* and the final fight with Clubber Lang, she could have done with some of Rocky Balboa's spirit. She walked towards the curtain as if she had no idea there could be an evil witch hunter waiting behind there for her and drew it back. The small room that served as a kitchen, storeroom and consulting room was empty, and she stopped in her tracks. So far so good, she thought to herself as she looked towards the small cubicle and its closed door.

'Why are you hiding? I could smell you as I walked through the door. You'd think after all these years you'd be able to do something about that rotting stench of death that follows you around.'

The door creaked open, and the blackness was almost all-consuming. Then Corwin stepped out. He looked devilishly handsome, but he always had. He was a good foot taller than Lenny and his hands were twice the size of hers.

'I wanted to surprise you. Turns out I'm the one surprised. Where is your sister?'

'Go screw yourself and while you're at it get the fuck out of this shop before I call the cops. You're trespassing, asshole.'

He threw back his head and laughed, a deep, throaty sound that vibrated his vocal cords, and it went right through Lenny. Then he stared straight at her.

'It never had to be this way. Why wouldn't you just take my offer to be my wife? The pair of us could have been such a powerful force to reckon with. The things we could have done, we would have been unstoppable.'

Lenny's instincts had been spot on when she'd spurned his advances. He'd still been a mortal back then, before he'd turned into this and become an eater of souls.

'I've never liked you, and I never will. Don't you think it's time you gave up all of this, are you not tired of the hunt? It's not as if you get a different result with each chase, is it? You find us, stalk us, hunt us, then kill us. It's kind of getting real boring, George. Wouldn't you rather be retired and enjoying fishing out on the lake with a six-pack of Bud or playing golf?'

'Fishing, what fun is that when I can hunt women for pleasure? I'm sorry, Lenny, but this lifestyle is way more exciting than fishing. Why would I drink cheap beer when I can savour souls that taste infinitely divine? I haven't tasted yours yet, but I like to think it will be like the finest wine, the sweetest chocolate and the creamiest desert all mixed together into one sweet ingredient.'

Lenny panicked. He didn't just want to kill them this time. He wanted to steal their souls and the thought made her feel faint. She slipped her right hand into her pocket; her fingers gripped the heavy stone inside the bag. She knew it wouldn't be enough, but it might buy her a little time. What was the binding spell Sephy had said they could use? She needed to summon Hecate and ask for her help but how was she supposed to do that when he was standing in front of her? When Dora took the fight to him, she would have already used the incantation that had been hidden for centuries in Lucine's spell book and called upon the dark goddess of all witches bringing the moon goddess powers to life. If Lenny could stall him long enough for Dora and Sephy to get their act together it might work.

'Okay, what if we came to a compromise?'

'A what?'

'What if I told you I'd be with you, so we could rule the world, that kind of thing?'

He stared at her, his dark eyes probing into the depths of her green ones so hard that she could feel tiny needles of pain as they reached inside.

'You're being serious?'

'I'm tired of running away, tired of all the fear. Why don't we give it a go, call a truce? Who knows, I might enjoy it.'

'What about Isadora and Seraphina? What about Lucine? Are they going to let you do this without a fight?'

'Lucine passed this morning, Sephy and Dora are grieving. I want your assurance that you'll leave them alone if I agree to go with you.'

He nodded. 'I only ever wanted you. I'm sorry about Lucine. She was a good woman.'

'We're all good women, all of the—' Lenny stopped herself, not wanting to argue with him and let him know she was still full of fight.

'That you were and I'm sorry for how it all turned out. I do have some regrets about what happened back then.'

She tried not to glare at him. Sorry didn't cut the pain and fear he'd caused them for centuries. He was lying, he couldn't be trusted, but she'd play this game for as long as she could to buy Dora the time she needed.

George walked towards her and held out his hand. 'Shake on it.'

Lenny swallowed hard; she didn't want to touch him. The thought of her skilled surgeon's fingers touching his repulsive dead ones made her cringe inside. Pushing her hand forwards, she gripped his as tight as she could, his fingers slick with perspiration, making it hard to keep hold of it. His other hand shot out and grabbed the back of her neck. His fingers squeezed so tight she felt her shoulders rise to her ears to try and protect herself. He pushed her forwards and she fell into the corner of the desk, hitting her head on one of the shelves containing Sephy's jars. She felt her skin split and saw stars in her eyes as the blood began to flow down the side of her face.

Anger pulsated underneath her fingers, and she rolled to face him. Pointing towards him, she sent a beam of electricity at his heart. It jolted him backwards and he looked shocked. Taking the stone out of her pocket before he could do anything else, she got to her feet and charged towards him. Taking a swing at his head, she heard the sound of her fist whooshing through the air, but it missed. Somehow it didn't land where it was supposed to and then she saw the jar of salt he'd thrown at her sprinkled all over the floor. She let out a scream of anger.

'You dirty bastard. I told you I'd come with you.' The salt showered her, and she fell to her knees as it covered her, taking away all of her strength. He stood and watched her fall then nodded his head. Taking some cable ties from his pocket he bent down and tugged her hands together; she couldn't fight him. The salt Sephy had made was too powerful. They'd never anticipated it being used against them and now she watched as he tightened the plastic straps around her wrists with a huge grin on his face, then straightened up.

'Come now, Lenora, don't be so angry with me. After all these years and all of our battles, did you really expect me to believe you would come with me so willingly? I am sorry if you truly meant it this time and I would work on making it up to you if you did but I can't trust an English woman and you shouldn't expect me to.'

Lenny's anger was so great she could feel it radiating from her in waves towards him. She bowed her head, unable to speak, realising that she had just walked straight into George Corwin's wicked plot and her own death sentence. Her only hope was that it would buy the others some much-needed time to prepare for the final battle. He bent down and scooped her into his arms, throwing her over his shoulder and carrying her out of the back door to a waiting limousine with blacked-out windows. He opened the door and tossed her into the back, climbing in after her.

43

The smell of charred peas lingered in the air, but Dora thought she might be getting the hang of it. Sephy was busy grinding herbs and more black salt behind her when she cried out loud.

'Lenny.'

A chill settled over Dora and she turned around to see her aunt's pale face.

'What's wrong?'

Sephy was swaying, her hand clutching the base of her neck.

'She's in trouble, he's got her, I'm sure of it.'

Dora didn't need to ask who. Corwin. 'How?'

She stood up and took hold of her aunt's elbow, guiding her to a chair and gently sitting her down.

'Are you sure?'

Sephy nodded. 'Quite sure. We have this bond. I suppose it's a bit like a psychic bond, but we always know when the other is happy, sad, in trouble or in danger, and she's in danger. He's hurt her, I'm sure of it.'

She stared at Dora. 'I sent her away and she walked right into a trap. Oh my, this is all my fault.'

Dora's heart was beating too fast, it was pounding against her ribcage so hard it hurt her chest. She thought of the damage Corwin had done to poor Katie. Lenny was much older than her friend, she might not be able to withstand a beating of that kind.

'What can we do? We have to find her, now.'

Sephy stood up and grabbed her cape off the hook. '*We* are doing nothing; you wait here until I come back.'

Dora shook her head. 'Absolutely not, I'm not letting you go out looking for her on your own. It's madness and he'll hurt you too. Can't we phone the police and report her missing? Actually, we don't know for sure if she is yet. Let's go to your shop and see if she's there. If she isn't then we'll call the police.'

'And tell them what, Dora, tell the cops a witch hunter has taken my sister who is a reincarnated witch? This is Salem and the cops are open-minded, but they won't believe that, and I'll get put in lockdown on a psych ward for at least forty-eight hours. You can't remember the lifetime when it happened to you, but it wasn't good.'

'We can check the shop, that's where she was going. If she's not there then I do whatever rituals I have to do, to gather everything I need, and I'll go looking for him.'

Sephy's bottom lip quivered as her eyes filled with tears. 'We're just not ready, if only we had a little more time.'

'There is never enough time to do the things you want if you don't even try. I'm willing to give it a shot. We can't ignore it. What about Ambrose, can he help in any way?'

'Maybe. We need to at least make the offering to the goddess Hecate if we're to seek her power and protection to make this work. I hate being rushed but we have no option but to do it now. Thank God you found Lucine's book, Dora, it has the most powerful incantation there is to draw her nearby. The moon is almost full, we have that to guide us. Dora, please go into the garden and find an apple, choose whichever flowers you are called to and bring them inside.'

Sephy began to clear the table, crying silent tears. Dora went outside and closed the door softly, leaving her aunt to prepare the altar. Dora had no need for a torch, the garden was illuminated with a silver light, so bright it looked as if someone had turned on a spotlight.

She stared up at the night sky, filled with so many glittering stars and the fullest moon she had ever seen. It was so near to the earth Dora wondered if she could touch it. There was a loud rustling in the oak tree and her heart began to race as she watched the leaves sway, and then she saw Hades take flight. He soared into the air and down to where she was standing. Without hesitation she held out her arm for him and he landed softly on it.

'Lenny's in trouble, we need your help. I'm sorry for hurting you.'

Hades looked up at her, his small eyes staring into hers. 'Bring Lenny home.'

She nodded. 'Yes, we have to bring her home. Do you think you can find her?'

He hopped from one foot to the other and gave her a curt nod. Then he pecked at her hair and took off again. 'Find Lenny,' he cried as he soared into the night and Dora felt a crushing love for the bird she'd never known could exist. He was as human as she was and even cleverer.

'Be safe, Hades, and find Lenny,' she called into the sky. 'Then come tell me where she is, okay?'

He let out a soft caw and carried on his journey. There was a thunderous flapping of wings and Dora watched in amazement as hundreds of crows took flight from the branches of the old oak tree where they'd been resting. There were so many of them they filled the night sky like a fluid black cloud as they passed across the moon on their quest to find her aunt. Corwin may be all-powerful, but he didn't have an army of crows at his disposal or the love of the English women.

She looked around in the garden and spied the row of apple trees. She scoured the branches for an apple that would be perfect and saw a crisp red one on a branch she could just about reach on her tiptoes. Dora plucked it from the tree and pushed it into the pocket of her dress, then she looked for some flowers. The kitchen was already full of dried herbs, so she passed by the herb garden, searching for something else. There was a small yew tree bordering the edge of it. Dora reached up and carefully pulled off a sprig of leaves. Underneath the yew were some delicate lilies of the valley. It had been their scent that had drawn her towards the yew tree.

She stared in wonder at the delicate, lacy white flowers. They only usually flowered for three weeks in May back home, but who was she to question the magic and beauty of Sephy's garden? She tenderly picked some, apologising to the plants, then turned around and spied another flower, one she knew of but had never seen before.

Belladonna or deadly nightshade with its shiny black berries that reminded her of Hades' glittering eyes. Dora knew she should get a pair of gloves to touch the leaves of the deadly plant, but she didn't have the time. Bending down, she picked a few stems and then rushed back inside with her offerings. There were two black candles lit on the table, along with a large, pearly-white moonstone crystal, a set of rusted old keys and a small engraved silver disc on a leather chain. Dora placed the apple and plants next to them. Sephy looked at them and nodded appreciatively.

'They are perfect choices for the queen of all witches, she will love those.'

'Hades has gone to search for Lenny with his friends.'

Sephy smiled. 'Of course, I was panicking so much I forgot

about his ability to seek out us English women far and wide. I'm sure he will find her, dear, he's always been as good at finding as he is at watching. Now repeat these words with me.'

Sephy quickly looked down at the open pages of the book and nodded, then poured out a little black salt and mixed it with a couple of drops of rosemary oil before dipping her thumb in the concoction and making a mark on Dora's third eye. She held out her hands to Dora and she clasped hold of them. They were so soft, such kind hands. Dora didn't want to let them go. Sephy inhaled deeply and exhaled, then standing straight she spoke out loud.

'Hecate, goddess of the night, come to us now and hear our plight, please send your vengeance to help our fight, in binding Corwin to the light.'

Dora wasn't sure if anything was supposed to happen, she didn't feel anything, and it seemed as if nothing had changed. They stood there, frozen in silence, holding their breaths. Then slowly out of the middle of the altar a black shadow began to form, swirling around and contorting into different shapes.

Dora watched, mystified and a little afraid of what they had just summoned. She stared at Sephy, eyes wide with fear, and hissed, 'Is it a demon?'

Sephy shook her head then lifted a finger to her lips. Dora stopped speaking, doing as she was told, and watched as the figure began to stretch and bend first one leg, then two, three, until it was standing on four legs. A body began to extend up from the legs and soon there was a tail and a huge head with pointed ears. Dora realised she was looking at a dog and glanced at Sephy, who smiled at her. The shadow dog turned to look at Dora and she felt a wave of familiarity. She knew this dog, not from this lifetime but from another, and she felt hot tears fall down her cheeks as she whispered:

'Caesar.'

The dog moved towards Dora, and she held out her hand to

stroke him. Her fingers slipped through the smoky blackness, but he looked at her with such pure love and devotion she wanted to cry.

'I've missed you, big guy, it's been too long.'

Sephy clapped her hands in delight. 'Thank you, Hecate, queen of the night. You sent Dora her protector and guide.'

The dog jumped down from the table and vanished from view, but they felt the ground vibrate as he landed on it.

'Where is he?'

'By your side, Dora. You don't need to see him to know that he is there. He will take care of you, of us, I'm sure it. Corwin was never fond of dogs, so when he sees Caesar, he will be scared, maybe enough to give you time to work the binding on him.'

Dora looked down at her legs. She couldn't see the dog, but she could feel his heat and the panting of his hot breath, his tongue lolling from his mouth just the way it used to.

'I can feel him, it's amazing. But how on earth?'

Sephy smiled. 'That's because he's never left your side. Even when a beloved pet passes, they are always with us in spirit. This makes me so happy, you two were inseparable. You brought him home one day in a battered cardboard box and told me you found him by the gate, and he was a Labrador puppy. After a non-starter of an argument with Lenny, we decided he could stay. He kept on growing, he was no Labrador, that's for sure, but he was so faithful to you and we all loved him. He was so human-like, especially his big brown eyes. I'm convinced he was a human soul who had come back as a dog. He loved you like I've seen no other dog love a human, so it makes sense that Hecate would send him to help protect you. He's probably been doing it for years, but you didn't realise because you had no idea who you were. How sweet. If this doesn't prove to you that magic exists, Dora, I don't know what will.'

As if to prove Sephy's point, Dora felt a big wet nose push

into her thigh and she giggled. Reaching down, she imagined how it used to feel running her fingers over Caesar's huge, soft, furry black head, scratching behind his ears like he loved.

'I believe more than you could ever know.'

'Good. Keep that belief strong in your heart because you're going to need it, Dora, we're all going to need it. Now, let's get to the shop.'

'Can I phone Ambrose and tell him to meet us there in case he's not home?'

Her aunt nodded. 'Yes, that's wise.'

Dora took out her phone and dialled his number.

'Are you okay?' Ambrose sounded anxious when he answered.

'No, Lenny is missing.'

'What?'

'We don't know for sure, but Sephy can feel it, that something bad has happened. She was on her way to the shop, could you meet us there in five minutes? We're on our way.'

'I'm on my way home, I'll go there right now. Margo is just about to serve supper. Even if Corwin doesn't get his hands on us first, she's going to kill the pair of us, the number of times I've deserted her the last few days.'

He hung up and Dora looked at Sephy. 'Let's go.'

'Hang on, I want you to have this.'

Sephy picked up the small silver disc and placed it in the palm of her hand.

'This was your mom's, it's very old and it's a protection amulet depicting Hecate. Lucine was very fond of this and treasured it. She would want you to wear it, Dora. Let me slip it around your neck. Every bit of protection we can gather is a good thing, wouldn't you agree?'

Dora nodded and turned so Sephy could fasten the leather cord around her neck. She tucked the silver disc inside the high neck of her dress to protect it. If her mum treasured it Dora didn't want to risk losing it when the time came to do battle. She felt ready, she had Hades, her power, Caesar and her love for her aunts to get her through this. They just needed to find where the bastard had taken Lenny and set her free then send him to the light where he would be bound for the rest of eternity. It was easy, nothing to worry about at all.

44

Sephy jumped in the front of the van and Dora the passenger side. Dora left the door open long enough so that her shadow dog could also climb in with them. Sephy, who never usually drove fast, sped out of the street towards the shop. She mounted the curb and abandoned the car at the same time as Ambrose came pelting around the corner, almost colliding with the small white van. Dora was already out of the van and pushing the front door of the shop open.

'Lenny, are you here?'

She prayed her aunt would answer her and make the pair of them realise how wrong they were, but she was greeted by silence and the earthy smell of rotting compost. Sephy came in behind her and her nose twitched.

'He's been here, I can smell him.'

'That's his smell? He came into my shop, and I thought he smelled of expensive aftershave. I never smelled anything like this.'

'You couldn't, dear, you were just a mortal back in London with no prior knowledge of your heritage and previous lives.

Now you've awakened your magic you can smell him for what he really is. Nothing but a fetid, decomposing piece of shit.'

Dora smiled at Sephy, tickled despite the gravity of the situation. Since she'd arrived in Salem, she'd hardly ever heard her swear.

Ambrose sniffed the air and shook his head, then he squeezed past both of them. 'Sorry ladies, I know you are both in charge but let me check the shop out first. I need to feel as if I'm of some use to you.'

He looked around then went through the curtain leading to the back room and stopped.

'Sephy.'

Sephy rushed to where he was standing. There was a pile of shattered glass jars on the floor and a streak of red along the corner of the whitewashed shelf. She strode towards it then leaned forwards to smell. 'Blood. He's hurt her – that doesn't smell of decay like he does. Damn him, please Lenny, be okay, don't fight him too much, we're on our way.'

The back door was unlatched and Ambrose pushed it open, Dora following him. The pair of them stood there surveying the area but could see nothing in the street.

Sephy joined them. 'He's gone, there's no scent, no trace. He had to have had a vehicle.'

'What do we do, call the cops?' Dora asked.

'No,' both Sephy and Ambrose said in unison.

'They can't help us,' Sephy added. 'They never have been able to and probably never will. It's too much for a mere mortal's mind to accept. I'm sorry, Dora, but that's the way it is and always has been. We fight our own battles. Win or lose, it's what we do.'

A look of pain crossed Ambrose's face. 'I hate him, I wish I'd never been born to the same family as him. My father was bad enough, but my uncle was always so much worse, always waiting around behind closed doors to make his move when he thought no one was looking. Only I could see him, I saw the blackness inside of him. I just wish I'd been brave enough to do something about it before he got this strong.'

Dora stared at Ambrose. With his floppy fringe and dazzling smile he did have a look of George Corwin. But whereas Corwin wore an air of cruelty around him like a cloak, Ambrose wore one of friendship and loyalty. She reached out and touched his arm and Sephy turned to him.

'You are nothing like him. You were also a child, he wasn't your battle to fight.'

'I feel as if he was, that I could have made the difference for you all, Sephy.'

She reached out and hugged him briefly. 'You have been here for us all since that terrible day and for that we'll always be grateful, Ambrose.'

Dora felt her heart fill with warmth watching her aunt soothing Ambrose when it was her who needed the soothing.

'Well then, I guess we go home and wait for Hades to report back.'

'Or we could go to Boston? Lenny said that was where he was, we might be able to use our powers to track him down. It has to be worth trying.'

'We can't, darling, we are unprepared and emotionally wrung-out. We could be wasting precious time driving around in circles. Boston is not Salem; everyone doesn't know their neighbours.'

Sephy ushered them back inside and bolted the back door behind them. She glanced at the mess on the floor and ignored it. Then they were out the front of the shop, where Dora was surprised to see the van still there parked across the pavement with the engine running. If this had been London, Sephy would never have seen it again, it would have been stolen and on its way to the other end of England. Once Sephy had secured the front door, all of them piled inside and they drove back to

Sephy's fairy tale pink house. They clambered out of the van and down the garden path, Dora scanning the sky for a sign of Hades and his friends, but there was nothing. Sephy led them inside where they took seats around the kitchen table. Ambrose took in the offerings and smiled.

'You invoked Hecate, you brought out the big girl?'

Sephy nodded. 'I fear I had no choice; she came and answered our prayers. Maybe a little too late for Lenny, but she is here and Dora is well protected.'

Ambrose stared at Dora, with her long black hair pinned in a messy bun, her grey linen dress with the tiny pearl buttons and high lace collar. 'Dora, you look so beautiful. You look just the way you used to. I remember you when I saw you walking through the woods to get to the village with your book under one arm and a handful of freshly picked daisies. I fell even more in love with you than I had when we were children.'

Dora smiled at him. 'I feel like that girl too. She was so innocent but there is something raw and untamed inside of me waiting to be unleashed. I need to find Lenny and Corwin then maybe we could start all over again, Ambrose.'

His eyes sparkled and his grin lifted his whole face into an expression of boyish charm. 'You would? Of course you would, that is amazing. What are we waiting for, let's get looking!'

As if summoned, the sky outside turned even darker and there was an almighty whooshing sound as the darkness moved towards them. They rushed outside and Ambrose took a step back but Dora stepped forwards. She opened out her arms and stood there waiting for Hades as the crows flew towards them and the old oak tree. Dora watched as they all took their turns to settle on the branches, the noise deafening, and felt a pang of fear in her heart when she couldn't see Hades among them.

'Where is Hades?'

She turned to Sephy, who was biting her lip and wringing

her hands. 'I don't know. He's probably watching Lenny and doesn't want to leave her.'

Dora called out into the night sky. 'Hades, come back, where are you?' The crows in the tree were watching her, then a smaller one flew down and landed on her arm.

Dora looked at it and whispered, 'Where is he?'

But she already knew; she had a crushing feeling of loss inside her chest that she couldn't explain. The crow bowed its head, unable to look her in the eyes, unlike Hades who had taken great pleasure in staring her out. It took off, soaring high into the night sky, and she knew then that something was terribly wrong.

'Is he hurt, is he dead? What happens if Corwin has hurt him? Isn't Hades the one who will protect our souls when we die?'

Sephy bowed her head. 'I don't know, Dora.'

Dora felt a burst of electricity explode from her fingers with a loud crack as she pointed towards a fallen branch and let it shoot from her, splitting the wood in two. She was furious, raging with lifetimes of pent-up anger and frustration towards George Corwin. She spun around and around, the electricity humming around her as a bright light enveloped her. She closed her eyes and pictured Lenny, tough, strong Lenny who had endured everything life had thrown her way and yet still strived to help the people around her. Images of her first life filled her mind: the cottage, the garden, the woods surrounding it, Gallows Hill looking down onto the town and the ledge below it where she, her mum and aunts had taken their last breaths.

She stopped and turned to Sephy. 'I know where they are. He's waiting for us to go there, to Boston; he's always been waiting for us to go there since the very first time. I need your van keys, please.' Dora held out her hand.

Sephy shook her head. 'You're not going alone; we're coming with you.'

'No, if I'm to do this, I'm to do it alone. I wouldn't be able to concentrate with you there in case he hurt you, Sephy, in case he hurt either of you. I need you to wait here, do what you have to do to keep Hecate and anyone else you can summon to help me, but I have to do this alone.'

Ambrose shook his head. 'I'm coming with you, no arguments.'

She took hold of his hand. 'No, I need you to keep my aunt safe. I need you to make sure we still have a home to come back to when all of this is over. I can't do what I have to if I'm worrying about him hurting you and Sephy. Because he will, I know that he will to get what he wants. He doesn't care about anyone except getting his revenge.'

A look of pain flashed across Ambrose's face. 'But Dora, I'm supposed to help you, I always do.'

'Things are different this time though, aren't they? I think we should try to do something we've never done before. You can be my research assistant; we can keep in contact by phone the whole time and you can guide me through the streets of Boston.'

He nodded. 'I could do that.'

'Yes, you could. But more than anything I need you to take care of Sephy.'

She wrapped her arms around him, pulled him close then stood on her tiptoes and softly kissed his lips. Then, before he could pull her in closer, she tore herself away.

'You're a good man, Ambrose, I thank thee from the bottom of my heart. Sephy, I need your keys.'

Sephy was dithering until she heard Dora speak and then she stopped and stared at her.

'What did you just say?'

'I said, I thank thee. Oh, where did that come from?'

Sephy smiled and Dora knew she was trying to work out if she should let Dora do this on her own. Then she handed the keys to her and from out of nowhere Dora was holding her close, burying her head into her neck and inhaling the wonderful lemon, vanilla and lavender scent that her aunt always smelled of.

'You're back, the old Isadora is home, and this makes me so happy. Now you have Hades, Hecate and Caesar by your side. Please call on the power and use your guide and protector the best that you can.'

Sephy stood up straight. No longer wringing her hands with nerves, she looked almost majestic as she stood tall and pulled a piece of old papyrus and a jar of black salt from her pocket and passed them to Dora. Then from her other pocket she drew out two small stones.

'Memorise these words, Dora. It's vitally important, for this is the binding spell that shall undo the curse and render Corwin defenceless. Make sure you cast your circle first and use the black protection salt to keep you safe. These stones are small, but mighty. You have haematite for strength and courage, chalcedony for power over dark spirits. It's what we've waited for, and I know you can do it. You must be fearless and remember that you are the magic, it's inside of you, flowing through your veins like a river of stardust that you can call upon as you need it. Be safe, my beautiful girl, and bring my family back to thee to stand strong for all of eternity.'

Dora nodded her head. It was true; she could feel the magic fizzing inside her, and she had a feeling if she didn't release some of the pent-up energy, she might burst into a glittering ball of this stardust that Sephy kept telling her ran through her body. She pushed the salt and stones into her pocket then looked down at the piece of papyrus and saw six lines of old cursive script in bold black ink. She read them through a couple of times, hoping when the time came she could remember them word for word, then she tucked the piece of paper into the pocket with her stones. She didn't tell either her aunt or Ambrose that she knew where Corwin was and that he was waiting for her to figure it out. She had no intention of driving to Boston, she was playing for time and hoping that they would let her go on some wild chase. She stopped herself from any further thoughts about it in case Sephy was as good at reading minds as Lenny. There was no way she was putting them at risk.

She turned and rushed down the path towards the small van. She could feel the floor vibrating with Caesar's heavy paws running with her, and she had never felt so glad to have an invisible shadow dog by her side willing to fight for her to save them all.

She opened the door and whispered, 'After you, boy.' She could almost hear the leather seat creak with the weight of the muscular black dog that had been an Italian mastiff in his mortal life. She turned and waved, then took off. She didn't know Salem now, but she could remember the Salem from centuries ago and she drove out of Chestnut Street towards where Corwin was waiting for her, less than a five-minute drive away.

It struck her how close to all the horrible memories and places Sephy still lived. Once she was almost there, she would find the rocky outcropping on the small parcel of land where they had hanged the innocent victims of the witch trials. Where her aunts and mum had been hanged, after being kept in squalor and tortured for days in the jail. Her insides churned with pent-up anger and sadness at the injustice of it all. Her phone began to vibrate and she saw Ambrose's name. She slid her finger across and could barely hear him; the van had no hands-free.

'Sephy said you need to find Proctor's Ledge; she knows fine well you aren't on your way to Boston.'

Dora grinned. So her aunt could read minds too. 'I'm on my way to Gallows Hill.'

'She thought so. Dora, it's not Gallows Hill, there is a low spot we used to call the crevice below Proctor's Ledge. It's where they dumped the bodies after they cut the rope around their necks, letting them fall. No one was hanged on the hill, it's the ledge, and below it is a memorial. It's a small, curved, walled memorial in between two houses. If Lenny's not there, then you can walk up the hill and a little farther up is Proctor Street. It runs directly behind the memorial, you can get to the wooded area that way. This is where you all died in case he's hiding somewhere a bit more discreet. I can be there in ten minutes if I set off running now.'

'No. Please don't, if I need you, I'll tell you.'

Dora ended the call and turned onto Pope Street, driving slowly until she saw the curved stone wall of the memorial sandwiched between two white clapboard houses. She shivered as she wondered if the people who lived there could hear the cries and wails of the innocent people who had been murdered in the spot between both properties late at night when there was no traffic around.

She stopped the van a little way up the street, not wanting to walk straight into Corwin's trap so brazenly and give herself a fighting chance. She got out and gave her shadow dog time to follow. She didn't even remove the key from the ignition so she could get away fast if she needed to. She couldn't see Lenny or Corwin at the memorial, but Corwin wasn't going to be somewhere so open. No matter how powerful he was, she doubted he would try to kill both her and Lenny in such plain view of neighbouring houses.

As she got closer, she spied a small black mound on the floor and felt her heart rip in two. No longer caring about the element of surprise, she ran towards the entrance to the memorial and saw Hades, his crushed, lifeless body on the floor. Dora had to stifle the scream that was bursting to erupt from her throat at the sight of her watcher, her friend, no longer able to be anything to her other than a memory. Dora fell to her knees, hot tears falling freely from her eyes as she gently scooped the bird's broken body into her hands and held him close. He was still warm. The pain in her chest was unbearable as it gripped like a vice, squeezing every inch of life out of her. She could feel Caesar next to her and wondered if Hades would turn into a shadow animal. She didn't want him to. She looked at the stone his body had been thrown under and felt a stab of anger begin to burn inside her stomach.

It read 'Lenora English'.

Dora looked up the hill to see if Corwin was there watching her from the cover of the trees. He would love to see her so upset and would be enjoying the show. She kissed her friend's head and carefully placed Hades on the wall. She clambered onto it, then stood up on the side of the hill that had been planted with trees and evergreen ferns.

It was fully dark, and the moon illuminated some of the hill but not all of it. She wanted to scream Corwin's name in fury, but was conscious of the two houses and their occupants. Instead, she made her way up the steep incline as far as she could go. There was only a narrow part of it accessible, the rest was fenced off. He wasn't here – she'd missed him but not by long. And then it hit her. She knew where he was. This place was far too public, but the field Giles Corey had been slowly crushed to death in over the course of three days wouldn't be. That's if it was still a field, she wasn't sure. All she could do was head in that direction and hope for the best.

As she part stumbled, part jogged down the incline with tears rolling down her cheeks, she almost ran straight off the edge of the memorial, and only just stopped herself in time. It was difficult in this dress, but she didn't care. She managed to get herself down and heard a small tearing noise as the seam gave way on one side. She could feel the air whooshing up through the slit but it didn't matter, it gave her more movement. She tenderly picked up Hades and put him in the hem of her dress, holding it up so he was covered in case any tourists walked past on a mission to see the memorial. They would be in for a treat with her dressed in a now damaged, stolen, seventeenth-century dress as she cradled her dead pet bird and talked to her shadow dog with snot and tears running down her cheeks.

She made it to the van just as a large group of tourists turned into the street. Once she was sure Caesar was in, she carefully laid Hades onto the back seat and shut the door, then got in and drove away just in time, a vision of the group turning on her and shouting, 'Witch, witch, witch.' Over and over the cries filled her mind, past lives colliding with this life. She had to push them away and tell herself they were not a mob of angry Puritan villagers baying for blood.

Her phone began to ring again. She swiped it but instead of managing a hello she let out an anguished cry and Ambrose's panicked voice filled the front of the van.

'I'm on my way, are you okay?'

'No, I'm fine. They weren't at Proctor's Ledge.'

She glanced in the rear-view mirror at the dead crow and decided not to tell Sephy until she had to. A dead crow was probably a sign of impending doom.

'Ambrose, where is the field Giles Corey was killed in?'

'It's a cemetery now, they built over it and he's supposed to be buried in there. It's called Howard Street Cemetery; Dora, I'm coming, I can't wait here.'

She heard Sephy in the background. 'We're both coming.'

Dora ended the call; she couldn't think about Ambrose or Sephy. She had to focus. If Lenny was dead then she was sure

Corwin would have left her body back at the memorial and not Hades'.

She drove way too fast for the streets of Salem towards where she remembered the field was. Turning onto Federal Street, she passed a building with a black-and-gold plaque on it that read 'Old Witch Gaol', and then made her way along Bridge Street until she saw the entrance to Howard Street, the cemetery filling one side of the narrow residential road.

Dora wasn't sure if there was any magic left to run through her veins because they seemed to be threaded with fury at Corwin and his senseless persecution of all women who were bloodline witches. She knew if he'd already hurt Lenny there would be no stopping her. She didn't care what happened to her as long as she broke the curse and got rid of Corwin for good.

She didn't bother being discreet and stopped the van outside the black, waist-high, chain-link fence that ran around the perimeter of Howard Street Cemetery. Dora opened the door and waited for her beloved dog to jump out.

She whispered, 'Don't show yourself until I ask you, please.' A wet nose pushed against the cold skin of her thigh where the dress had torn and she felt her love for him begin to fill her heart, as it pushed away a little of the sadness.

The gates were closed but it didn't matter. Thank God Dora had her Doc Marten boots on, they equipped her for all eventualities. She ran at the fence and in one swift swoop found herself on top of it. She balanced for a minute before landing on the other side, the ground thumping as Caesar landed next to her. She scanned the old graves, looking for a sign of Lenny, and then got the faintest smell of something gone bad carried on the wind and knew Corwin was hiding out of sight. The dog next to her stood on edge, his silent growls only she could hear echoed inside her head and she patted his head.

Walking further in she called out, 'I can smell thee, I know who you are, George Corwin. Why are you hiding from me when thou foul disposition gives thee away?'

She strode in the direction of the far end of the grassy cemetery where the moonlight didn't cast its glow, leaving it shrouded in darkness and shadows. She saw a figure on the floor, and knew it was Lenny. She was lying underneath an old tombstone that was far too heavy for her slight figure and a rush of fury filled Dora's veins, so intense she could hear the crackle of static. Corwin stepped out of the shadows, a large boulder in his hands.

'What took you so long, Isadora, and look at you. Give a girl the right dress and she's right back where she came from.'

He shook his head. 'One move and I'll drop this onto your aunt. It took that stubborn bastard Corey three days to die, but your aunt is a lot smaller than he was and she's already looking a bit peaky from the weight of the tomb that is crushing her slowly to death.'

Dora tensed; she couldn't look at Lenny but at least she knew she was still alive, which was something. She had to distract Corwin without letting him drop the extra weight onto her aunt's chest. Or if he did, she would need to move quick to get it off her.

'What exactly do you think you are doing?'

'What I always do, taking the English sisters' lives one by one until you are all obliterated from this life.'

'Why? We'll just be back the same as we always are.'

'You're forgetting one thing; did you not visit Proctor's Ledge before you came here, Isadora?'

His voice was cold, taunting, and she wanted to rip his voice box out of his throat with her bare hands so she no longer had to listen to it.

'You did, of course you did. Any self-respecting English would have gone to the ledge before even thinking of coming here but you're not going to admit it, are you? You don't want to ask me why I killed that stupid crow that has followed you around for centuries because you know that I know he was more than just a bird.'

He stepped towards Lenny.

'Keep away from her.'

'Or what, you'll turn me into a frog, a cat?'

'I mean it, you don't want to know what I'll do to you.'

'Shall I tell you how you have kept evading me and reliving your lives? I'm angry with myself, you know, for taking so damn many centuries to work it out. I suppose it's better late than never.'

Corwin was so busy talking he didn't notice the black cloud of birds, filling the air as they silently flew towards the ancient tree behind him. Dora watched them from the corner of her eye, wary of alerting him to their presence.

'That bird or whatever he was saved your souls. Every time you died before I could claim them, he took them somewhere far away. I have a bit of bad news for you though, dearest Isadora, he's dead. I caught him snooping and turned the tables before he could fly away. It took very little to crush the bones in his neck, they snapped so easily.'

Dora let out a scream of anger and pointed her finger towards him, sending a surge of bright blue sparks in his direction. They hit the boulder, which she realised was made from marble with a brass plaque attached to it, but it was too late. The stream of light flew back and hit her in the chest with such force it took her off her feet and threw her into the air. She landed with a loud thud on the hard ground and let out a grunt of pain. She was winded and furious with herself; Sephy had warned her about reflective surfaces, she needed to control her magic and concentrate. Corwin was laughing at her, which made her even more angry. She felt Caesar next to her, straining to get at him, but she lifted a hand in front of him in a *wait there* gesture. She crawled to her knees and then to her feet. She was dusty, and her beautiful dress was not only torn, but singed.

'For real, you want to carry on when it's useless? Give it up, Isadora, you left it too late to be in with a fighting chance, but I do admire your spirit. You are so like your aunt Lenora – she was always a fighter.'

Dora noticed her aunt move slightly under the heavy slab of concrete and realised she was listening. She'd thought she was unconscious. Dora took a deep breath in and glanced up at the glowing white moon and remembered Hecate, the binding spell and the salt in her pocket. She smiled at Corwin, and he frowned, it was now or never while his hands were full.

She lowered her hand and commanded Caesar, 'Now, boy.'

The shadow dog leaped forwards and she watched in awe as he came into full view. Corwin let out a yell and dropped the heavy stone on top of Lenny. Dora had minutes to make this work, her hand had uncapped the salt, and she began to turn, spreading the black salt as she moved to form a protective circle around her. George held his hands up to protect himself from the dog and at the same time sent a flash of white electricity in the dog's direction. Caesar let out a yelp and fell to the floor.

Dora began to panic as she felt in her pocket for the papyrus, it must have fallen out when she jumped over. She turned and saw it near to the fence, she couldn't remember the spell that Sephy had given to her and she felt all the strength drain from her legs, making it hard to keep her body upright. The crows began to caw and they all took off at the same time, the beating of their wings deafening as they rose majestically from the branches of the oak tree. Corwin turned to them and sent a beam of light their way, but it didn't stop them as they flew towards him. She heard the singular beating of wings as a lone bird swooped down to pick up the piece of papyrus and then it was flying towards her, landing on her shoulder with the paper in its beak.

She stared at it. 'Hades.'

The crow nodded once, then pushed the paper towards her. The murder of crows were distracting Corwin, flying around him like a black tornado, while Caesar was up on his feet and growling at him, stopping him from moving towards Dora. She heard a voice so soft and light whisper in her ear and she felt a love so strong that she knew it was Lucine.

'I'm here, Dora, you can do this, we'll do it together. Just read the words.'

Dora nodded, her voice was dry, and she wanted a drink of water more than anything.

'I cast this spell into the night.'

She heard Lenny's voice in her other ear and carried on.

'And bind George Corwin into the light.'

Sephy's voice was behind her. She turned and saw her aunt standing there with her arms up in the air, she nodded and smiled at her.

'No longer can he thrive from pain, his action and desires he can no longer gain, in Hecate's name.' Dora paused as she saw a tall woman wearing a cloak step forwards from the darkness, holding a torch in one hand with a snake wrapped around the other. She was standing with Caesar staring at Corwin and she knew in her heart this was Hecate, the mother of all witches. She was here to help set them free.

'I end this fight and free all witches back into the night.' Dora yelled the words in Corwin's direction.

Corwin let out a strangled scream as the birds attacked him, pecking at his face, his eyes, his fingers. She watched in horror and awe as the holes in his skin left by the birds began to leak a black, fetid substance that filled the night air with its vile smell. He fell to his knees, screaming and writhing in pain.

Dora's voice was no longer hers, it belonged to a thousand women who had been persecuted and tortured by Corwin.

'Get them off me,' he howled.

She shook her head. 'For what is a witch without her familiars?'

She realised she was no longer standing on the ground but hovering above it. The tall woman turned to Dora and removed the cloak from her head. She was beautiful, there was a crescent moon drawn on her forehead and she had the bluest eyes. She smiled at Dora and nodded her head, then stepped forwards and took hold of the cowering Corwin. She lifted her hand and a brilliant white light, the same colour as the moon above them, wrapped itself around him. It was a rope made of moonbeams and it circled him so tight that he couldn't move. He screamed in Dora's direction and the light filled his mouth. There was an explosion of darkness that was sucked into the light and then he was gone. There was nothing left, not even the lingering stench that emanated from him.

At that moment in the intensive care unit in St Thomas' Hospital back in London, Katie's eyes flew wide open and she sat up in her bed.

'Lenny,' Dora screamed and ran towards her, terrified that she was too late and her aunt was already dead. She pointed her finger at the chunk of marble and the heavy slab, careful not to hit the shiny part, and sent a burst of power towards it. The stone and marble shattered into a thousand tiny pieces, leaving her bruised and bloodied aunt's body lying on the cold, hard ground. Dora fell to her knees and scooped Lenny up into her arms. She turned to see if Hecate would help her, but she was gone, along with her beloved Caesar. Ambrose and Sephy came running towards the pair of them on the ground.

Dora kissed Lenny's forehead. 'Open your eyes, please don't be dead.'

'If you kiss me again, you'll be dead.'

Lenny was staring at her through one bloodshot open eye.

'Oh my God, you're alive,' Dora breathed.

'Only just. What took you so long?'

Sephy looked down at her sister and her niece. 'Same old salty Lenora, thank God for that.'

Dora looked at Lenny then Sephy. 'Lucine was here, so was Hecate?'

Lenny squinted her one eye. 'Did you get knocked on the head, kid?'

Sephy smiled. 'No, she did not. She is quite right, Lucine was here as I knew she would be and we asked Hecate for her guidance. I didn't realise she would actually put in an appearance.'

Lenny sighed. 'Where's Corwin?'

It was Dora who answered. 'He's gone. I think we did it, we ended the curse and we're free.'

Sephy was smiling. They stood for a moment, wondering if the curse really was broken. It must be. Sephy sighed with relief. For once maybe they could get to live out their happy ever after.

'Dora, be a dear and go and close your circle. All you have to do is stand there and turn anti-clockwise. We don't want to leave it open in a cemetery of all places, we have no idea who might come through and we've had quite enough excitement for this lifetime.'

Dora grinned and walked back to her salt circle. Pointing her finger, she turned anti-clockwise.

Ambrose was standing there watching her. 'Dora, your hair.'

'What about my hair? I know it's a mess, it got a bit singed, but it's nothing a quick trim with some scissors can't fix.'

She walked towards him, and he shook his head. He reached out his fingers and touched it.

'It's silver, like your aunts'.'

Dora patted her head. The messy bun she'd fastened it in this morning was much diminished, there were more strands of hair out of it than in it.

'What do you mean?'

'It's beautiful, it really suits you.'

She turned to Sephy, who had helped Lenny to her feet. The pair of them were watching her.

'Is my hair...?'

'Whiter than the driven snow, my dear. An English trait, I'm afraid, when we go into battle. If it's any consolation you look stunning, darling, and it will save you a fortune on hair dye when it started to go grey.'

Ambrose took out his phone and turned the camera on, snapping a quick photo and turning the screen for Dora to look at. She stared in wonder at the beautiful white hair that fell about her dirty, mud-flecked face. Her eyes were also the most vivid green she had ever seen, even brighter than Sephy's.

Lenny smiled at her. 'Well, there is only one way for an English woman to come to terms with this kind of shock.'

Sephy began to laugh. 'Of course there is. We all need a little black magic to celebrate our freedom, don't you think?'

Lenny clapped and let out loud, 'Ouch.'

'Don't be so dramatic, dear, it's just a few cuts and bruises. A little bit of my arnica salve and some black magic, you'll be as good as new in a few days.'

Dora reached out and took hold of Ambrose's hand, and they watched as Sephy helped Lenny to the van. The gates were open.

'Did you cut them open?'

'No, they never lock them. Sorry, I should have told you.'

'They don't?' She smiled at him, and he grinned back.

'Dora, I have no idea how we're going to get that dress back to the museum. Have you seen the state it's in?'

She looked down at the filthy, singed, torn dress and laughed.

'We might have to get Sephy to work a little bit of magic on it before we do.'

Lenny's voice called out. 'Get a move on, I'm injured and need medical assistance.'

They looked at each other and smiled again, then ran to help Lenny into the rear of the van.

'Why the hell have you got a dead crow on the seat?' Lenny asked when Dora opened the door.

'I thought it was Hades.'

At the mention of his name, he appeared in the sky, soaring above their heads and circling.

'Well, I can assure you it isn't, he's alive and well. It must be one that went rogue, and Corwin thought it was our beloved bird.'

Sephy gently took hold of the crow and carried it to the cemetery where she bent down and dug at the earth with her fingers. She placed it in the shallow grave and said a prayer while they watched. Dora still felt sad that it had died at Corwin's hands, but she was grateful it hadn't been Hades. Tired, aching and looking as if they hadn't had hot baths in a year, all three English women got into the van. Even Ambrose, who hated cars, climbed in and sat next to Dora. He clasped his fingers around hers and she smiled at him. Maybe now they could get to live their lives as they should, together. Maybe there would even be kids somewhere in the near future. Dora had never thought about that before, but someone had to carry the English line on, and she would love to share all of this history with a little girl of her own one day.

Lenny let out a sigh.

'This lifetime was the hardest. Can we make a pact or something not to let it get to this stage ever again? You know, a pinkie promise or something would do. I don't want to go through this next time around.'

Sephy nodded. 'Let's get you and Dora cleaned up, make those cocktails and then we'll stand around the fire naked in the back garden and make a pinkie promise under the moonlight while chanting to the goddess.'

Dora stared at her aunts, horrified. She wasn't doing that for anyone.

Both Sephy and Lenny turned around to look at her with huge grins on their faces. 'Gotcha.'

And then they all began to laugh, Dora a little slower than her aunts who she had decided were crazy, wonderful, magical, but above all the most beautiful human beings she had ever met, and she was never going to let them go ever again.

EPILOGUE

The bookstore had been left open. The priceless first editions were there for anyone to find. In her haste to return Lucine's book of spells to Sephy, Dora had forgotten to shut the door. So it stood, uncloaked, unable to vanish again.

The woman had been sitting on her porch with an ice-cold glass of peach tea, rocking back and forth in the chair that had been in her family since she was born. The wood smoothed to a silky finish by all those hands that had gripped the arms as they rocked in it for hundreds of years. She loved this chair and thinking about her ancestors all sitting doing the same thing on a warm, muggy New England day made her wonder what they had been like.

She was tired. The recent stress she'd been having was taking its toll on her, even though she knew she was better off alone than being married to *him*. At least she had this house for now. He had packed his bags and left two days ago without saying a word, but she knew his silence wouldn't last and he'd be back to fight for what was rightfully his. She was his wife of ten years; she *should* be entitled to half of everything including this house that they had got into debt over their heads for.

Anger bubbled inside her. She'd found the messages on his phone from another woman.

She felt herself drifting off and, as she slipped into a deep slumber, she found herself walking into the forest that backed onto her property. She felt as if she was being called into the dense, dark woods by something that whispered to her in hushed tones she couldn't understand. She had to see what it was.

Her bare feet were crunching through the dropped pine needles and twigs, but it didn't hurt – dreams were like that, you could cut your head off and walk around with it in your hands and not feel a thing. But she couldn't help thinking that if she was dreaming would she be having conscious thoughts? There was a tugging sensation in her chest, it felt as if an invisible rope had been tied around her and she was being dragged towards something, she had no idea what until she saw the small wooden shack. The door was sagging badly and was slightly open, showing how dark it was in there, and she heard the whispering coming from inside.

You should get the hell out of here, do not go inside of that building, a clear voice of reason told her, but this was a dream, and she could do what she wanted, so she did.

She walked closer to the cabin, or whatever it was. It was old and the roof was covered in leaves and there were brambles all around it. It looked like the kind of place a fairy tale witch would live in, cooking over an open fire with a huge black cauldron, green smoke coming out of the chimney.

She paused outside the door; it was too dark in there; her flesh had broken out in goosebumps yet still she felt no real fear, only a need to go inside.

'I'm coming inside, is that okay with you? I won't hurt you.' She laughed, what if whatever was in that cabin wanted to hurt her? She had no cell phone or flashlight with her, but she knew she was going inside and she did. Stepping over the threshold, she inhaled the deep earthy smell of the forest, but she also smelled books, paper and ink.

It smelled as if she had stepped into Barnes and Noble.

Her eyes adjusted to the dark and she smiled to herself to see the shapes on the shelves all around her. Books, there were lots of books. She liked reading but wasn't obsessive over it and wondered why of all things she would dream up a bookstore in the middle of a forest.

The whispering stopped and she turned to see a cold blue light glowing from the pages of a book in the far corner. The light pulsated and she reached out to it. As her fingers touched the light the air around them crackled with static and she pulled her hand back, afraid she'd been electrocuted. She had never seen anything like it and if a book could do that in the middle of the forest on its own, she might have just found the answer to her problems, it might be worth a lot of money. Stepping closer, she jabbed her hands into the light and watched as tiny red and purple fireworks began to fill the air. Grabbing the book, she held it tight to her chest and ran out of the cabin back through the trees.

She jolted awake and was sure she could smell singed flesh; she was still in her rocking chair on her porch but what was that smell?

Lifting her fingers, she saw that the tips of them were red, the skin burned with little blisters. She wondered what the hell she'd done in that nap to have caused this and then she looked down at her dirt-covered feet. There were pine needles between her toes.

As she bent down to brush them off, she noticed the thick, heavy, leather-bound book on the floor beneath her chair. Etched into the cover in blood red were the words 'The Book of Black Magic'.

A LETTER FROM HELEN

I want to say a huge thank you for choosing to read *The Vanishing Bookstore*. If you did enjoy it, and want to keep up-to-date with all my latest releases, just sign up at the following link. Your email address will never be shared, and you can unsubscribe at any time.

www.bookouture.com/helen-phifer

I cried so much writing this story and again as I went back and edited it. I never truly believed I could write something so poignant, warm, funny, magical and beautiful as well as a little dark and I feel so honoured that the English sisters chose me to write their story. I'll let you in to a little secret: I didn't want it to end.

Salem is a wonderful place that I hold dear in my heart, and I literally can't get enough of it. I was always drawn to it from first hearing about the Salem Witch Trials in a history lesson at school – or maybe it was an English lesson, I can't remember, it's a long time ago – but until last year I had never been able to visit. The moment I got out of the Uber outside the Hawthorne Hotel I just felt as if I was home, and the entire stay was one of pure joy.

I feel so grateful and quite frankly awed that I even came up with this story. The aunts feel like a part of my family, and Dora too. Ambrose is a complete sweetheart and I'm so glad that they all found each other again. To me, the English sisters are very real, they have been in my mind for such a long time.

My favourite witchy movie is *Practical Magic* and oh how I wanted to go live with Aunt Frances and Aunt Jet. Alice Hoffman's books are some of the best I've ever read and were a huge inspiration to me. Ever since I watched that movie all those years ago, I've been yearning to create my own magical, spellbinding family and here they are.

There were no English sisters executed in 1692, but the other names are those of major players in the Salem Witch Trials. Judge Jonathan Corwin who presided over many of the accused witch trials and his vile nephew High Sheriff George Corwin unfortunately did exist. The Witch House that I am drawn to every time I visit Salem and even had tattooed on my arm on my last visit there was the judge's house and the only building standing in Salem that has direct ties to the witch trials. It is now a mecca for lots of visiting witches and tourists, which I love.

I wasn't lying when I said I hope Judge Corwin truly is turning in his grave. His nephew George was a brute who delighted in torturing many of the innocent victims. The only saving grace was that he died young, so he could no longer abuse and torture anyone. Bridget Bishop was the first innocent woman to be hanged on 10 June 1692, and so followed another eighteen hangings. Giles Corey was indeed pressed to death in a field that is now Howard Street Cemetery and five more died in the atrocious conditions inside the county jail. There were over two hundred people accused of witchcraft in what was then a relatively small area of colonial Massachusetts by a group of girls who claimed to have been afflicted by them, alleging their spectres would hurt and taunt them.

I have taken as much history as I could and used it as realistically as possible, but I am a writer and this is a work of fiction so I may have used a little of my creative licence to make this story work. But I hope that I have done the victims justice.

There are a great many fabulous books on the Salem Witch Trials. *A Storm of Witchcraft* by Emerson W Baker and *Six Women of Salem* by Marilynne K Roach are two I highly recommend.

There are also quite a few fabulous museums too. The Salem Witch Museum and the Peabody Essex Museum are just two of the many wonderful places to visit in Salem if you want to know more about the history of the trials.

The witch trials memorial next to Charter Street Cemetery is a very serene, thought-provoking place to visit. I visited early one summer morning, when there was nobody around, and as I silently stood in front of each stone with a victim's name carved into it, I said a little prayer for them. Proctor's Ledge Memorial below the actual site where the hangings took place is another very heart-wrenching place. To know so many innocent people were executed on a parcel of land directly above it was very surreal, not to mention desperately sad. I felt very honoured that after all these years of reading about the victims I was able to finally pay my respects to them and let them know that I hear them, their voices have never been silenced.

10 June 1692
Bridget Bishop

19 July 1692
Sarah Good
Elizabeth Howe
Susannah Martin
Rebecca Nurse
Sarah Wildes

19 August 1692
George Burroughs
Martha Carrier
George Jacobs, Senior
John Proctor
John Willard

19 September 1692
Giles Corey (pressed to death)

22 September 1692
Martha Corey
Mary Easty
Alice Parker
Mary Parker
Ann Pudeator
Wilmot Read
Margaret Scott
Samuel Wardwell

Salem today is a wonderful place, a thriving little city, so steeped in history and beauty that I left a piece of my heart there after my first visit and now I'm drawn there almost every day. If I could move there I'd go in a heartbeat. The people are warm and welcoming and the history tours are a great way to learn about the witch trials. There is a fabulous podcast all about Salem I love hosted by two local tour guides, Sarah Black and Jeffrey Lilly, called 'Salem the Pod' which is full of the history of the city and the witch trials. The shops are a witch's dream come true, so many beautiful witchy shops and of course there are many other fabulous shops – it's not all about the witches but if you're anything like me then that's what you love.

Chestnut Street is in the heart of the McIntire Historic District, full of beautiful, Federal-style mansions, and Sephy's pink house, although not strictly a mansion, did in my mind's eye fit beautifully in that area. The actual house that Sephy's was inspired by is near to Salem Common and I saw it in a real estate agent's window when I was strolling past on the way to Derby Wharf on a gloriously sunny day. I knew immediately that this was the kind of house the English sisters would live in.

If you've read any of my other books then you will have heard Caesar mentioned, he is our beloved family dog that we lost, and I like to keep him alive this way. He is all of those things that Dora loved about him, and he would have protected her against Corwin in a heartbeat.

I can't thank you enough for coming on this magical journey with me and I hope that you enjoyed it as much as I have.

If you'd love to listen to the music that gave me the inspiration and helped me write Dora's story then you can here: https://spoti.fi/3Vai1oR

All my love and blessed be,

Helen Xxx

www.helenphifer.com

 facebook.com/Helenphifer1

X x.com/helenphifer1

ACKNOWLEDGEMENTS

This book is a work of love and would not be in your hands if it wasn't for all the hard work and tireless input of my brilliant editor Jennifer Hunt. Her insights, additions and kind words of encouragement have made this story so much better, and I can't thank her enough for believing in this as much as I do.

I'm so grateful for the whole Bookouture team, I count my blessings every day that I get to work with you all. I never expected to blurt out about this story on my visit to Bookouture HQ last February in London, but I'm so glad that I did because it just flew from there and now here we are and I'm so excited to see this published. Thank you!

A huge thank you to Kim Nash for sharing that wonderful day with me and holding my hand.

Another huge thank you to the fabulous Noelle Holten and the rest of the amazing publicity team.

Thank you so much to the wonderful Jen Shannon for all her help and hard work, you are very much appreciated Jen!

A big thank you to Rhian McKay for her brilliant copy edit.

A huge thank you as always to my eagle-eyed dear friend Paul O'Neill for his final surveyor's reports.

A very special thank you goes to my lovely friend and favourite witchy woman Donna Trinder for answering my questions. You inspire me every day and I can't wait for you to read this.

A special thank you to my friend and 'Witchy Wednesday

Book Chat' podcast host Sharon Booth for helping to make it so brilliant. If you haven't listened to it you're missing a treat!

Thank you to all my fabulous witchy readers who inspire me every day.

A big thank you to the lovely KrisTina Petty at the Hawthorne Hotel for making our last trip so wonderful that I didn't want to leave. The Hawthorne is beautiful, steeped in history and the perfect location to explore Salem from.

Another thank you to the beautiful Amanda from Ascend Get Lifted on Essex Street for giving me my very first aura reading and making me feel so seen and heard. She is one of the most beautiful souls I have ever met and if you are lucky enough to go to Salem, make sure you go get an aura reading off Amanda. Plus, she gives the best hugs too!

Thank you to Sarah Black and Jeffrey Lilly from 'Salem the Pod' for the inspiration and hours of entertainment. It was so amazing to meet you, Sarah, outside Witch Pix and to take Jeffrey's tour. Next time we'll take your tour, Sarah, I can't wait.

A very special shout out to all the wonderful historic sites, museums, stores, restaurants and people of Salem. I have never been to a place so beautiful and welcoming, it was my dream to visit for so long and now I can't stop thinking about it.

Finally a huge thank you to my family, especially Steve who accompanies me on my research trips and who has fallen in love with Salem as much as me. My gorgeous grandkids make my heart so happy every day and I'm so blessed to have them. Gracie, Donny, Lolly, Matilda, Sonny, Sie-Sie and Bonnie, you are all amazing and so special to me, I love you all so much. I also love their parents too, but you know grandkids are extra special. Jess, Josh, Jerusha, Jaimea and Jeorgia, thank you for turning into amazing humans, I love you all too, not forgetting Danielle and Deji and Roley!

Lots of love to you all, Helen Xx

PUBLISHING TEAM

**Turning a manuscript into a book requires the
efforts of many people. The publishing team at
Bookouture would like to acknowledge everyone
who contributed to this publication.**

Audio
Alba Proko
Sinead O'Connor
Melissa Tran

Commercial
Lauren Morrissette
Hannah Richmond
Imogen Allport

Cover design
Lisa Horton

Data and analysis
Mark Alder
Mohamed Bussuri

Editorial
Jennifer Hunt
Charlotte Hegley

Copyeditor
Rhian McKay

Proofreader
Elaini Caruso

Marketing
Alex Crow
Melanie Price
Occy Carr
Cíara Rosney
Martyna Młynarska

Operations and distribution
Marina Valles
Stephanie Straub
Joe Morris

Production
Hannah Snetsinger
Mandy Kullar
Jen Shannon
Ria Clare

Publicity
Kim Nash
Noelle Holten
Jess Readett
Sarah Hardy

Rights and contracts
Peta Nightingale
Richard King
Saidah Graham